PRAISE

SITA AND THE
PRINCE OF TIGERS

"In *Sita and the Prince of Tigers*, Winona Howe has given us a transfixing story of love and redemption. Fans of *The Jungle Book* will appreciate the feminist perspective and how it changes everything. This debut novel is not to be missed."

—Sari Fordham, author of *Wait for God to Notice*

"A great story about the improbable relationship that develops between a woman and a tiger, and the challenges and opportunities that ensue. It delves into their lives in the jungle and how it affects other animals, villagers, and even a maharajah. It's unexpected, heartwarming, and inspiring."

—Sonee Singh, award-winning author of *Embody*, as well as *Embrace, Embolden,* and *Lonely Dove*

"*Sita and the Prince of Tigers* is a magical tale that deeply embraces not only the elements of the natural world around us but also the power of love that resides within."

—Puja Shah, author of *For My Sister*

"Unlike the reporter who came to find a lost legend and fell asleep, I was entranced from beginning to end. A truly unique story, *Sita and the Prince of Tigers* keeps on surprising at every unexpected turn. As folklore with a touch of magical realism, it is as real as it gets, deeply grounded in the values of love, family, and place.

"Independent of spirit, Sita finds the love of the tiger prince and creates a world where fantasy and folklore merge in the heart of the jungle, awakening within all of us the dream of living in harmony with nature. The character of Sita stands out as one of the gifts of literature, a female protagonist who has a choice. In choosing love over fear, she becomes one of the wise ones whose wisdom is sought after even by the highest in the land.

"Beautifully written. Winona Howe has given readers of all ages something truly magical."

—**Eleanor McCallie Cooper, author of *Dragonfly Dreams* and *Grace in China***

"The tale of *Sita and the Tiger* challenges and moves the reader in enjoyable and unexpected directions. This engrossing narrative offers alternating glimpses into Indian daily life in the palace, the village, and the jungle, and shows that these places are more alike than different. In each there is cruelty, kindness, loyalty, and most of all love. Most memorable, however, is the unique familial relationship between the Prince of Tigers and the outcast village girl Sita. She is ferocious and vulnerable, and their bond is both magical and believable. I was captivated by this book."

—**Linda Strahan, Emerita, University of California, Riverside**

"I, like Sita, have fallen in love with the Prince of Tigers."

—**Sharon Churches, copy editor**

"The lush landscapes and rich characters stayed with me long after I finished reading *Sita and the Prince of Tigers*. This is the kind of book you curl up with on a lazy Sunday afternoon or take with you on vacation."

—Pandora Villaseñor, life coach and host of *The All Gifts* podcast

"*Sita and the Prince of Tigers* is an amazing book, filled with wonderful writing and beautiful descriptions. I've never been to India, but in reading the book, I could almost imagine I was there with Sita and her prince. This book is one I would definitely recommend to my friends; it is an amazing fantasy book with lots of emotional moments and a strong theme of diversity. *Sita* is a beautiful book, and I loved every minute of reading it."

—Natalie Brooks, tenth grader

Sita and the Prince of Tigers
by Winona Howe

© Copyright 2022 Winona Howe
ISBN 978-1-64663-802-4

All rights reserved. No part of this publication may be reproduced, stored in a retrieval system, or transmitted in any form or by any means—electronic, mechanical, photocopy, recording, or any other—except for brief quotations in printed reviews, without the prior written permission of the author.

This is a work of fiction. All the characters in this book are fictitious, and any resemblance to actual persons, living or dead, is purely coincidental. The names, incidents, dialogue, and opinions expressed are products of the author's imagination and are not to be construed as real.

Published by

 köehlerbooks™

3705 Shore Drive
Virginia Beach, VA 23455
800-435-4811
www.koehlerbooks.com

SITA *and the* PRINCE *of* TIGERS

Winona Howe

VIRGINIA BEACH
CAPE CHARLES

*To Stephanie, who has always been there for me
in more ways than I can mention, and who has believed in
Sita and the Prince of Tigers from the beginning.*

Hindi Proper Names

MAJOR CHARACTERS

NAME	CHARACTER	MEANING
Anila	Sita's friend	air
Arun	Ashok's twin	reddish brown
Ashok	Arun's twin	without sorrow
Bala	Hari's younger brother	young
Bhima	Sita's aunt	formidable
Chandra Devi	reporter's interview subject	moon goddess
Farah	Farha's daughter	beautiful
Farha	a young tigress	happiness
Gokul	Neelam's father	generosity
Hari	Bala's older brother	tawny
Jaya	the maharajah's son	victory
Kartik	a son of the village	courage, strength
Maharajah	ruler of Sundara Pradesh	–
Mitali	Anila's sister	friendship
Nagaiah	Sita's neighbor	king cobra
Neelam	a newcomer to the village	sapphire
Prince of Tigers	ruler of the jungle	–
Priya	sister of Hari and Bala	beloved
Runa	Sita's mother	origin
Shira	a jungle tigress	variation of *sher* (lion or tiger)

Sita	a daughter of the village	furrow
Suhani	Neelam's mother	pleasant
Vanada	Vasu's twin	rain-giver
Vasu	Vanada's twin	excellent

MINOR CHARACTERS

NAME	CHARACTER	MEANING
Aditi	maid at Sita's house	boundless
Akshat	man of the village	cannot be injured
Bharata	man of the village	maintained
Bhasker	man of the village	sun
Bhalu	jungle animal	bear
Bikram	Neelam's brother	promise
Chaaya	woman of the village	shadow
Cheel	jungle bird	black kite
Dhruv	man of the village	firm
Dilip	child of the village	one who gives
Drupada	man of the village	wooden pillar
Duleep	head of the maharajah's household	protector
Gauri	man of the village	white
Gotama	Neelam's brother	best ox
Gurdeep	Anila's husband	lamp of the guru
Haathi	jungle animal	elephant
Harish	the maharajah's "prime minister"	ruler of monkeys
Indira	the maharajah's second wife	beauty

Kali	the maharajah's first wife	dark-colored one
Kanika	woman of the village	black cloth
Kunti	man of the village	spear
Lord Rama	a Hindu deity	pleasing, gives peace
Manju	a jungle tiger	pleasant, sweet
Meher	Indira's childhood nurse	blessing
Mor	Sita's neighbor	peacock
Mudit	village shopkeeper	happy
Navya	young maid at the Primrose Palace	young
Parth	shopkeeper in the city	always hits target
Prabu	headman of the village	powerful
Sanchit	man of the village	brought together
Shekhar	man of the village	peak or crest
Tabaqui	a jungle jackal	name taken from *The Jungle Books*
Udit	village bullock driver	awakened
Vinay	village cowherd, son of Kunti	good manners

PROLOGUE

The reporter would come to rue the moment he had listened to his friend. "You say you need something new for your paper, something unusual?" his friend said. "I don't know what you're looking for, but I've got a suggestion for you."

The reporter was young and had dreams of advancement. "What I'd really like is to find a story that no one else has told, a story that could only come from the heart of India."

"Well, old man, that sounds a little ambitious, but I suggest that you visit . . . oh, I forget the name of the village, but it's about the fourth village east of Balaghat—well, I think it's Balaghat anyway, but it may be some other place that sounds the same. You can get a train as far as Balaghat, at least, but I'm not sure how you would go on from there. Walk, I suppose, if it's that important to you. The village is slap up against the jungle, and seems to have a rather strange history."

"I low so?"

"I suppose I was drunk when Murchison told me about it; in fact, I'm sure I was. It does seem, though, that the village had some sort of special connection with the maharajahs of the district. I'm almost sure Murchison said some of them visited the village. Of course, it might have been forty or fifty years ago, maybe more, maybe less, but I don't have to tell you how unusual it is for a maharajah to have any connection with, or interest in, a specific village."

"Unless it was for tiger drives. Was that it? Or could it have been to obtain more elephants?"

"I'm pretty fuzzy on the details, but those reasons don't sound familiar. I just know that some strange stories have come out of that village. If you can find it, just ask about Mita? Bita? Sita? Something like that."

So the young reporter had come. Or rather, he was trying to get there, wherever there was. He had taken the train to the end of the line at Balaghat. Then he had hired a car, hoping that he would get a good enough story that his editor would pay for the rental. But the road was bad and so was the driver, who crept along when there were no obstacles and refused to slacken his speed when there were. Now, at the least, the car had a flat tire. He fervently hoped the axle was not broken. He cursed when that thought crept into his mind.

He suspected the driver had borrowed the car without permission from an absent employer and hoped to profit from his passenger's errand before the employer returned. The reporter knew very little about cars. He knew there was nothing he could do to help and felt he was wasting time, sitting on a rock and shooing flies away, while the driver poked about the car, raised the hood, and lowered it again. Then he lay down on the road, trying to peer under the car, tut-tutting all the while. It was clear that the driver knew no more about how a car worked and what needed to be done than did the reporter.

A man was walking down the dirt road; his feet were bare, and a puff of dust rose around them with every step he took. He was clearly interested in the unusual sight of a broken-down car, slowing and turning his head to watch as he passed by, not wanting to miss a moment of this spectacle. He came to a halt, and the reporter suddenly grasped at an idea. He approached the barefoot stranger and offered the man money to guide him to the village.

The arrangement was a little loose because the reporter did not really know what village he wanted to be taken to. Nevertheless, the stranger seemed happy to become his guide, so the reporter took his leave of the driver, saying that he would be in touch with him later. The two men strode along the road—a track, really—the reporter becoming more and more impatient. Before the car had come to grief, he had passed two villages. Now they had passed two more.

"Is it much farther?" he asked the man who had become his guide. The unknown village had become almost mythical in the reporter's mind. It was late afternoon, and he was tired. He had removed his jacket, but he was still sweating and felt the blisters forming on his feet.

"Not far," the man intoned in that singsong accent the reporter found so annoying.

"Will we get there before dark?"

"Maybe."

Great, the reporter thought. *I hope I can find a place to stay. And I really hope this story, whatever it is, is worth it.*

They arrived in what he hoped was the right village just after dark. His guide was able to locate a widow who was willing to feed this stranger supper and provide him with a charpoy in her shed. He would be sharing the shed with a couple of goats, a fact that did not improve his temper.

The woman brought him a dish of dal, and chapattis to scoop it up with. She was clearly curious about this stranger and viewed his unexpected arrival as an unusual and very interesting event. The reporter queried her about the names he had been given.

"Do you know a Mita?"

"Mita? Who is that? There is no one in this village named Mita."

"What about Bita?"

"Why do you come here to ask about people who do not exist?"

The reporter was growing desperate. "Have you heard of a Sita?"

The woman was silent at first. Then she said slowly, "My great-grandmother used to have a friend called Sita."

"Can you tell me about her?"

"Me? Of course not. I didn't know her. But you might be able to speak to her great-granddaughter tomorrow. If she will talk to you."

"Why wouldn't she?"

"People say the women of this family are strange. She might decide to talk to you, and she might decide not to talk to you. But you can ask tomorrow."

The reporter did not sleep well. Three times during the night, he had to get up and take his shoes away from the goats; they seemed to feel strongly that the shoes had been provided for their dinner, and they were delighted that the leather was edible. In the morning, he ate lentils and chapattis again for breakfast. Then his hostess led him through the village, a fairly large cluster of small houses made of mud bricks, expounding on the way to everyone they met: "This man wants to learn about Sita. I am taking him to Chandra Devi's house. Is that not the right thing to do? She is home, is she not?"

Nearly everyone she spoke to apparently felt a response was required.

"No, you should take him to Prabu."

"Chandra Devi has gone away into the jungle. She may not be back for some time."

"Yes, Prabu must decide."

"No, she is at home, but she is sleeping."

No one explained that Prabu was the headman of the village, and nothing the villagers said made sense. The walk was interminable. The reporter's feet still hurt, and five people and three dogs were following him. The parade finally reached the edge of the village, but his guide did not stop, and they continued until they had left the village nearly half a mile behind. Crops were planted on one side of the path, but the tilled land was not extensive enough to support the village where he had spent the night. Also, there were no women working in the fields or small boys chasing away the birds that came to feed on the crops.

"Why are these fields separate from the village fields?" he asked.

"You will have to ask Chandra Devi" was the answer.

Then he saw a house that was quite different from the ones he had seen in the village. This house was larger, for one thing, and sprawled nearly to the edge of the jungle. Part of it was stone, part of it wood. An elderly woman sat on a straight-backed chair under a mango tree that shaded the yard.

"This man wants to talk to you," announced his guide.

The woman turned towards him, her eyes assessing, as if to determine whether talking to him was worth her while. He noted that she was small and thin. Her face was pale, and her green eyes gleamed. She was clearly old, yet her face was unlined.

"I will pay you to talk to me," he said, but she made a dismissive gesture. Then he noticed the many bracelets she wore and the necklace that certainly was set with precious stones, and jewels in her ears that he thought might be diamonds, although he could not tell for sure. The necklace was a string of moonstones with a huge emerald hanging from the end, and colors flashed from her bracelets. The silk of her blue choli and sari was shot through with different shades of blue and green and further enhanced by embroidered borders of flowers. Her house was by far the biggest in the village, and she had her own fields. Clearly, if Chandra Devi did not want to talk to him, he could offer no inducements that would change her mind.

"Please tell me about Sita," he said.

The woman sat very still, looking at him with those assessing green eyes. When she finally started speaking, her narration was punctuated by long pauses, as though she were trying to remember things that had happened to her, even though the stories she told sounded like legends she had heard about people who had lived and things that had happened long ago.

CHAPTER

1

After Bhima, Sita's elderly aunt, died, the village was insistent that Sita leave the hut at the edge of the jungle where she had lived all of her life and move into the confines of the village. The village men did not want anything bad to happen to a girl of their village; this would reflect badly upon their manliness and their ability to protect the females they were responsible for. The village women said that there was no telling what a young girl might get up to if she was not guided by those older and wiser than she. There were also a number of practical reasons why Sita might be better off and safer in the village. If she lacked food, someone would doubtless help out. She would be less likely to step on a *naja naja* or run afoul of a hungry *tendua* or even a *baagh*. Yes, everyone was agreed on Sita's future. Everyone except Sita herself.

Sita was adamant that she would not leave the hut. The village had presented somewhat the same arguments to her aunt every year since Sita could remember. They had omitted the parts about being a young girl, saying instead that an aging woman would not be able to defend herself against the dangers she might encounter—but Bhima had refused to move. Sita's aunt never cared much what people thought about her. No one remembered what her real name had been before she decided to rename herself. It had been somewhat shocking because Bhima was a man's name; it meant "formidable or terrible," nothing like what a woman should be or be called. But Bhima had decided that she had no interest in marriage, and she took a man's name to show that she was capable of taking care of herself. She liked living close to the jungle; she said she wanted to be close enough to hear its voice and feel its heartbeat. Sita felt the same way.

She finally told the village that the only way she would move was if she were carried forcibly, and that this would be unpleasant and unbecoming to all concerned.

"She is truly the daughter of her aunt," the villagers said as they shook their heads at her intransigence. "She is surely the same stiff-necked woman who would always go her own way."

Of course, Sita once had a mother, but Runa had died when Sita was only a few months old. Bhima, Runa's older sister, had come to live with Runa during her pregnancy, and she stayed to be a mother to Sita. Although she was not a woman the villagers would have described as motherly, Bhima was devoted to her niece. In fact, Bhima was the only adult who was a constant in Sita's life. No one knew who her father was; certainly, no man from the village ever stepped forward to declare that the small, squalling bundle was his child, and Runa had never spoken, even to Bhima, about who Sita's father might be.

When Sita was a baby, Bhima wrapped her in a cloth and strung it up like a hammock. Bathed by the air of the jungle and rocked by its breezes, Sita listened to its birdsong lullabies while Bhima worked in the garden. When Sita grew larger, she helped Bhima plant seeds and carry water, and form chapattis with her small hands. When she grew older still, Bhima taught her how to grind the roots of the *shatavari* and prepare the medicine to treat ulcers. In the evenings, particularly if Bhima's last candle was exhausted, she would teach the child how to speak the language common to all dwellers in the jungle.

"Who knows, it may be useful someday," Bhima said when Sita asked why she should learn all these strange words she never heard anyone else say. After that, Bhima often spoke in the jungle dialect to make sure that Sita was not forgetting what she had learned. When she felt that her niece had absorbed a working vocabulary, she also began to teach her tiger talk, showing her how similar the two dialects were but how they were different as well. These lessons ceased, however, as Bhima focused more on passing down her knowledge of wild plants in the locality and how they could be used. Runa had had some knowledge of herbs, and Bhima's understanding of traditional medicine was fairly comprehensive; she was happy that Sita was both interested and quick to learn which plants were helpful to heal various ailments and which should be left alone.

Because of Sita's history with Bhima and the lessons she had learned from her aunt, it was not surprising that the girl wished to stay in her familiar surroundings despite now being alone. Furthermore, once the village capitulated, deciding that Sita could live by herself, she was alone and happy. Of course, she missed Bhima. The knowledge that Bhima had always been there to help her had given Sita a feeling of security, but now Sita realized that she would have to learn to live without that warm feeling of comfort and support. In many ways, however, her life went on as usual.

She cultivated her small garden, pulling out the stubborn weeds and bringing water from the village well when there was no rain. The village clearly considered her of no account, but they did not shun her for refusing to follow their demands. Sita would occasionally take a coin from her tiny hoard to buy some necessity (of which there were very few), and she would participate in village celebrations and rituals. She also continued to search the edges of the jungle and deliver the spoils to Mudit in his small shop—fruit from the bael tree, neem leaves, or perhaps a beautiful butterfly. Mudit, in turn, would sell these things to others: merchants, women of the village, perhaps even strangers who might be travelers from the city—whoever wanted or needed the fruit to eat, fresh or dried (or perhaps to use in religious rituals), or the leaves to treat various skin diseases. Sometimes people wanted to buy a butterfly that looked different from any they had seen before.

Thus had Sita and her aunt supported themselves, and now Sita was supporting herself on her own. She was not sad when she picked the fruits or leaves, but she felt sorry when a butterfly floating through the foliage was suddenly caught by her, because she knew that all too soon, it would be laid out on a board or pinned up on a wall, never again to feel the soft currents of air that it rode so effortlessly. She realized she was denying it the freedom—in a very final sense—that she craved and demanded for herself.

"I am sorry," she whispered to a butterfly with lacy black-and-yellow wings. "I would rather see you free and happy, drifting and weaving among the jungle breezes." Still, she must earn a living. Her saris were thin and limp, and occasionally she needed to purchase a few things she could not grow in the garden.

One day while Sita was hoeing the groundnuts in her tiny garden, she felt something—a presence, but of what? At once, every one of her senses came alive, and she sought to identify the source of this sudden awareness. Sita remained alert as she swung the hoe up and down until she reached the end of the row. She felt no change in the currents of air caressing her cheek; she smelled no unfamiliar odor, only the humid combination of everyday scents drifting from the jungle. Although she did not turn her head, she saw nothing to disturb her, no movement of grass or leaves that might have indicated a cobra or leopard in the area. But something was there.

Sita didn't actually think of it or call it a "presence"; she just knew that someone or something was there that did not belong in her garden and was not a part of the jungle she knew. *Perhaps it is the spirit of the maharajah or even a god*, she thought. But there was no answer to be found, and Sita felt no sense of danger, so she gathered the groundnuts her hoe had unearthed. As she often did while working, she hummed the wordless, almost tuneless song she had learned from her aunt—Sita had heard it from the time she was still in her hammock, being rocked by the breeze.

Although she noticed nothing out of the ordinary, she continued to be alert for any hint of what (or whom) might be nearby. Before long, the presence faded away; in the following days, however, she felt it often—not just in the garden but also when walking the trails at the edge of the jungle, seeking and harvesting the plants that provided her with the healing medicines she made for herself and to sell to others. Once, she saw the grass quiver very slightly as if something or someone had just passed that way, creating a faint ripple in the air, but she saw nothing more.

CHAPTER

2

Sita became accustomed to the presence and to its absence. She never felt it when other people were around, and if her friend Anila came to her hut for a chat when the presence was there, it would slowly dissipate until there was nothing except the palpable absence of whatever it was. Sita had never been lonely before; she did not know the meaning of the word. Perhaps missing Bhima had made Sita restless, but now she found herself wishing that the presence would return. What was it, and why had it selected her to observe?

Sita had never heard of anyone else having this experience—having some contact, however slight, with a being that was definitely not part of the everyday world. She had to admit, though, that never having heard of a similar situation was not much of a test. After all, she had not told anyone about her recent experiences. Sita spent a lot of time thinking about them, however, and realized that she drew a certain comfort in the presence, though she could not understand why this should be so.

She began to explore a little farther into the jungle. The flowers, plants, and trees she knew mostly preferred to grow near the edge, where the jungle and cultivated land came together. But Sita wanted to explore, to see what she could find that was new and different.

Once, she spotted a cluster of rose-purple flowers surrounded by bright-green leaves and what appeared to be bare gray roots, sprouting high above her in a sal tree. Sita hitched up her sari to climb the trunk. She wanted to see the colors at close range and to run her fingers across the petals that looked like silk. The flowers were even more beautiful when she was sitting on a limb close enough to touch them; she could now see the small dots of darker purple in their throats. Sliding down the tree was more difficult than climbing up, but Sita counted the exchange of a few scratches for the close-up view of the flowers a fair trade. She brought one of the flowers back to her hut, but it was wilted the following day.

She also saw more animals past the strip of familiar forest. The first was a sambar stag lazily chewing his cud as it lay peacefully in a clearing. Sunlight through the trees dappled his coat so that he looked like a larger, stronger, more muscular chital. When Sita approached him, he suddenly jumped up, his jaws still moving but his body tense, preparing to flee.

"Brother, I mean you no harm," Sita said softly in the universal dialect of the jungle. The sambar studied her intently, and then stalked slowly away. He realized it was not necessary to flee, but he also did not want to be that close to a human, even one who was not armed with a *laathi* and therefore did not appear to be a threat to him.

A *cheel* soaring above the treetops laughed at Sita's statement and the sambar's response. "Why should he trust you?" he called. "Your kind have hunted his since the beginning of time."

He was obviously surprised when Sita called back, "The sambar has no more reason to fear me than I have to fear him. We are both peaceful dwellers on this bit of earth." The bird did not answer but wheeled away into the blue.

One day Sita went into the jungle to look for *vasa bach*. Mudit had told her that his sister-in-law was having trouble sleeping, and Sita said she would bring him some leaves of this plant as a sedative. She knew she would most likely find these plants near water, so she directed her steps to a stream where she had collected them in the past. It was a hot day, and when Sita reached the stream, she bent down to scoop up the cool water and lap it from her hand. She picked a few handfuls of the leaves but decided not to dig for roots until she had eaten.

Sita had tied a few groundnuts into the end of her sari and now settled on a log, slowly chewing them. She had almost finished when she felt it, the presence; it was near—nearer than ever before. She did not move her body, but her eyes swept from side to side, searching for a physical sign of the mysterious presence.

One thing had changed dramatically. The clearing had been empty and deserted when she arrived. Now a baagh, a large, male tiger, was sitting by the end of the log. His coat was dark, closer to auburn, strongly marked with black stripes. The cream fur on his face and ruff was also striped, and he possessed a fine spray of whiskers. His eyes were a deep, glowing green, and they watched her intently. Sita's heart thumped fast and she sat very still. She did not feel she was necessarily in danger (if the baagh had wished to harm her, she might already be dead by now), but it would be extremely silly to scream or run.

At last, the tiger spoke; not surprisingly, he spoke in tiger talk. "I have been watching thee," he said.

"I know," responded Sita. She was surprised she could still remember the words her aunt had taught her long ago. She recalled that it strongly resembled the common jungle language, but its structure was more formal and its vocabulary more extensive.

The tiger was also surprised, but his astonishment sprang from a different cause. "Am I so clumsy, then, that thou couldst hear my footsteps that followed thee on the trail, or did the grass wave so that my tail caught thine eye when I slid through the grasses like water that flows around a stone without sound?"

"No, Sir Tiger, not at all. I have never seen thee nor heard thee."

"Then how didst thou know I was near thee?"

"I felt thy presence. I felt thee when thou came, and I felt the void when thou departed."

"And wert thou not afraid?"

"No," said Sita, calmly. "Thy presence did not disturb me. I know thou art so strong that a blow from thy paw would make me cease to exist. But I do not believe thou came here in order to kill me."

The tiger rose, his muscles rippling as he took two steps and sat down again, this time facing Sita, who looked fearlessly into his eyes, even though she had been told that a direct stare was a sign of aggression. "It is true," he said. "I have no evil designs against thy life. I was merely curious about those who call themselves 'humans,' and as thou hadst chosen to live out of the village, thou wert the easiest to observe."

"I do not seek thy life or wish it to be ended either, but I speak truly when I say that many men in my village would be glad to boast that they had killed a tiger; furthermore, they could sell thy skin for enough money to live on for a year and far beyond."

The tiger had appeared inscrutable, but now he smiled, although Sita did not think her words humorous. Perhaps it was not a smile but a sneer, accompanied as it was by a dismissive motion of his paw.

"I have no fear of those *gulams*," the tiger stated. "They are not strong or wily enough to injure the Prince of Tigers, even though a *khalanayak* may be among them . . . and should probably be removed," he added thoughtfully. "They do not realize it, but it is only through my munificence and forbearance that they are not harmed. And why dost thou refer to this group of people with a hedge around their habitations as thy village? If I am not mistaken, thou hast chosen to live away from them."

"It is true, O Prince of Tigers. I have refused to live in the village. I chose to live at the edge of the jungle because I have lived there my entire life and I like to be alone. It seems more home to me than always having people around me and having the smoke of thirty fires constantly in my nose. I would rather smell the scents and perfumes of the jungle."

"Perhaps thou wouldst like to know the jungle better," said the tiger.

"I would, but I have no guide. I am a small person, and I could not walk so far."

"Thou dost not have to walk at all. Thou shalt ride on my back. Come."

It only took a moment for Sita to decide. Then she stood on the log and slipped onto the tiger's back. "I want to know the jungle," she said.

"Then thou must put thy arms around my neck and hold on. We will be moving very fast."

Sita put her arms around the tiger's neck. The vasa bach leaves lay on the ground, discarded and forgotten.

CHAPTER

3

Sita could not believe how quickly and how silently the tiger moved. The jungle rushed past her in a blur of emerald green. Soon they had passed the crooked tree that marked, for her, the end of where she felt safe when she explored by herself. But the tiger did not stop. He ran on and on until Sita was breathless. The only thing she could feel (or maybe hear) was the pulse of the tiger's quickened heartbeat under the hands she wrapped around his neck and chest.

Finally, he stopped. "Thou canst get down now. First, look around and tell me what thou thinks of the jungle. Thou thinks, perhaps, that the jungle is already known to thee, but where thou lives is only the borderland. I have brought thee to the real jungle, *my* jungle."

Sita looked around her. The trees were taller, and their branches spread wider; some were covered with vines, through which a greenish light filtered down to the fern-covered jungle floor. A lacy white butterfly slowly fluttered along, high up in the canopy. She heard bird songs that were new to her. Sita turned to the tiger, who was watching her.

"Thou art right; this is not the jungle I know. It is far more beautiful than what I have seen before. But why dost thou call it thy jungle?"

"Because I am the Prince of Tigers. A tiger always rules the jungle, and this jungle is mine. It belongs to me, and it is my responsibility to rule it well."

"What does it mean to rule the jungle? I had not thought of the jungle as a place of rules at all."

"As I am its ruler, the rules in the jungle are made by me. I decide who can live here and who should be driven away; if those return, I may decide to take more serious action. When I hunt, I am removing from the herd those chital or sambar who do not contribute to the vigor of the group: the old who cannot keep up; the young when the herd is overgrazing; and a stag, now and then, when there are too many battles between the males, yet the losers refuse to leave the herd. I determine the limits of many predators' territories. If thou dost not see Bhalu about, it is because I have informed him that his territory lies farther north. He sometimes refuses to accept this, but after I remind him that I am the Prince of Tigers, he plods northward again."

"If thou rules the jungle, why art thou not called the king?"

"I cannot say. It has always been thus. The title is of little consequence. The important thing is that I am the jungle's ruler."

"If the jungle is thine, then thou dost not have to fear anything in the jungle."

"That is correct. And as thou art with me, thou art also safe." The tiger smiled in his own way—it was not a sneer nor yet a grin. "The only thing in the jungle that could cause thee hurt at this moment is I, the Prince of Tigers. And I will not harm thee. I only wish to talk with thee, and learn from thee. I want to learn the ways of man, as thou seeks to learn the ways of the jungle."

This exchange seemed fair to Sita. "What is thy name?" she asked.

"I have already told thee who I am. I am the Prince of Tigers. I have no other name, nor do I need one. When I roar, all the inhabitants of the jungle say, 'There goes the Prince of Tigers—I hope he is not hunting tonight.' But what is thy name?"

"I am Sita. I am not a princess; my neighbors do not talk of me with respect. I am merely Sita—a stubborn, motherless girl who refuses to do what she is told by those who have no right to force their rules upon her."

"Thou shouldst not sound so humble, but perhaps I do not hear humility; perhaps what I hear is arrogance."

"I assure thee I am both poor and humble. Even my name, Sita, is humble. It means 'a furrow,' like the one I make in the ground when I am ready to plant beans."

"Names are relatively unimportant," said the tiger. "As I said, I am always referred to as the Prince of Tigers, or sometimes as 'my lord,' by the jungle folk. But if thou should feel the need for a different and better name, choose another. From the observations I have made as I listen at the edge of the village, I am aware that people feel the need for names and that, apparently, many names are available. Choose one that fits thee better."

"Sita, just Sita, fits me. What I am called does not matter, but I wish to keep the name Sita, as it is the name my mother gave me. She died when I was a baby. She had nothing to leave me, but she gave me my name."

"Very well, Sita shall still be thy name. It is time to take thee back to thy home now, lest thy neighbors should think thee lost and start searching."

Once again, Sita got on the tiger's back. He did not run this time; still the jungle passed in a blur until he stopped and she slid off his back. They were near her hut but just inside the jungle where the tiger would not be seen by boys driving the village's three water buffalo home from a day of grazing. It was nearly dusk, and Sita heard someone walking down the side path leading to her cottage. The tiger said, "I will come again. I look forward to our next meeting." Then he faded so easily into the shadows that Sita wondered if the entire afternoon had been a dream.

Her visitors were the two sisters, Anila and Mitali, coming to see Sita in spite of the late hour. They had brought her two coconut balls. "We had too many," Mitali said.

"We thought you would like a treat," Anila said, and added, "If you moved into the village, you would be with us all the time."

"We could work together," Mitali reasoned. "We could talk about what is important to the three of us. And you would be safe."

Sita was angry. *Does the village think I can be bribed to do their bidding by two coconut balls?* She liked Anila and Mitali, especially Anila. But she did not want to live near them, work with them, and spend all her time with them. She did not want her life to be limited to confidences about which young man might be considered a good match, or which young girl was no better than she should be. Sita was happy enough where she was; she did not want to change her solitary life for one of gossip and tittle-tattle, or to be pitied because she was alone and seen as needing help.

She wanted to be free and independent from the village as always—as Bhima had taught her to be. Furthermore, although Sita had known Anila and Mitali all her life, she was much more anxious to spend time with her new friend, the Prince of Tigers, than to see these old friends. She hardly dared to believe that he would come back, but conversation with him would be more stimulating than discussing what Chaaya had been cooking when she burned her hand, and whether or not little Dilip would ever learn to walk.

"Thank you very much, my friends," Sita said. "I am well content here, and here I shall stay. But it is almost dark, and you should return to the village quickly. I will walk with you part of the way."

"You seem anxious to get rid of us," Mitali observed. "Is there a reason for this? I thought you seemed nervous and excited when we arrived. Is something going on that you do not want to tell us?"

"Don't be silly," Sita responded, rather more sharply than was usual for her. "I am just tired. I dug up *suran* today; the ground was too hard, and my back hurts. Also, I am thirsty. I probably won't even eat supper, just drink some mango juice and go to sleep."

Sita hoped the sisters would believe her, but her attention was not on them. She wondered if the tiger was still nearby. All her senses were alert as she strolled to the village with her friends, but she heard and felt nothing. She told herself it was because Anila and Mitali were chattering so much and so loudly. *Be quiet—I want to listen!* Sita thought, but she said nothing.

An early moon rose as she walked back to her lonely hut, revealing nothing except the usual and the familiar. Disappointed, Sita decided to eat after all, and ladled cold curried rice onto cold chapattis. It might have been an unappetizing meal, but Sita did not notice. She thought about the tiger and how swiftly he had moved through the jungle, even when she was riding on his back.

CHAPTER

4

After that day, Sita was often in the tiger's company. Sometimes she met him in the jungle, running joyously along the trail until she saw him waiting for her with a smile on his face; or he might be sprawled under a tree, his coat turned russet in the deep shade. The breeze on her cheeks felt so good as she ran; she wondered why she had not run places before, but then, the Prince of Tigers had never been waiting for her before.

More often, however, the tiger came to Sita. She never heard him coming, but suddenly he would be there, sitting at the end of a row of beans in her garden, or under the mango tree if he knew no one was about.

The prince rarely entered her hut. He took up most of the space when he came inside, but he also mentioned that he felt confined. "I understand that animals from the jungle are sometimes captured and put in small places like this where they can hardly move around. There are locks on the doors so that they cannot escape; then humans come so they can safely gape at them, and even poke at them or tease them if they are so minded. I also hear that these animals are never allowed to come home to the jungle again. Bah! I would not like to live a life like that. I could not endure it."

"I had not heard of these places," said Sita, "but I do not doubt that they exist. I know that humans are often cruel to animals and do not care if they cause them harm. They even kill those of the forest, sometimes with laathis or great knives. If the animal is a big one like thou, O Prince of Tigers, a man with white skin sometimes comes; he carries a long hollow stick that spits out death. This stick makes the man very powerful. I always hope that all the jungle folk stay safely undercover when a hard-hearted man like this chooses to walk on their trails."

The conversations between Sita and the tiger continued. The tiger learned why each village had a headman, what the people kept in their houses, whom they worshipped, and what they feared. Sita learned which deep-jungle plants and fruits were poisonous, why she should be afraid of the dhole (even though they had not hunted in this part of the jungle for many years), how to interpret the calls of the langur (or *bandar-log*), and that not all tigers were to be trusted.

Sita was quite surprised when the Prince of Tigers calmly stated that many tigers were untrustworthy. Of course, Sita had heard of man-eaters all her life; if a tiger was seen in the vicinity of the village, someone always said, "What if he is a man-eater? What will we do then?" This tended to be on some villagers' minds, even if there was no reason to think that a particular tiger was interested in anything in the village other than the occasional goat that strayed away from the rest of the herd or refused to enter his owner's shed at night.

She had grown to trust the Prince of Tigers, however; it seemed to her that he was extremely unlikely to be dishonest or needlessly cruel. Sita knew he was a predator and that predators live on those weaker than themselves. She asked him about hunting, how it felt, and how it related to the rest of his life. He was not annoyed when she asked those questions, but she did not feel that his answers necessarily helped her to understand.

"I am a tiger," he said. "Therefore, I am a hunter. It is natural, and I can imagine no other life." Then he shrugged.

Sita found the shrug a little disturbing. She could not imagine a life other than the one she was leading either, but she did not see her life as one that brought harm to others. She had to admit that the prince was right—a tiger was born to hunt (and kill)—but he had not answered as completely as she would have liked. And then there was the shrug. She also wondered if he was keeping something back, perhaps about other ways a tiger might be untrustworthy, but the notion was fleeting and soon passed from her mind. In spite of these questions and qualms that occasionally troubled her, Sita continued to spend as much time as possible with the tiger.

Their conversations flowed freely. "It makes me angry when men beat their wives!" Sita burst out one morning when she had seen a woman with a bruised face outside Mudit's store.

"Why do you think this happens?" the tiger asked, which led to a discussion of what made individuals of both species angry and dangerous.

Another day, both had been quiet for some time when the tiger suddenly announced, "It is said that there are one hundred five shades of green in the jungle. I, however, have personally identified only sixty-three." Sita laughed and confessed that although she realized there were many shades of green in the jungle, it had never occurred to her to count them or keep track of how many she had seen.

Often they were silent, content to merely be in each other's company. Sometimes Sita sat on a giant teak log and the tiger lay at her feet. If the circumference of the log was so great that her feet did not reach the ground, she rested her feet on his back. If she sat on the ground, the tiger would sit or lie close beside her; occasionally he put his head on her lap.

The physical closeness they shared made their conversations ever more personal. Sita confided in the tiger that she did not know who her father was, whether he had been a husband to her mother or whether she had been conceived during a passing encounter. He told her that the latter was not strange or shameful to him; in fact, that was the way of tigers. However, he had noted that some people chose to remain together, for years even, and seemed to value this extended relationship. Sita was a little puzzled. Was he trying to make her feel better about possible abandonment by her father, or did he feel that was the way life was supposed to be? Perhaps he merely mentioned lasting commitment as a surprising fact he had discovered.

Sita found their jaunts on jungle paths the most enjoyable part of their time together. Sometimes she rode on his back, or she might walk beside him with an arm thrown over his shoulders. At times like these, she felt that they were in complete harmony, as was the rest of the world. It was inevitable, however, that someone, somewhere, sometime would become aware that there was a tiger in the neighborhood of the village, even if they did not realize that he stayed in their vicinity because of Sita. A tiger in such close proximity to the village would create an atmosphere of uneasiness. People would be more nervous, they would jump to conclusions more quickly, and they would become more dangerous—to her as they became more irritable with her refusal to fit into the life pattern they desired her to follow, and especially to the tiger as their fear encouraged them to seek ways to permanently remove him from the area.

Sita did not care how they treated her, but she could not bear to think that the tiger might be injured or killed because of the friendship that had developed between them.

CHAPTER

5

The Prince of Tigers had killed, eaten, and slept. Now he groomed himself so that every hair lay silkily in place on his shining coat. He knew he must make a decision; the care and attention he paid to his grooming was merely a way to postpone that decision a little longer. His original plan, as he had told Sita, was to learn about the world of humans—how they thought and why they acted the way they did. He had selected Sita as his tutor in these matters because she had more of an appreciation for the jungle than any of the other people he had observed as he prowled the edges of various communities.

She seemed to be a calm individual; furthermore, she had an independent spirit, defying the village customs and going her own way. The tiger's assumptions about Sita had been correct. Not once had she screamed hysterically at his approach, a common reaction when people (especially women) were startled or frightened. In addition, she had never spoken of him to another, thus keeping a secret that was important to him but that he had not even demanded of her.

Sita had also been a good tutor, expanding his mind in many ways. He found some things she told him surprising, but others merely supported what he had personally observed during his silent comings and goings in the vicinity of the village. He now understood quite a lot about people—their likes and dislikes, why they behaved the way they did, etc.—so perhaps it was time for the experiment of learning about people to be concluded. But the tiger had discovered that he did not want it to be concluded.

Tigers are more analytical than other animals, and the Prince of Tigers realized that he wanted to spend more time with Sita, listening to what she had to say and finding out what more he had to learn. He was amused when they disagreed on the reasons behind certain attitudes and actions, but he enjoyed those spirited conversations; he did not try to force Sita to accept his perspective but believed that time would prove which interpretation was correct. He liked hearing Sita "purr" (his word for her tuneless humming), which she did often whether he was present or not. He had never heard another person purr, and Sita's ability to do so was one more thing that set her apart from other humans. The tiger routinely closed his ears when people made the noises they called singing; he had noticed that people tended to appreciate these sounds, but the Prince of Tigers regarded them as more akin to the harsh, screeching noises that Mor, the peacock, made than anything else.

Tigers could not purr, of course; they chuffed instead. But chuffing was really a series of sounds, while purring was more continuous, like Sita's humming. She told him that she fell into the habit of humming because her aunt had done so for as far back as she could remember. The prince was not particularly interested in this bit of family history. He only knew that when he was padding silently down the trail, drawing nearer and nearer to Sita's hut, he liked hearing her purr. It was as though she were welcoming him home, although there was no way he could ever have viewed her small, enclosed (and to him, stifling in its sense of enclosure) hut as home.

The tiger also liked his role as Sita's teacher of jungle ways, just as she was his teacher about people and their ways. He liked to have her sitting on his back, gripping his ruff with her small hands or with her arms around his neck so she would not fall off. Although she acknowledged his standing by calling him the Prince of Tigers, Sita did not always agree with him and the way he set about his business—but he respected her all the more for her ability to challenge him when she believed that he was in the wrong.

The question before him now was this: as he did not want to leave Sita, how could he ensure that she was always near him? He did not know how Sita felt about him. Clearly, she enjoyed his company and was delighted that their friendship had given her an entry into the world of the jungle that she had not possessed prior to his appearance in her life. Sita had distanced herself from her people even before he met her, but would she be willing to essentially cut her ties to the village and choose the Prince of Tigers over the entire context of her life up to this point?

The prince lay silently in a great clump of lantana, considering the question of Sita's future, and whether he should seek a future together with her, considering all the implications that an alteration this extreme in his life would bring. His auburn coat with its black stripes and cream accents blended into the golden-orange flowers; only the occasional twitch of his ears or switch of his tail would have revealed his presence . . . had anyone been watching.

Sita had searched all day for a honey tree but had not found one. Mudit had indicated that several villagers were requesting honey and he had none. If she could bring him some, he would pay her more than he had last year.

Sita rarely spent time in the jungle without seeing at least a few busy bees searching for nectar-producing flowers; she was confident she could provide the honey Mudit had asked for, as well as keep some for herself. So Sita entered the jungle, expecting to bring home a bucket full of honeycomb, but the day had not unfolded the way she expected. She found nary a bee's nest, brown and bulbous like an outgrowth of the tree to which it was attached.

She located and pursued a number of bees. She ran through the grass, jumped over fallen branches, and pushed her way through thickets, but she lost them as they flew more swiftly than she could run and finally disappeared in the canopy overhead. She sat on a log to rest, and it suddenly occurred to her how very foolish she had been. In her headlong dash, she might easily have disturbed a naja naja or stepped on a krait; furthermore, in her quest for honey, she had ventured farther into the jungle than was safe when she was alone and unaccompanied by the Prince of Tigers.

Tired and discouraged, Sita was trudging home when she saw the tiger sitting by the path.

"I want to take thee to a place thou hast not seen before, a place that is farther away and may take us much of the night to explore."

"I am tired today, O Prince of Tigers," Sita responded. "Could we not go another evening?"

"Thou wilt like this place—I am certain of it. As I said, it is at a distance, but of course thou canst ride."

Too tired to argue, Sita said nothing further. She stood on a log and stepped onto the tiger's back. At once she felt happier, more alive; she wondered how much of her melancholy and discouragement had come from not having seen the prince for several days. She leaned forward and tightened her arms around his neck. It suddenly occurred to her that this felt more like an embrace than just holding on. She wondered at her boldness but said nothing. Information about and words for physical signs of affection were not yet in the tiger's knowledge or vocabulary.

"Thou must hold me tightly, but not that tightly!" the Prince of Tigers admonished Sita. "I must be able to fill my lungs with air if I am to be able to run carrying thee on my back."

Sita smiled at the tiger's solemn tone, which made him sound rather old and stuffy. She relaxed her grip enough that he could breathe deeply, but not so much that she would fall off his back if he suddenly swerved. His gait was so smooth that Sita could have gone to sleep and not fallen off if not for his occasional leap over a log or small stream. No matter how thick the mat of vegetation under the tiger's feet was, Sita did not want to risk the fall, so she stayed awake.

The tiger hurtled through the shadowed jungle as the late afternoon darkened into dusk, and Sita rode on his back, happy with both the physical contact and the emotional closeness she felt when she was with her greatest friend, the Prince of Tigers.

CHAPTER

6

Sita was feeling sleepy again when the tiger's pace slowed and he came to a stop. She slid off his back and looked around. The prince had stopped in a clearing; at its edge, a large stone building with tumbling walls peered out of the underbrush. Trees and vines at the edges of the clearing were in bloom, the flowers gleaming in the light of an early moon, and the very air was like perfume.

"We will explore it another day," the Prince of Tigers said easily as Sita glanced at the stone building. "I do not think there is time now. See, the moon has already risen."

Sita had not thought of the time, but now she was worried. "What will happen if the people of the village miss me?" she queried. "Will it put thee in danger?"

"I rarely think of danger in connection with thy village," said the tiger suavely. "But look, thou hast not noticed one of the chief pleasures of this spot."

"What is it?" Sita asked. Then she saw where the tiger was looking—a pool of water, faced with the same stone as the building. A stream flowed into one end of the pool and out the other. Even in the shadows, the pool appeared crystal clear, reflecting the moon rising over the jungle.

The two sat side by side, gazing into the clear water. At first,

Sita examined her own reflection. She did not own a mirror, and looking into the well when she drew water did not provide her with an accurate picture of her appearance. She had occasionally (and self-consciously) looked into a brook, but the ripples distorted her reflection. This pool was the closest she had come to looking into an actual mirror, but instead of focusing on herself, Sita turned her gaze on the Prince of Tigers. As she examined the tiger she saw in the pool, she realized that he was also watching her reflection. In the semidarkness, his eyes glowed green, and he was looking at her without any trace of the intensity he sometimes showed (always reminding Sita he was a predator), or the mockery in his smile when she attempted to defend the actions of humans. Instead, there was a caressing quality in his gaze. Sita shivered but could not look away from his mesmerizing eyes.

The tiger lowered his head, lapping the water, and Sita dipped her hand into the cool liquid and drank too; it tasted fresh and sweet.

"This water is always good for drinking," the tiger said, "but it is good for other things as well."

"What?" Sita started to ask, but he suddenly took a gigantic leap. Water flew in all directions, splashing Sita, who leaped to her feet, watching him with astonishment. Then, sensing his enjoyment, she laughed with pleasure at seeing him acting more like a half-grown cub than the prince of the jungle. She remembered Bhima once saying that tigers liked water, but the villagers had scoffed at her words, and she never spoke of it again. Sita's own observations had convinced her that all cats hated water, but now, watching the tiger splashing happily, she realized again that her aunt had possessed insight into most things. She felt fortunate to have lived with Bhima and been given the opportunity to learn from the older woman, but this was merely a passing thought.

Now Sita's entire attention was focused on the Prince of Tigers. He swam across the pool and back again; he dipped under the surface and came up spouting water in Sita's direction; he jumped up and down, flinging drops of water everywhere. When he leaped up with his back straight and his front paws thrown out to the sides, the drops of water sparkling like diamonds on his glossy fur in the moonlight, he looked an imposing prince indeed.

"Why dost thou not come in?" he shouted. "The cool water always feels refreshing."

"I am sure thou art right; I can see thou art enjoying it, and it looks inviting," Sita agreed, "but I do not know how to swim."

"That is no problem at all; it will be easy to teach thee."

"My sari will get wet," Sita objected. She wondered how she could explain a wet sari when she had clearly not been washing clothes.

"Take it off," the tiger suggested. "There is no law in the jungle that says thou must wear clothes. Jungle people can wear clothes or not, just as they choose."

"Really?" Sita asked. "Dost thou, then, have that choice?"

"Regretfully, no. I am condemned to always wear a fur coat. Would that I could abandon it at will, although I must admit I am very attached to it."

Sita laughed and the tiger looked puzzled. "I will explain why later," she said quickly. "The word *attached* is one that has two meanings."

The tiger continued. "Snakes, for example, shed their skins. And birds often lose many of their feathers; sometimes they cannot fly until their new feathers grow in. But thou art fortunate. Whether to wear clothes or not is thy choice."

The whole scene seemed strange and fantastical to Sita—the moonlit glade, the deserted palace (because surely that was what it was), the playful Prince of Tigers (she had never seen him in this mood before), and now his suggestion to disrobe. She must be dreaming, and she would wake at any moment to find this lovely dream gone forever. She unwound her sari and removed her choli, folded them carefully, and stepped into the shallow end of the pool.

CHAPTER

7

The Prince of Tigers was correct—swimming was easy to learn. She enjoyed the new experience immensely. They frolicked in the pool for a long time. He ducked her under the surface, and she came up sputtering. He sprinted across the shallow end; she grabbed his tail as he went past, and he towed her into the deep end. She crawled onto his back, and he swam in circles until she was dizzy. He lifted her between his paws and tossed her into the air; she splashed him when she hit the water. She was smiling broadly when her mouth suddenly filled with water as the tiger took a wild leap and water spurted in every direction. Sita could not remember ever laughing so much.

At length, both were tired and left the pool. Sita suddenly realized how much time had passed since she had climbed onto the tiger's back; she had already been absent from her home for several hours. Though she was not so worried that she wanted this magical evening to end, she knew she would need to put this fantasy behind her and return to the real world.

"I must get dressed," Sita said. "It must be time to go home now." She suddenly remembered that Mitali had said she would drop by for some bael leaves Sita had promised to give her. *Has she come? How long did she wait? What will she think or say?*

"This is one of my homes," the Prince of Tigers responded. "We will stay here tonight."

"But . . ." Sita began.

"I will lie here on this mossy spot. Thou canst lean against me, and I wilt keep thee warm."

Sita did not argue. She had been tired before the prince appeared; though energized by their games in the pool, she was completely exhausted now. Sita curled her slight body against the tiger, feeling his breathing as she leaned against his side; she heard his gravelly chuffle. The moss was thick and velvety, and she quickly drifted off to sleep, forgetting about her clothes that still lay folded at the edge of the pool.

※

When Sita woke up in the morning, the clearing was filled with sunbeams, making the day appear bright and hopeful. The deep-orange *choola* flowers glowed in the early-morning sun, the grass was a brilliant green, and the bamboo leaves shivered in the slight breeze; even the gray stone of the ruins seemed less dull and dusty than it had the evening before. Sita put on her choli and was just knotting the sari around her when the tiger pushed his head out of the bushes and smiled at her. "We need to talk together, thou and I," he said.

"We talk together all the time. I am sad when two days go by without the sound of thy voice."

"That is precisely what I want to talk about. I want thee to leave thy hut, move into the jungle, and live with me. Then we could always hear each other's voices, always be close to one another—could rejoice that although we are of two different races, we understand one another and are happiest when we are together."

"Dear Prince of Tigers, I also love thee," Sita began.

The tiger looked a little confused. "What is this love you mention?

This is the first time I have heard the word, so it means nothing to me. It seems as though it must be important, so why have we not discussed it? What is love and what does it mean?"

"It is merely another way of speaking about what you have just said to me. When two people want to always be together, to talk together, to play together, to breathe the same air, to have the other's voice be the first thing they hear in the morning and the last thing they hear at night . . . that is love."

"Never have we talked of this love in our previous conversations," the tiger said, "so I did not know what it is. Nevertheless, it sounds like a good thing to me and describes what I want our future to be. If that is what love is, then I must love thee. And if thou love me also, what is to hinder us from living as one?"

"Only Kartik," said Sita.

CHAPTER

8

Sita had not thought about Kartik for a long time, but thinking of a future with the tiger brought him to the forefront of her mind. Although he was Sita's oldest friend, Kartik had neglected her during the very time she would have been grateful for some understanding and support after Bhima's death. When Kartik and Sita were young children, they often played together. Their mothers had been friends, and after Runa's death, Bhima had continued the friendly contact between the two families. As the children grew older, however, Kartik spent his time with boys like himself who hoped to earn a few rupees by chasing monkeys away from the crops but who actually spent most of their time mock fighting with each other and bragging about their bravery.

Now Kartik considered himself a young man who was far superior to any girl of the village, and Sita had actually not seen him for some time. The complication for Sita was two-fold. Kartik was her old playmate and the male individual in the village to whom she felt the most closely tied because of their childhood friendship. More important than this, however, was the fact that their mothers had been friends. There had been some talk between the two women, when both were pregnant, of the possibility of their children marrying if one woman bore a son and the other produced a daughter. Nothing had come of this because of Runa's death so shortly after Sita's birth; nevertheless, it was commonly known, and there had been many jokes in the village over the years about the children whose destinies had been decided before they were born. Sita did not know if the talk between the women had been only casual or if a definite agreement had been made. Kartik's mother had also died early (from typhoid), and Bhima never addressed the issue with her niece.

When Sita arrived back at her hut after the Prince of Tigers suggested they live together, she was surprised to find Kartik in her yard, lounging on a charpoy under the mango tree. It had been nearly a year since she had seen him alone. This was partly because he was working for a man in the next village, but it was largely because Kartik had a disdainful attitude towards everything related to his background and boyhood and preferred to be at the heels of his employer, doing anything he could to advance himself favorably in the man's eyes.

"What is this I hear?" Kartik demanded. "You have not moved into the village, even though you have been ordered to do so."

This was not a good beginning, and Sita's look of welcome changed immediately to an expression that could only be described as mulish. "It is my business where I live. I cannot see why I should base my actions on what a few people think. They do not have the right to tell me what to do."

"I have the right, as your future husband, to do so. You should do nothing without consulting me. It is for me to decide what you should do, and I will tell you when it should be done."

Sita was extremely taken aback by Kartik's words and haughty air, and in addition to being surprised, she was also angry. Although she had admitted to herself that some complications might be present if indeed actual marriage negotiations had occurred, these were hazy in her mind; furthermore, Kartik had never given her any reason to think he was considering her as a bride.

In point of fact, Kartik had only recently viewed her in this light.

The thought had come into his mind after his employer mentioned that Sita's old aunt had never spent any money, so it was possible she had a hiding place for the coins she had earned through her medical advice and herbal remedies—and only Sita might know where the coins were hidden. Therefore, he had a much more tangible motive for seeking her hand than either memory or affection would dictate.

Sita had planned to ask Kartik if he was aware of actual marriage negotiations between their mothers. But he was not referring to anything like this; he was arrogantly announcing himself as her future husband and clearly expected her to obey his stated desire without his providing any explanations.

"We are not affianced," Sita answered. "Therefore, you cannot tell me what to do. I do not accept your authority over me."

"I also hear that you are behaving improperly, walking into the jungle by yourself at all hours. A tiger has been seen near your hut on many occasions. Whether this tiger is an animal, a man in disguise, or an evil spirit, you will take care to stay away from him. If you do not, I will beat you and kill him." Kartik was carrying a stick, and carried away by his own dramatic rhetoric, he raised it threateningly.

"You must leave now!" Sita did not flinch from the expected blow. "If you wish to live, leave now. But be assured of this: I will not obey you, and I will never marry you."

Kartik dared not mention a probable hoard of coins, but he thought that Sita might still be malleable if he appealed to her acquired knowledge of her mother's wishes. Perhaps she would see their union as a way to honor her mother. "Both our mothers . . ." he began.

". . . are long dead." Sita finished Kartik's sentence for him. "I do not know whether their talk was idle fancy or a way to commemorate their friendship. But I do know this. My mother would not want me to marry someone whom I do not like, and certainly she would not wish me to marry someone who threatens to beat me."

Sita had not meant her discussion with Kartik to become so

confrontational; nevertheless, as a result of this meeting, she felt freed from the possibility of becoming the wife of such an arrogant, and perhaps even violent, man. She did not even care to consider what Kartik's feelings would be if she rejected him as a possible husband. They might have waded in the stream together and made mud chapattis in the yard, but the small children and friends who had been Kartik and Sita had grown up to be very different people. He wanted nothing from her (she was unaware, of course, of the "buried coins" theory) besides obedience to his will; she wanted to make her own decisions, without being countermanded by someone who felt superior to her in every way. Kartik would no longer be an emotional obstacle in her mind when she thought about living in the jungle and the kind of relationship she and the Prince of Tigers might have. Any feelings, even friendly or sisterly ones (although those only consisted of memories and what-ifs), had vanished. Their relationship was over.

For Kartik, however, it was not over. It had been years since he and Sita were friendly, but now that Sita had refused to consider him as a husband, it suddenly seemed very important that she become his wife. He had a job conveying his master's *uple* and sheaves of grain to the area market and selling them. Sita could cut and tie up the sheaves and help dry the uple, thus increasing the amount that he would be paid. And then there was—or might be—the pot of coins. If Sita would only marry him, he could dig up every square inch of the hut floor and the garden Sita cultivated around the hut. But first, Kartik must do something amazing that would force Sita to see him as a man who was capable of great things. Even he could see that threatening to beat Sita had been the wrong approach. Beatings could wait until after they were married.

Kartik turned over in his mind the various acts that would make Sita respect him. He could kill a wild pig and hold a feast for the village. He could cut down a teak tree and make a fine house. Or he could kill the tiger. This might possibly save Sita's life. He did not really believe that the reported tiger was a man in disguise or an evil spirit. No, it must be a real-life baagh that the villagers had seen. And if a tiger was prowling around near Sita's hut at the edge of the jungle, it was only a matter of time before it killed her, a defenseless woman. The act of killing such a large and dangerous beast would certainly make everyone, including Sita, recognize that he was a man to be respected, even admired.

So Kartik took his charpoy, *bhaala*, and laathi into the jungle, not far from Sita's hut. He climbed a tree, settled the charpoy in its branches as a machan, and waited. For three days he did not see a tiger at all; he also realized he had not brought enough food for an extended stay. He climbed down and went back to the village for more food. Then he moved the charpoy to another tree and waited some more. Once, he saw the tip of a tiger's tail vanishing behind a tree; he threw his bhaala, but even if his throw had been accurate, it would have fallen short. On another day, when he awoke after dozing off, he became aware that a tiger was sitting near the tree, watching him.

Kartik knew nothing of the Prince of Tigers, but he could see that this was an exceptionally large and handsome male. It also seemed to Kartik that the tiger wore a mocking smile. The tiger's expression filled Kartik with a sudden, unreasoning anger. *If only I had a gun.*

CHAPTER

9

In his obsession with hunting down and killing the tiger, it did not occur to Kartik that checking Sita's hut might bring him closer to his quarry. He imagined that when he paid his next visit to Sita, he would be dragging a tiger skin. She would be amazed at his strength and power and would easily, perhaps even enthusiastically, agree to become his wife.

Sita had other plans. While Kartik sat in a tree, dreaming of becoming a hero, she communicated her decision to the Prince of Tigers when he came to her hut.

"As we love each other (and the complication I mentioned will no longer deter me), I will be thy wife and thou shalt be my husband . . . that is, if thou art still of the same mind."

"We are agreed then," the tiger said. "However, there is something I should tell thee. Thy foolish suitor hath determined to kill me, which means that sooner or later I will have to kill him. Dost thou want to watch?"

"I do not want you to kill him at all—and I certainly do *not* want to watch," Sita said in a definite manner. "Although I want to be always at thy side wherever thou art, can we not move deeper into the jungle for at least a time, until Kartik abandons his foolish plan? I am also loath to leave the only home I have ever known. Cannot we spend some of our days and nights here and some in the jungle?"

"I do not know whether the village will allow me to live in such close proximity to them," the tiger said, running possible scenarios through his mind. "We will explore this option, however. I do not wish thee to be unhappy, which thou might be if taken away from all thou hast held dear—until thou met thy lord and husband, of course."

His grin when he said the last words showed that this statement was to make fun of Kartik and that young man's belief in his own superiority. "But for a little while, let us confine ourselves to the jungle. If thou art known to be no longer in residence, perhaps the village will stop gossiping about thee, and thy suitor will stop hunting me. I know that Kartik does not feel at ease in the jungle by the way he stands and moves and how he does not listen to the sounds that are all around him. As his quest can only take place in the jungle, perhaps he will tire of it and give it up quickly. Perhaps he will even find another woman to marry."

"Your plan is good, O Prince of Tigers," Sita said. (She was always a little surprised at how analytical the tiger was.) "Let us then go into the jungle together, as we shall be always. We can return to my hut from time to time, but with thee in the jungle is where I desire most to be."

"It is good to know," said the tiger, "that I wilt be thine and thou shalt be mine forever."

"It is good. Forever," echoed Sita. "Let us then go."

※

Both Sita and the Prince of Tigers were wrong about Kartik; he did not give up his quest. He did not see the tiger again, but Sita was not to be found in her hut either. As she was absent, Kartik felt free to dig a little in her garden (because the ground was softer there), and around the roots of the mango tree (because he thought the earth between the roots looked disturbed). All he discovered in the garden were some suran Sita had neglected to dig up, while among the mango roots he found a small *chuha* that, resenting his home being destroyed by this careless or malicious giant, chittered angrily at the intruder. Kartik was afraid to search further; he did not know how he would explain his sudden urge to dig up the ground surrounding Sita's hut if someone should walk by and notice his activities. So he went to the village, reporting that Sita was missing and that she had likely been killed by the same tiger several people of the village had seen prowling around the general vicinity of Sita's hut.

"The poor, poor girl, to come to an end like this," someone said.

Another voice chimed in, "I told her not to stay in her aunt's hut. This is what happens when a young girl disobeys her elders."

"I knew she would come to a bad end, although this was not the end I had foreseen," said an old woman who always thought the worst about everyone.

"I offered her lodging if she would stay with me," the headman's wife said.

A villager standing at the back of the group said something derisive in an undertone, and several others snickered, because the headman's wife never volunteered to help anyone unless she was paid handsomely—whether in coins or menial labor.

"Who said that?" the woman rasped out, but all had straight faces by then, and no one answered.

Kartik offered a strong argument for the village's active involvement in this tragic situation. "We cannot assume that just because the tiger has killed and eaten Sita, he will go away. No, he will have marked this village as a place that he can safely raid, whether his victims are people or goats. We should all band together and hunt him until he is killed or has conclusively left the area."

"What good will it do to hunt the tiger with laathis?" asked an older man.

"We need a gun," shouted two or three together.

Kartik was glad that the village had come to this conclusion before he had to introduce the word himself. Although he would never speak of it to anyone, he remembered how frightened he had felt, crouched on his makeshift machan, when the tiger was sitting below him and smiling. He had wondered if the tiger could leap up to his perch.

But he did not have a gun. Nobody in the village had a gun.

"I know a man in the next village who has a gun," Kartik offered cautiously. "Would you like me to speak to him?"

And so, it was agreed. Kartik would be responsible for obtaining a gun with which to hunt the tiger, and the village men would join in the hunt.

In fact, the man in the next village who owned the gun was Kartik's former employer. Kartik had lost his position when he became obsessed by the idea of killing the tiger and started ignoring his duties; he felt strongly that the tiger was to blame for the change in his prospects. He also thought that a tiger skin on one side of the scales was more than equal to loaning a gun on the other. If they made the trade, Kartik doubtless would be restored to the position he had once held and clearly still deserved. A tiger hunt that ended successfully—in other words, with a dead tiger—would make everything right again.

Kartik visualized the scene, gloating over the details. He saw himself standing proudly with the dead tiger stretched on the ground in front of him. He wondered how long the tiger would measure from the end of its nose to the tip of its tail. It was by far the biggest tiger he had ever seen, perhaps the biggest one seen in the entire region. What a trophy it would be!

It was time to stop dreaming and time to act. Kartik left the village, walking down the dusty path towards the field where he knew he would find his former employer working. He turned over a number of approaches in his mind, trying to decide which argument would be most likely to secure the cooperation of the man who owned the gun, the man who could make Kartik's future the happy and successful one he envisioned. It was too bad the man did not have a daughter.

CHAPTER

10

"**M**y little wife," the Prince of Tigers said one sunny afternoon as the two lazed by a stream. "I am going to have to break my promise to thee."

The day seemed suddenly darker. Did the tiger mean he was going to leave her? After months of companionship, conversation, sharing, closeness, laughing, and playing, Sita hardly knew how the days would pass without the Prince of Tigers. They would indeed pass, but they were certain to be dark, miserable days. "My lord," she choked out, "have I offended thee in some way?"

The tiger looked surprised and puzzled. (It was always amazing to Sita how he could indicate his emotions by the slightest muscle movements—turning his ears slightly or shifting his whiskers almost imperceptibly, for example.)

"Thou has not offended me, but another has. I fear that I will be forced to kill thy old suitor after all. I thought he was merely impetuous, but he has not learned wisdom and has become even more focused on his quest."

"What has Kartik done?" Sita demanded. Given her last interchange with the friend of her youth, who had most surprisingly become an unpleasant, overbearing individual, she found she could believe anything of him.

"Art thou not aware that he has tried to kill me multiple times? He has stalked me through the jungle; he has sat up high in a tree, hoping to spear me unawares; he has set out poisoned bait; and he has dug a pit holding wicked, sharpened stakes pointing upwards, across one of my favorite hunting trails."

"My husband, thou hast not shared all this with me."

"Because thou cared for him once, I sought to shield thee from his blackhearted deeds. But he has gone too far. He has sought to bring a man with a gun to the village. The village men are to act as beaters, forcing me in the direction they choose where the man with a gun will be waiting. Dost thou think I am justified in bringing about his death?"

Although saddened on one level, Sita did not waver a moment. "Thou art justified, my lord," she said. "He has called down death upon himself, by seeking the death of the Prince of Tigers—not once in anger, but many times, with much cunning and with many deadly weapons. Also, he has made many people *co-conspirators* in this."

"I do not know the word co-conspirators," the tiger said thoughtfully, "but do not concern thyself further. Kartik will not bother us again."

✗o

The man with the gun was coming to the village as soon as he returned from his weekly visit to the area market. In a few days the tiger would be no more. In the meantime, Kartik decided to make one last effort to kill the tiger on his own. Why should he share the glory unless it was necessary to do so?

He wondered why he had come to view the tiger as a rival. An amusing thought: more correctly, the tiger was an obstacle that had to be overcome—well, removed. Then, Kartik could obtain his desired end: marriage to and ownership of Sita (which included, of course, anything that might be in her possession)—if by some miracle Sita was alive.

So, he would make one more solitary attempt. What should he try this time? Digging a pit had already taken a lot of time and effort, and accomplished nothing. Sitting in a tree was easy, but he had wasted many an hour trying that already with no result. It would have to be poison again. The tiger had ignored the bait before, but perhaps the bait itself was not attractive. Kartik had killed a rooster that had wandered too far from its owner's yard. It was old and thin and undoubtedly stringy. Or perhaps the tiger preferred to eat what he had killed himself. But even a tiger had to drink, and Kartik found a spot that he thought might work.

Two large streams came together in a pool that ended in a waterfall. The streams ran so swiftly that the waterfall shot out over the stone lip and leaped and foamed and sprayed all the way down to the rocks at the bottom. At one side of the pool, a small channel of the foaming water led to a wide bowl where the water was placid. Kartik knew that jungle animals came there to drink because a trail led directly to the edge of the bowl, where it stopped. If he was fortunate, the tiger would come and drink there . . . and die there. Perhaps some other animals would come, drink, and die too, but Kartik could not help that. It was nothing to him.

When he came to the pool above the waterfall, Kartik thought once again, as he had when he discovered it, that it was a pretty spot. The trees overhung the pool, the streams murmured more softly than the waterfall, and the bowl of water was so still that it was like a mirror. Kartik knelt and leaned forward to pour the poison into the water. He was struck by how clearly his face was reflected. He had a handsome one and could not understand why his masculine beauty held no appeal for Sita. It would be different when he was a hero.

He poured the poison into the water and paused to examine his features once again. Then, suddenly, he was not alone in the mirror of the pool. A great tiger was looming over him. Was it the tiger he had been stalking? In the reflection, it was hard to tell, and he could not turn around; he was frozen in his awkward position. Like lightning, two very different but parallel thoughts rushed into his brain: he had never discovered where the coins were hidden, and he should have waited for the man with the gun.

CHAPTER

11

That night, when the Prince of Tigers came, quite late, Sita was waiting quietly for him. "And is all accomplished, my husband?" she asked, softly.

The tiger looked sad. "This is the first time I have killed for a reason other than hunger," he explained. "I would have had my reign as Prince of Tigers, the ruler of the jungle, unmarked by this kind of killing."

"Kartik forced this situation upon thee," Sita said softly as she rubbed the tiger's shoulders. "I, of all people, know thou hast always, when possible, chosen peace."

"*Always* may be too strong a word. As a growing cub and a young, male tiger, I thought no more of peace than anyone else. It was only when I reached my prime that I began to wonder about the constant warfare between man and beast and whether understanding of each other could be achieved."

"What happened tonight?"

"I was coming to the small pool above the waterfall," the tiger said, "when I smelled him. He was kneeling at the edge of the pool and pouring poison into the water. He was looking into the water as he watched the poison swirling and saw my reflection for just a moment before my paw smote him with great force. He fell forward into the water, and I gave the body a push so that it went over the waterfall. I watched as it spun down and down, but I did not see it resurface at the bottom."

"I share thy sadness, my husband," Sita murmured, as she continued to knead his mighty muscles, "but it is for the best. Kartik will no longer seek thy life. We can only hope that none other in the village takes up his bloody quest."

Sita's hope was, however, not fulfilled. The villagers were at first concerned about Kartik's absence and then, after his body was found a short distance below the waterfall, outraged by his death. The tiger had not used his claws when he struck the mighty blow; every mark on the body could have been made as Kartik slipped over the lip of the waterfall and was battered by rocks during his long descent. Nevertheless, many assumptions were made, and the few clucking voices were soon augmented by others as the village tried to make sense of Kartik's death.

Everyone knew that Kartik had been tracking a great tiger—not a few of the men had helped him in various stages of this project—and they slowly came to believe that Kartik must had been killed by the very same tiger he had sought to slay. They had thought of Kartik as a young man who was smart and would doubtless be a success in life. An example of this was how he had gone to another village, when there was no work available in their own, and quite quickly found a good job—they were unaware that his employer had dismissed him because he had not been a steady worker. At some point, superstition became part of the puzzle. Perhaps the tiger Kartik had been tracking had possessed special powers, like in some of the old myths, and he had used these powers against the man who had shown enmity towards him. Furthermore, many believed that Sita must carry part of the responsibility for Kartik's death because she had been as unwilling to follow his directives as she had theirs.

The villagers were both right and wrong in their assumptions. They convinced themselves that Sita had indeed been killed by the tiger; from their point of view, Kartik was merely attempting to avenge her death. Sita was, of course, alive and had nothing directly to do with Kartik's death, yet she had released the tiger from his promise not to harm her old playfellow. Even had the villagers possessed that information, they would neither have known nor understood the forbearance of the tiger who had survived several murderous attempts by Kartik before he decided that enough was enough . . . and took lethal action against his adversary.

No, the village blamed Sita because if she had listened to reason, moved into the village, and married (all things that an obedient girl of the village would have done), Kartik would have had a focus; then he would not have been so irresponsible. He would not have had the time and energy to attempt the quest that ultimately took his life. It was fortunate for his posthumous reputation that he had never provided a complete explanation about why he was so anxious to kill this particular tiger—that jealousy had figured into his state of mind nearly as much as the fact that his need for control had been thwarted by Sita's obstinate refusal of his suit, and that if he could only have found the mythical hoard belonging to Sita's aunt, he would have been a rich man.

So the village was actively unfriendly to Sita when she appeared some time later and they learned that she was not dead after all, merely absent on a visit to relatives previously unknown to the village. They passed her without speaking. When she brought some herbs to the local merchant, he refused to buy them and did not meet her eyes as he told her that he already had more than he could possibly use or sell. This attitude concerned Sita, who knew that Mudit was not overstocked and was only taking this position out of a wish to punish her for Kartik's death.

More worrying was that five or six men had decided to avenge that death. By now, they were certain that the tiger was to blame; therefore, they must take action against him. They thought of various ways to kill the tiger (the same options Kartik had previously explored), but they were no more successful in their goal than he had been. It was an unfortunate but undeniable fact that Kartik's demise did not bring Sita and the Prince of Tigers the peace and security they craved and had expected.

CHAPTER

12

When Sita and the Prince of Tigers decided to live together, they had not totally considered the practicalities of their situation. Though Sita had learned some tiger talk from Bhima when she was a child, the first issue was that of communication. She had looked on tiger talk as a game, a way she and her aunt could talk to each other with no one else understanding them. But Bhima discouraged Sita from playing this game; it only made the village more suspicious of the woman who chose to live apart, and who appeared to be teaching her niece to exhibit the same independent spirit. So she had not taught Sita enough! Every day, Sita wished that Bhima had had the time and energy to teach her more, although she realized that Bhima must have been exhausted, working to support the two of them by herself.

But now Sita wondered if she was to blame. Could she have learned more if she had paid more attention to her aunt, instead of climbing the mango tree to look at a bird's nest or chasing her favorite butterfly (the black-and-white-and-crimson one) that fluttered among the white-and-yellow flowers of the *maniphal* tree?

Sita had learned rapidly under the tutelage of the tiger. He also confirmed something her aunt once said—that although tiger talk was more formal and structured, it was quite close to the jungle language common to all jungle creatures. She did not need to worry about becoming fluent in the common tongue; she already had some knowledge that, combined with tiger talk, meant she would be able to communicate, to a certain extent, with all the jungle creatures.

Nevertheless, Sita desired to speak correctly, no matter whom she was addressing. She felt pride when she and the tiger were walking down a trail and saw a *siyaar* approaching them. It did not run away, but it left the trail and edged around them, keeping its eyes fixed on the tiger.

"Greetings, my friend," Sita said. "Is it a good day for thee?"

The siyaar gave her a slanting glance. "Well enough, I suppose, for sambars and chitals as long as the Prince of Tigers is not hunting." He flirted his tail and disappeared into the bushes.

The tiger looked quizzical. "I am not certain why thou wouldst go out of thy way to be friendly to Tabaqui, the siyaar. Siyaars can be amusing, but they are also cunning and deceitful."

"I am practicing my new vocabulary," Sita replied.

"I understand that," the tiger said, "and it is a good idea, but thou shouldst probably leave it at that. Siyaars do not make good friends."

Because they spent so much time together, talked so much, and Sita wanted to learn, she learned quickly. The tiger, on the other hand, had some trouble making the sounds that comprised human speech. He understood it well but spoke slowly and carefully in his efforts to speak correctly. Sita had no trouble understanding him, but other humans might find it more difficult. Sometimes, in conversation, they switched from one language to the other, although their verbal communications with each other tended to be largely conducted in tiger talk.

A more serious problem was that of food. The tiger was a meat eater, a predator, and he only ate meat of animals he had slain himself. Sita, on the other hand, was essentially a vegetarian. She mostly ate what she grew in her garden or edible plants she found in the jungle. When the Prince of Tigers suggested that she witness a kill, he was acting as a male who wishes to demonstrate his strength and skills to impress his mate. Sita agreed to view a killing because he asked her to, but after she complied that once, she vowed never to repeat the experience.

Sita sat high in a tree that stretched its limbs out over a game trail; the tiger was almost hidden from her, lying to the side among some clustering ferns. He was as silent as the mossy stones scattered in the clearing. His breathing was slow and even; his tail did not twitch. From the branch Sita had selected, she had a good view of the trail and of the animals that were using it. A *nevala* ran by, constantly darting this way and that as it investigated a hole in the ground and a rotting log. A troop of langurs swung silently through the trees. Sita sat so quietly that they did not notice her; their silence indicated that they had not seen the tiger either. Then she spotted a sambar walking down the trail, his antlered head held proudly, his nose twitching, his eyes darting in every direction. A streak of flame like a jungle fire suddenly enveloped the sambar, who bellowed once, kicked a few times, and then lay still.

The Prince of Tigers raised his head, jaws dripping with the sambar's blood, and called to Sita. "Come down and eat with me, wife. See, I have provided a meal for thee."

Sita was almost frozen with horror, but she followed the branch back to the trunk and worked her way down to the ground. She stood watching as the tiger tore at the carcass.

"What is wrong with thee? Art thou not hungry?"

"I have rarely eaten flesh, and it has always been cooked."

"Then we will take some home and cook it for thee."

"I would like to go home now," said Sita.

"I will bring thee some meat to cook later," the tiger said as he returned to his meal.

Sita slowly walked back to her hut, where they were staying for a few days. She was revolted by what she had seen. She found it profoundly disturbing to watch the life drain out of a beautiful animal.

Only moments before, it had been in the prime of its life, healthy and vigorous; next came sudden panic, followed by helplessness, and finally the dulling of its eyes that signified the end. At the same time, she realized that her husband was acting in a way that was perfectly natural (and indeed necessary) to him.

As he had promised, the tiger brought home a large piece of meat for Sita to cook. She roasted it over a fire, but she did not like it and neither did he. He tasted her dal and suran and did not like them either. Food was something they learned to compromise on—they ate separately. He killed when he needed to eat, and he ate where and when the kill happened. Sita did not accompany him or eat his food. She prepared her own food and ate when she was hungry.

Home was also a concept that had different meanings to the two, and at first, they operated rather like nomads. Some nights they slept at Sita's hut, the tiger only arriving after dark so as not to be discovered and alarm the village. Sometimes they slept at the roofless, gray stone building by the pool in the jungle. And sometimes, they curled up together in a clump of bamboo, under a bush or tree with low branches, or wherever they happened to be in the jungle. The variety of these sleeping arrangements had some appeal, although Sita disliked lying outside in the rain because sleep seemed especially long in coming, while the tiger felt confined and uneasy in the small space that Sita's hut offered. Even Sita saw the one-room hut as stifling and cramped when it contained the tiger (who tended to stretch in all directions) as well as herself.

"I know thou hast a feeling for this home of thy youth," the Prince of Tigers murmured to Sita one spring night. "But it does not seem to be a friendly place to thee now. Furthermore, I doubt that I will ever feel truly at home so close to where people continue to plot against me."

"You are right, my husband; my feelings for the village have undergone a great change since my former friends have directed their hatred against thee. I can no longer feel that I belong to them as I once belonged, even though I have always lived apart. Now I belong to thee and only to thee." The tiger smiled and pulled Sita closer with a big paw.

"However," Sita continued, "I need a place that is not wide open to wind and rain; I do not feel comfortable without a roof over my head. I do not totally understand this need myself, and I do not expect you to, but it is a part of being human that I do not believe I can leave behind."

"Thou dost not have to, my Sita. The answer to this problem is obvious. We should move permanently to a location that lies in a somewhat different direction, a little more northeast than the pool you know. In that spot lies an entire city, not just the one building where we have stayed from time to time. It is a deserted city. I have never investigated it, but there are many habitations to choose from. Surely, we can find a dwelling there that suits us both, as well as puts us beyond the reach of those who would do us harm."

Sita nodded sleepily. "Thou hast solved the problem, O my . . ." she murmured.

13

Early the next morning, before anyone stirred in the village, Sita and the Prince of Tigers headed down the trail that led to the deserted city. Sita had wound her extra sari around her and carried some pans and kettles. The tiger had offered to carry them on his back, but Sita felt that conveying them herself, all the way from her hut to the deserted city, needed to be done—that this act was somehow symbolic of her shift of allegiance from the village to the Tiger.

Though the locations were not markedly different in distance from Sita's hut, it took much longer for the small procession of two to reach the city than it had taken to arrive at the pool when Sita rode on the back of the tiger on her first visit there. Furthermore, on that occasion both of them had been filled with the joy of freedom and being newly in love; now a feeling more closely akin to defeat and rejection colored their move. Sita felt that her village had turned its back on her, and the tiger knew they had done so because of him. Even if the villagers did not know about the Prince of Tigers specifically, they knew that Sita was different. Yes, she had been independent and recalcitrant and had insisted on having her own way when they urged her to move into the village, but now she truly seemed apart from those who had been her people. They did not know how to deal with this change except by rejecting her as they felt she had rejected them. When she first disappeared, they had mourned her to a certain extent, but that turned to active resentment when she returned whole and healthy, while Kartik, a son of the village, was dead.

When Sita and the Prince of Tigers arrived at the deserted city, they worked on selecting the dwelling that would be their home. Many of the buildings were habitable—so many, in fact, that it was two or three weeks before they made their decision. First, they surveyed the expanse of stone buildings, many of them half ruined, that crouched and tumbled here and there, partially covered by vines that played about the openings and trailed down the steps. Then they explored more thoroughly an acre or so of rooms and houses and palaces that one or both deemed candidates for their new home. Sita rejected one possibility because there was no roof, while the tiger would not hear of calling any place "home" that he felt was too small and cramped for the Prince of Tigers. They would stay in one place for a couple of days, then test another. It was fun at first, but before long, both wanted to feel more settled.

What they settled for was a palace at the edge of the city with two levels aboveground and one below. The tiger was pleased to find a pool near the palace, larger than the one he and Sita had long enjoyed. This pool was fed from a nearby river, and the water made pleasant gurgling sounds as it flowed in and out. Like most of the buildings in the deserted city, the palace was made of stone, but it was larger and in better repair than many of the others. Images of animals and people and what surely must be gods were carved into the stone, although some of the carvings had partially worn away over the ages. Both the upper and lower floor had wide stone verandahs looking out over the jungle. All the rooms were spacious and opened to others, so the tiger did not feel too enclosed. Sita marked one room for sleeping and another for other activities. Cooking would take place in yet another area so that the smell would not be too disagreeable. The stone floor and walls were colder than her old hut, and she wished she had rugs to brighten and warm these new living quarters. All the floors were littered with dry leaves and dust that had blown into the palace over the years, and Sita was anxious to begin the massive cleaning job awaiting her.

It was not long before the palace seemed like home to her in spite of its size and many rooms. She swept the floors vigorously with a broom made of twigs and long grass that she tied together with vines, humming as the dust flew. Sita took her kettles to the pool, brought them back filled with water, and scrubbed the stone floors as well, washing away the dirt that had resisted the broom. She explored nearby dwellings to see if they contained any objects she could use, and found various items of brass and pottery (vases, bowls, lamps, and the like), along with other items (knives and one knife-like object so bulky and long that Sita decided it must be a sword).

The prince found, in the palace itself, some rugs that had been rolled tightly and stored where they had been untouched by rain. Damp had not improved them, but Sita was happy to discover that they were mostly intact. Moving them was not easy. Sita was little, and the tiger was not built to carry anything too large to fit in his jaws; nevertheless, they managed the task with a lot of pushing, dragging, heaving, and grunting. Sita was well pleased with the effect when they were spread out, and the tiger rolled on them contentedly.

The tiger cautioned Sita against searching the cellar rooms of the palace.

"Thou might meet a *naga* in the dark," he said solemnly.

"Why there more than any other place?"

"Of course they can be found anywhere, but tales have always been told of how nagas suddenly appear in old temples and palaces (particularly underground), and then seek to defend territory they have come to believe is theirs alone."

"My husband, I will be careful. I will not go there except in thy company."

"It is well, my Sita."

ℓσ

Sita and the Prince of Tigers were well pleased with their new home. They decided to call it the Ananta Palace because it had been waiting quietly for them in the jungle—from their point of view—forever, since time began. And surely their happiness would last forever. They knew they would live together happily in the Ananta Palace for the rest of their lives, at least until Sita's hair turned gray and the Prince of Tiger's joints stiffened so that he moved more slowly and deliberately. But that time was far in the future. Now, Sita purred often; she greeted the prince when he came home from hunting with a choola flower in her shining, black hair.

"Thou art turning orange like me," the tiger teased. "Soon thou wilt be a tiger too."

They often sat together on the balcony, admiring the sunset and watching the *camagadaras* boiling out of caves and hollow trees and wheeling about in their pursuit of insects.

"I feel completely at peace in moments like this, but it takes thy presence to make it so. I cannot imagine having this happiness without thee," the tiger said. The air was turning cool, and a curtain of rain swept across the jungle; they watched its progress and knew the downpour would soon approach the palace.

"I, too, am happy," Sita responded, "and I know full well that my happiness would not be complete if we were not together. Every minute apart seems wasted. I know that I exaggerate, but when thou art absent, I long for thy return."

Because of their different eating habits, the two spent some time apart, but much more of their time was spent together, investigating the deserted city, wandering through the jungle, and exploring in different directions. Sometimes Sita rode on the tiger's back, but often she walked beside him with her arm thrown across his shoulders or around his neck. She called him "my husband" or, if she was being formal, "my lord." Sometimes she used his title, "Prince of Tigers." He usually called her "my Sita" or "my wife," although occasionally he referred to her as "my most precious pearl." As it did not seem that the tiger had any knowledge of or interest in gems and precious stones, Sita asked him where he had acquired this phrase and how he knew when it should be used. He replied that when he was attempting to learn about humans, he had once heard a man address a woman with these words and they had made the woman very happy. He did not think, however, that the love this man and woman apparently had for each other exceeded the feelings he and Sita shared.

They were very happy.

CHAPTER

14

Sita had enjoyed the process of setting up her new home very much. It seemed extremely luxurious to her. In size and original workmanship, this was the case; however, age and neglect had caused much deterioration. Furthermore, many of the things she had found to furnish the rooms with, although usable, were hardly in good condition. The metal utensils were dented, the pottery was chipped, and the rugs were frayed and worn, even mildewed in places. But it was all beautiful to Sita. Her previous belongings had been minimal and of the very cheapest quality. Yes, the Ananta Palace was indeed a palace to her.

Getting to know other jungle dwellers was interesting, and sometimes rewarding. Sita enjoyed standing or sitting on the balcony, either looking directly into the trees where birds were hopping about and langurs playing (or brawling) or watching animals going about their business on the ground below. She particularly enjoyed watching the *val kuruvi* as he darted among the trees, pursuing and capturing insects. At first, she merely watched as he fluttered and swooped; then she became entranced by his beauty—his rufous back and tail, his blue-black crested head, and the bright-blue rings around his eyes. At last, she tried to speak to him, but the conversation was brief.

"How are you today?"

"Busy, of course. I must feed my nestlings." And the bird flew off.

She could admire the beauty of the val kuruvi, but it was obvious that the bird thought conversation with her was a waste of his time.

Probably the friendliest jungle dweller was also a bird. Mor, the peacock, along with his harem of wives, was usually somewhere about the clearing or perching in nearby trees, if not on the verandah itself. He displayed curiosity about many aspects of life that most animals either ignored or avoided.

"Why do you live here instead of the village?"

"Because I like it better."

"Humans like to live closely packed together like fish at spawning time. Are you sure you are a human? Perhaps you are some kind of spirit who appears in human form."

Sita enjoyed these conversations. She had never talked about this sort of thing in the village, not even with Anila and Mitali. Their conversations were always about their daily tasks, food, their futures as wives, etc. Sita had never had a conversation about life and values (with anyone except Bhima) until she met the tiger. The two of them had shared many of those conversations, but they were few and far between lately; anyway, it was hot, so she enjoyed sitting lazily in the shade and talking with Mor, who perched with a favorite wife on the low wall edging the balcony.

Sita had been feeling more tired than usual, so when the peacocks flew away, she lay back, turned her face up so she could feel the breeze on her cheeks, and thought how unpleasant life was when she and the prince disagreed.

Conversations with the Prince of Tigers had not gone well lately because, for the first time, the two were not united in their views; in this particular instance, their values were even opposed. Sita's body had been swelling, and her time was growing near. She would soon give birth, and she had told the tiger that she wanted to return to the village.

"I need to be with women who have knowledge of childbirth," she said. "I would feel easier when I give birth if I have a midwife with me."

But the tiger disagreed. "Thou art of the jungle now," he said. "I have observed that humans make birth far more complicated than it should be. Birth is natural in the jungle."

Sita did not believe the tiger was right in this matter. This was the first time she longed for familiar faces from her childhood home. Sita wanted to be with women she knew, women who had experienced birth themselves, and who would understand and be able to explain what was happening to her. Whether she would go to the village or stay in the jungle was still unresolved when the birth pains began.

Sita was entirely alone when she gave birth to twin boys, but as the tiger had predicted, the process was both natural and relatively easy. She cut the *garbhanaal* herself and cleaned her sons, marveling at their tiny fingers and toes, at the way their heads were shaped, at the lusty, squalling sounds they made. They looked exactly alike, and for a moment, Sita wondered how she would ever be able to tell them apart. Then she saw that the second man-cub to be born had a birthmark on his chest, shaped roughly like a *prashn chinh*; she felt relief that each man-cub would be at least somewhat separate and distinct from the other.

"O Prince of Tigers," Sita said when she heard her husband's soft footsteps at the door, "come look upon these, thy sons."

The tiger looked long upon the two baby boys that Sita had wrapped in lengths of soft cloth cut from her extra sari; she held one baby in the crook of each arm. He touched each baby with a gentle paw. "Are these indeed my sons?" he asked. "I see no vestige of myself in them."

Sita said nothing, but she was rigid with anger; the tiger noted this and was anxious to calm her.

"It was only a joke such as people make, my dear wife, but I can see it was not a fortunate thing to say. It had not occurred to me that thou wouldst not bring forth tigers," he said, almost sadly. "These are more thy sons than mine."

"How canst thou look on them as mine and not thine?" Sita spat. "Who they may look like is of little moment. They are man-cubs; they have the blood of both thee and me. This is what is important, what they *are* like, not what they *look* like."

The conversation was not totally acrimonious, but it was troubling to both parents. They had never spoken in disappointment or anger to each other before, and it forced them to confront differences that were far more fundamental than, for example, the refusal of each to eat the food preferred by the other.

The tiger said he needed to hunt and was gone for several days. Sita knew he had not been truthful with her. He had just returned from hunting; that was why he had not been present when the man-cubs were born. She could not help wondering where he was now and what he was doing. She wondered if he regretted that he had married someone so different from himself. It sounded to her as though he had wanted and expected tiger sons and now was unhappy with the man-cubs because they were not tigers.

Sita wept a little, then straightened her back and nursed her baby boys. "I am a mother now," she said to herself as she crooned to her sons and watched small Ashok and Arun drift from drowsiness into sleep. "I am sorry my husband is disappointed, but that does not change anything. These boys are both children and cubs. He and I must do everything in our power to protect them and take care of them."

She knew already that life would not be easy for the man-cubs. Their divided heritage was certain to cause them difficulties. She hoped that she and the tiger would be able to help them through the difficult times that inevitably lay ahead.

CHAPTER

15

One afternoon when the boys were around a year or so old, Sita heard a loud, hoarse miaowing near the palace. She knew it was not the Prince of Tigers. He would never have made a sound like this—a guttural wail that was squalling, strident, and demanding—no matter the circumstances. Furthermore, he was away, hunting, and the caterwauling coming from the clearing did not sound as though it was made by a male tiger at all. Cautioning the boys to stay inside, Sita went out to see what was happening.

A tigress was pacing restlessly, her tail lashing back and forth. Sita was surprised. No tiger had invaded her husband's territory that she was aware of, certainly not to the extent of appearing at his home. Tigers tend to be solitary. Sita had only seen one or two others, and that was when she and the prince had been exploring well beyond the borders of his territory. This tigress seemed to feel at home as she stopped to sample a leaf and scratch the bark of a tree; she had an exotic look, her coat a paler orange than was customary, and her stripes dark brown instead of black. She would have been beautiful, except for her unpleasant expression. This expression was so constant that Sita imagined the stranger must have been born with a permanent sneer. The tigress ceased pacing and came to a stop when she noticed Sita standing quietly in the doorway.

"I seek the Prince of Tigers," the tigress spat scornfully. "I want nothing from thee, thou puny thing. I refused to believe it when I heard."

"When thou heard what?"

"O, thou canst speak tiger, canst thou?"

"Yes, I can," said Sita gravely. "I do indeed speak tiger, but what is that to thee?" Although she had never seen the tigress before, Sita realized she must be speaking to Shira, a beautiful cat who carried a bad reputation with her, or created one, wherever she went. Shira had moved to a faraway section of the jungle shortly after a rumor emerged that she had eaten of man meat; clearly, she had now returned. Sita could not help thinking that Shira's return was unfortunate, as it was highly unlikely they would ever be friends. She could not picture the two of them sitting on the verandah and discussing jungle news, like how many baby elephants had been born in the southwest herd this year, or whether it was true that many hectares of jungle were to be cleared in a neighboring province because a high-ranking official wanted to build some jheels for shooting.

Shira lowered her head and curled her lip, staring up at Sita as though the object of her inspection had not proved worthy, resulting in contempt. Shira's sneer became more pronounced; it was certainly scornful. It occurred to Sita that perhaps this was the prelude to a physical attack, but she stood still, not even trembling. Shira's attack, however, was of a different nature.

"Perhaps that is why . . ." Shira said contemptuously, paused, and then spoke again, her eyes mere slits. "To speak our language was such an uncommon gift that he must have been impressed. I can think of no other reason why he would consort with thee. Thou hast no beauty; he can only see thee as small and ugly, puny even for a human."

"What dost thou want with my husband?" Sita did not want to tell this menacing tigress that she was alone; she certainly did not want to let her know that she had young and defenseless man-cubs in the palace.

"Why, to father my cubs, of course. For what other reason dost thou think I have come here? None better for that task than the Prince of Tigers."

"The Prince of Tigers is wed to me," Sita began. Shira let her sneer grow into guffaws that made her entire body shake, but they were suddenly drowned out by an earth-shaking roar.

Both Sita and Shira turned to see the Prince of Tigers enter the clearing. He was holding himself very tall and walking slowly with great dignity. To Sita, he had never appeared more princely.

"Leave this place at once," he ordered Shira. "Thou hast no business here."

"Thou didst not always speak so roughly—"

"I am painfully aware of that, to my folly. I was young, but I am different now. I have family ties and responsibilities, and I will have none of thee. Thou art a disgrace to the race of tigers."

Neither Sita nor the tiger had noticed, but Arun, the younger son who was always daring, had crept to the upper story and was stretching out to see what was happening when the tigress's eye was caught by the movement. "So thou art willing to father man-cubs with this puny little gulam, but not true tiger cubs with me?" she whined.

Shira said nothing further; if she had, it would not have been heard, because the roar from the prince was not only loud, it was very comprehensive. It gave his opinion of Shira (he, as well as all jungle animals, found her and her actions distasteful, even repulsive, at best) and contained a direct threat of what would happen should she disobey his order to leave the clearing instantly, an order which also forbade her to ever return.

Shira slunk past the garden and melted into the edge of the jungle while the Prince of Tigers turned to Sita.

"My wife," he said gently, "I am sorry thou had to encounter this one. I would not have thee troubled by her. She speaks correctly in that I was once briefly enamored of her long ago, but the time was indeed short, and my true heart was not involved. I did not love her, Sita. I did not even know the word or what it meant then."

"Please do not concern thyself," Sita said lovingly, running her hands gently over the tiger's whiskers and softly pulling his ears. "We will forget her as though she never existed. What thou speaks of is long ago. I had not even felt thy presence then. I know thy heart is with me now."

"Thou hast spoken truly," agreed the Prince of Tigers.

CHAPTER

16

At some point during this time, Sita decided she must have salt and cloth, but she had no money. She also needed some seeds. She had transplanted plants from the jungle so that flowers bloomed around the entrance to the Ananta Palace, and the flowers were a constant delight to her. She had also brought seeds from her old garden; however, the bean crop had failed, as some sort of mold had attacked the plants. As a result, Sita was running short of the foods she preferred. Oil for the lamps was quite low also. She would have liked to go to the village, but she had no money to purchase what she needed.

When she told the tiger of her dilemma, he thought for a few minutes, then said, "I think I can solve thy problem."

"How can that be, my husband?"

"I do not understand the human need for what they call money, although it seems universal, at least among the humans I have observed. However, I have also observed that they sometimes trade one thing for another, which is more understandable."

"I have nothing I can trade. The *kaddu* that I grow are also grown by others. And it is too far to convey flowers and still have them fresh enough for barter."

"I believe I can show thee something that will have value in the village, or perhaps anywhere. Come with me."

Sita followed the tiger as he led the way to a part of the palace she had never explored. It was more in ruins than the section where they lived. They climbed down a level, though the stairs were uneven and in some places completely broken away. It was not fully dark. Part of the roof was missing, and some of the ceiling timbers had fallen down.

"Look around," the tiger said, "and see if anything you find might be of use."

Sita peered around the dimly lit room. Nearly everything was in shadow, and the corners were even darker. Her eyes were suddenly drawn to a tiny sparkle of light. She stooped down to examine the object more closely, then pried carefully beneath the rubble. When she slowly and cautiously drew it out, she beheld a necklace of red stones; it might have shimmered had it not been buried for many years under layers of dirt turned to a muddy paste by rain, slivers of wood from the broken timbers, and the dried leaves that had blown into the ruins.

"What is this? Where did it come from?" she asked the tiger.

"Perhaps it belonged to the humans who lived here long ago but went away for some reason—I do not know. I never found it interesting enough to think about."

Sita held the necklace in her hand. It was beautiful, but it was nothing that could be exchanged in the village. There would be far too much curiosity about how she had something of such value in her possession. Everyone would believe that the valuable object could only have been obtained through some great crime. No, she would have to venture farther away than the village, perhaps to the city. Yes, that might work if she could find a merchant who was not overcareful about whether things were stolen or acquired honestly. She then realized the necklace was far too valuable for even this sort of transaction. It might attract attention to their life together.

The tiger tired of the search and wandered away, but Sita

continued to rummage in the cellar room, pausing briefly and returning to their quarters to fetch a lantern; now the search was illuminated, although the light cast menacing shadows that constantly moved and shifted. Digging through the dried mud and leaf litter, Sita found several more items she deemed too valuable for her purpose. Finally, she selected a bracelet; the plain metal surface was scratched and tarnished, while the single stone was unfaceted and appeared dull compared to the other pieces of jewelry.

Sita left the other jewels where she had found them and stood up, the bracelet in her hand. She was brushing the leaves and dust from her sari when she heard a long, soft, drawn-out sound. Whether inhalation or exhalation, Sita was not certain, but she knew instinctively who was making the hiss, and that her danger was very great.

"What are you doing?" a soft voice inquired. "Why are you taking my treasure away?"

"I am truly sorry, Nagaiah." Sita also spoke softly, struggling to control her voice. She knew she must make no sudden motions or disturb the king cobra any further. "I did not know this treasure hoard belonged to you."

"Did you think it belonged to you?"

"I thought it belonged to no one; therefore, no one would mind if I took this small piece to trade for the things my family needs. But as it belongs to you, I will replace it on the spot where it was lying before I came into this underground room. I did not know I was an intruder in your home."

"You may take it if you desire to do so. But you take it at the risk of incurring my displeasure. Perhaps I should say my extreme displeasure."

"I have no wish to displease you, Nagaiah." Sita laid the bracelet carefully on the stone floor. At once it sank into the leaf litter, the litter that had concealed Nagaiah so well, until he decided to reveal himself.

"Before you leave my domain," the great snake said, "I require that you answer some questions I will now ask."

Sita watched his coils revolving and weaving into new patterns. She remembered the tiger telling her to be careful and not to go belowground alone lest she meet a naga in the dark. She had obeyed him, and she had not come to the underground room alone. But the Prince of Tigers was no longer with her. *Where are you, O my husband? I need you now.* She watched without moving as the top half of Nagaiah stretched upward and grew taller. His hood flared dramatically, and his baleful eyes were level with her own. Sita had always been told not to look directly into a snake's eyes, but she found she was incapable of looking away. Then the questions began.

"Why are you here in this deserted palace?"

"It is no longer deserted; I live here with my husband, the Prince of Tigers."

"You must answer truthfully. Men and jungle creatures cannot coexist as the former are always trying to kill the latter. Even I, who live belowground, am aware of this."

"I have spoken to you in truth. I have chosen to live in the jungle with the Prince of Tigers. I have no wish to harm any of those I have met here."

A dry rustling sound—perhaps laughter—came from the great snake. It was a sound like death itself, but Sita would not allow herself to dwell on this; instead, her thoughts were fixed on her sons, who needed her, and on the Prince of Tigers. *Please come quickly, before it is too late.*

And then he was beside her, saying suavely, "I knew that we must be neighbors, Nagaiah, but I have not had the pleasure of your company until this moment. I trust that you have not alarmed my wife. Sita, this is the great Nagaiah of whom I have often spoken. Nagaiah, this is Sita, the only human I have ever met who does not judge those who dwell in the jungle by human rules, and who has chosen to separate herself from the human race in order to live here with me. I love and respect her beyond all others. It would go hard with anyone, *anyone*, who brought harm to her or our sons." The tiger flexed his paw so that his claws sprang forth, and he scowled in a way that revealed his teeth in a quite threatening manner.

Nagaiah considered the tiger's words and slowly lowered his hood. "I am honored to see you and meet your wife," he said in the same soft voice. "I was just about to suggest ways in which we could be useful to one another. Your wife tells me that she needs a piece of treasure from my hoard. I am willing to surrender this, but I would like something in return."

"And what is it you wish? Is it something we can supply?"

"Once, I was near a village when I came across a small bowl filled with an elixir that I have never seen before or since. It was delicious, and although this was years ago, I have never forgotten its taste and how it flowed smoothly down my throat. All I can tell you is that it came from the world of men and its color was white. If you can provide me with more of this elixir, I think we can coexist quite peacefully."

"We will do our best to supply your needs as you will help us with ours," the tiger said. "But we will need this small treasure in order to procure the elixir for you."

Nagaiah nodded. "You may take the bracelet," he said to Sita. "Do not fear to pick it up; I will not strike you. But I will be waiting for you to bring me what I desire." He curved away into the darkness.

Sita carefully picked up the bracelet and the lantern and held both in her left hand. She rested her right hand on the back of the Prince of Tigers and walked very close to him as they slowly picked their way up the broken stairs. She was still frightened, and the feel of the tiger's warm body under her hand and against her side was immensely comforting.

The tiger decided to take a nap, and Sita went outside to dig up suran in the garden. She had found this kind of work useful when she had a problem and needed time to think about it. *What is white and could be called an elixir?* She continued to slide her wooden fork into the ground and then push it upwards to nudge the suran out of the earth. *What can it be?* Just as she finished the row, a memory wriggled into her mind. She could actually hear her aunt's voice as Bhima told her that it was common at shrines, and even at many homes, to set out a bowl of milk for any passing cobra—that it was a fine way to indicate one's respect for the great snakes that were both gods and killers.

So the mystery of the white elixir was quickly and easily solved. Once again, Bhima's wisdom had helped Sita know what to do. She only wished that Bhima had explained how it might be possible to keep a goat in the midst of a family headed by a tiger.

CHAPTER

17

"Canst thou take care of the man-cubs for a few days, my husband?" Sita asked.

"I think thou canst depend on me for that," said the tiger, looking down his nose and speaking in a rather stuffy manner. "I may not be their mother, but I am certainly their father."

Sita cast a sideways glance at the Prince of Tigers. His eyes twinkled and he was grinning. He had immediately retracted the statement he made regarding the boys' parentage shortly after their birth, and Sita knew he had never truly doubted her love and loyalty, but it was a scene that still rankled.

The next morning, Sita left for the village. The prince did not accompany her; he was keeping the boys safe at the Ananta Palace. It was a long walk—Sita had forgotten just how long. She had often ridden on the tiger's back, and they sometimes divided the trip into two sections by curling up together and napping for a few hours. Now Sita was alone and had to remember to listen to the langurs and chitals, to stay alert for their alarm calls and to understand what she heard.

Once, she stepped to the side of the trail as a krait slithered away; she had almost stepped on its resting coils, and the movement had disturbed it. She realized she had come to depend on the Prince of Tigers in so many ways, not least as the interpreter of the jungle—a place and system so complex that it was easy to overlook some detail that might result in harm. Sita felt she had only scratched the surface of what there was to be discovered. She still had much to learn and wondered if she would ever feel fully confident in her acquired knowledge.

It was late in the afternoon, and Sita was tired when she emerged from the jungle. She did not stop at her old hut but could see that it had a run-down look. It was half covered with vines that had snaked out from the jungle to conquer this evidence of humans who had, perhaps, encroached on a world they did not understand.

In the village, she went directly to where Anila lived, but a stranger came to the door and said that Anila no longer lived there. "She married Gurdeep; she lives with his family now."

Sita knew she should not be surprised. She herself was married and even had children. Why should silly little Anila not have matured and moved on in her life as well? Sita was tired and wanted to sleep, but she had to talk to Anila tonight, so she trudged to Gurdeep's home, hoping that Anila would listen and be willing to help her.

The next morning, everything looked brighter. She had found Anila, and her friend had listened as Sita talked about the necessity of getting to the city quickly and how she could hardly make the trip in rags. Sita's sari could best be described as threadbare. Anila looked like she was bursting with questions about Sita's life and where she had been for so long, but after Sita deflected her first two attempts, Anila asked no more. Instead, she talked to her mother-in-law, who grudgingly allowed Sita a mat to sleep on. Anila was more sympathetic—she gave Sita one of her old saris (still far more presentable than Sita's own), and then ran down the lane to ask Udit if Sita could ride in his bullock cart to the city, where he was planning to go this very day.

Udit was happy to grant Anila's request. Like everybody else, he was very curious about where Sita had disappeared to and where she had spent the last few years. Also, like everybody else, he assumed that she had married somebody from another village, perhaps even a man from a primitive jungle tribe; if this were the case, of course she would not want her old community to know of her further decline in station. When he saw Sita waiting by the track for him, she looked poorer than ever. He wondered why she had not moved back to the village where life would certainly have treated her better.

The bullock team moved slowly, and Udit knew he would have plenty of time to ask questions and get answers. Sita was more silent than ever, though, ignoring some questions and barely addressing others. In spite of his curiosity, revealed by the questions he asked, Udit learned nothing about Sita or her new life, like where or how she lived. When the bullock cart reached the city, she merely thanked him for the ride and disappeared down a busy street.

In an hour, Sita had found her way to a merchant who she felt would suit her purpose. Parth was known in the area as being a little unscrupulous about business, more concerned with how much money he could make than with being strictly honest. He politely welcomed Sita and listened quietly to the story of her family, who had possessed this old bracelet for several generations but now were forced to sell it because of unforeseen financial reverses. It pained them to give the bracelet up, but realities were realities, and they could no longer keep it, even though it reminded them of a time when they had been respected and looked up to by their entire village.

Parth had heard very similar stories many times over the years. He could certainly see that the young woman talking to him was poor, but he was willing to listen for as long as she wanted to talk, as long as he ended up with the bracelet—even in its battered condition, he recognized quality when he saw it. Because the woman had such a downtrodden look and was dressed so poorly, he did not expect her to be such a hard bargainer; he knew, however, that he would still come out ahead. But he was curious because he knew with total certainty that nothing about the story she had told him was true. She had given him the name of her village, and there was no village of that name in the area. Also, the story was just too commonplace to believe.

Parth could figure sums and amounts and the profit he would make, all in the time it took to clear his throat. But he couldn't count the number of times he had heard the story of a family who had lost their money, who had lost everything except whatever they had placed on the counter and were trying to sell him. Nine times out of ten, the object had been stolen—not that he lost any sleep over that, unless he had a reason to think the police were hovering nearby. But what if this woman, poor though she seemed, had somehow come across a secret cache of jewelry, things she would feed to him little by little? The possibility was worth looking into, anyway.

The beads hanging in the doorway rattled as Sita passed out into the street and turned left. Parth snapped his fingers, and his nephew rose from where he had been dozing in the open window. "I want you to follow this woman, but discreetly. She must not know that you are following her. Only return when you can tell me where she lives." His nephew nodded, pushed the beads aside, passed out into the street, and turned left.

CHAPTER

18

The people of the village were worried; nothing seemed to work as it used to. Vinay, the son of Kunti, had been searching for some cows that had strayed into the jungle when he encountered a tendua—with fatal results. Two woodcutters had seen the great spotted cat slinking away as they carried bundles of wood back to the village. When they dared to investigate where the leopard had emerged from under a bush, they found the body of the boy lying in the grass.

It had been a long time since a predator had been bold enough to attack people in the area. When they'd seen the large male tiger on a regular basis, they had been filled with anxiety about whether or not he was a man-eater, but in the end, he had disappeared and had not now been spotted for some time, probably a number of years. Now, because the villagers were afraid of the leopard, they did not go to the fields to tend their crops, as the path ran alongside the jungle. Those neglected crops were now dying, and it looked as though there would be hunger in the village soon.

There were other problems as well. Drupada's house had burned down, and his baby had been badly burned. A messenger should have gone to the next village for help; there was someone there who acted as a midwife and nurse, although she had no real training in either area. No one was willing to leave the village, however, especially after dark when the leopard was more likely to be on the prowl, and the baby had died after a few days of constant whimpering and crying, her little face screwed up in pain. There were other problems and complaints as well, but it was agreed that the killer leopard was the chief problem.

Not only had he killed (and partially eaten) the young cowherd, but he was also blamed for the death of Drupada's baby. This blame was probably misplaced as the baby's burns were extensive, but the village believed it anyway. In any event, the village concluded that their misfortunes had been multiplying for a long time. No one had really seen a pattern until the death of the cowherd.

The men met to discuss the situation, hopeful that one of them would offer a solution. Every one of them was able to cite a problem—whether or not it was connected to the main issue of what to do about the man-eating leopard—but when the headman said, "Enough of this complaining. What can we do?" no one answered or had anything to suggest.

The women were standing in the shadows, around the edges of the space where the men sat. When one of them said, "We should ask Sita," it was not at once obvious who had spoken. Then someone was pushed forward into the light; it was Anila, who felt all at once rather like a silly child to whom no one would listen, except perhaps to tell her to be quiet.

The headman turned to her. "Why do you, a woman, speak?" he asked. "And why do you say that? What does Sita have to do with this? I saw her creeping along the path not long ago. She looked like a beggar. How could she possibly help us?"

"Anyway, she deserted us," someone cried, while another added, "We tried to help her, and she would not be helped."

"She came to me because she needed help," Anila said slowly. "She said she would repay me, although I would have been glad to help her anyway."

"Really!" said a voice from the darkness. Anila shrank a little because she recognized the voice of her mother-in-law.

"She came back a few days later, late in the afternoon. I had given her a sari and choli, and she gave me cloth for new ones, and money besides."

Gurdeep's mother moved forward and held her daughter-in-law firmly, just above the elbow. "No need to tell everyone our business," she hissed.

"She gave me these things and then just walked away. I think she took the path towards the jungle, although I didn't really notice."

"She stopped at my house and bought two goats," old Bharata put in. "I started to ask her where she was taking them, but she just looked at me, then walked away."

"Where is she living now?" the headman asked Anila.

"I do not know, but I think it is a long ways away. I had not seen her for a couple of years—not until she asked me for help, that is."

"You have told us that you have seen Sita and that there was business between you, but you have not answered my question. Why did you suggest that we should ask Sita what to do?"

Anila looked down and shuffled her feet a little. "I'm not sure," she said. "It just seemed to me—"

"Trust a woman," a voice boomed. "Trust her to tell you what to do but not be able to tell you how or why."

All the men laughed, and Anila shrank in embarrassment. She knew her voice was smaller than ever. "Please listen, Prabu," she said. "Please let me finish. It just seemed to me that the tendua is a jungle animal, and no one knows more about the jungle than Sita. She might know something that could help us."

Anila's suggestion was not received favorably by all. There were mutterings of complaint and disagreement. "I don't think a stupid girl knows any more than we do about leopards," a man scoffed, and his neighbor agreed, saying, "She hasn't hunted like we have; she can't throw a laathi."

The headman wrinkled up his forehead and waited for more suggestions, but no one volunteered another one.

"All right, then," he said. "If no one else has a suggestion, this is what we'll do. First, we must all be extra vigilant. If anyone sees anything out of the way, please report it to me. And we will try to get in contact with Sita. I don't see how she could help us, but no one seems to have any other ideas. So, is anyone willing to search for her?"

"I am," said a young man. He had come to the village only a week or so ago. No one could offer him any work, so the village did not know why he stayed. He was sleeping at Gauri's house and paying him a few annas for the use of a sleeping mat and two meals a day, meals which were little more than chapattis and whatever Gauri's wife could scrounge from her mostly dead garden.

"Is anyone willing to go with him?"

No one spoke.

In the morning, the stranger came out of the house, carrying a package of chapattis that Gauri's wife had handed him. "I am ready," he announced. "I will find this woman for you."

"Be careful of nagas," a woman cried, and a man snapped, "I wouldn't worry about cobras. Look out for the tendua! Do you have any sort of a weapon?"

"I have a knife," the stranger said. "If the tendua comes, I will climb a tree." He turned and followed the path towards the jungle.

A murmur arose from the assembled villagers, and many different voices rang out.

"He is clearly from the city!"

"Didn't you notice his hands?"

"I would not hire him even if I needed a workman and could pay one."

"Even in the city, they must know about tenduas and that they can not only climb trees but spend much of their time among the branches."

"Will he come back?"

"Will we ever see him again?"

In fact, they never did see him again. It was as if the jungle had swallowed him whole. Whether the leopard had eaten him or his bones were still sitting in a tree somewhere was not known, and back in the city, Parth waited long for a report that he never received about the mysterious woman he had bartered with for an old bracelet. Eventually, Parth shrugged. What else was there for him to do? He did not think he would ever see the woman again. And he was fairly certain that he would never see his lazy nephew again, either.

CHAPTER

19

It had made Sita happy to see Anila again. The silly girl had grown up and shown compassion to her old friend. She had not expected anything in return either—Anila had been genuinely surprised and grateful when Sita returned to pay her debt as she had said she would. Sita decided to visit her old friend again, even though it meant going to the village, which she did not particularly enjoy. So, in the end, they did not need to seek her out. She came to them.

❧

When she returned to the Ananta Palace from her visit, her eyes were brimming with laughter. "Where art thou, my husband?" she called. "I have something to ask thee."

"And what is it, my wife?" asked the tiger, who had been watching the man-cubs play. He enjoyed this duty. It was not something that a tiger father usually did—male tigers do not traditionally interact with their offspring—but he was interested in watching their growth and progress. Their favorite game at the moment was kicking and batting at round gourds, and then chasing them about the courtyard. The tiger had noted the man-cubs' increased speed as they pursued the jungle version of balls, and how much more easily they manipulated the gourds than they had a few months (or even weeks) earlier. The man-cubs liked the time they spent with their father, too. They wrestled and tumbled over the Prince of Tigers, sometimes pulling on his ears or nipping at his tail, while he patiently endured these undignified "assaults" by his sons.

"O Prince of Tigers, canst thou tell me why the affairs of the village used to run smoothly, and why they do not run smoothly now?"

"That is a simple question and hardly requires an answer from me. I think thou should already know the answer to that question."

"I think I do, but I would like to hear it from thy mouth."

"Very well. Because it was thy village, and because I took an interest in it for thy sake, I put the village under my protection. Dangerous leopards and other tigers stayed away because it was my territory. Only wild hogs bold enough to meet me would root in the village garden, but they were rarely willing to take that chance. Even the *bhalu* did not want to be on my bad side. I made that part of the jungle safe for those of thy kind, but appreciation is not in their nature."

"I think it might be now, my husband," said Sita. She told him what she had learned from Anila, and they talked long into the night concerning the village's troubles and what could be done about them.

Anila had told Sita when the next village meeting would be, and Sita was standing in the shadows beside her friend when the headman once again asked for ideas.

Again, there was silence, but when it had gone on awhile, Sita spoke up. "Although this is no longer my village, I ask permission to speak," she said, softly but clearly.

Heads craned around. "Who is speaking—identify yourself," Prabu, the headman, called out.

"I am Sita, who grew up next to the village at the edge of the jungle."

"Continue. Say what you want to say."

"The village used to be protected."

A single gasp came from many throats. Then the shouting started.

"What do you mean?"

"Who protected us?"

"Who paid for this protection?"

"Why did it stop?"

Sita held up her hand. "I cannot talk when you are all shouting," she said calmly, and the meeting space grew quiet. "There used to be a tiger in these parts who was curious about people and how they lived and what they were like. Because he wanted to observe man, he took this territory for his own. When it became known that this was his territory and that he would not allow interference, life became easier for you. Man-eaters decided to go elsewhere, snakes crawled away when they felt your footsteps approach, and wild hogs went to other villages to dig up their crops instead of yours. But you chased this tiger away, and that is why you are in trouble now."

Again, there was a buzz of many voices. Men shouted:

"It was not me!"

"I was not responsible!"

"It was Sanchit who stepped on an adder the following year. It must be his fault."

The headman lifted his hand for quiet. He asked the women to leave the circle so that the men could talk among themselves without interruption.

He called Sita back, however, and the rest of the women trailed back also. "Do you know this tiger?" the headman asked. "How do you know him? Are you in touch with him?"

"He is well known in the jungle," she responded. "I could try to send him a message. The cheel might be willing to take one to him."

"We would like to have his protection restored, but we would also like to know what his conditions are. What does he require from us?

What if he wants us to give him something in return that we are unable to provide?"

"This is becoming a complex message," remarked Sita. "I hope it will survive translation."

"Will you be seeing the tiger soon?"

"Whether the message comes from me or whether it will be passed through others is something I cannot know. This tiger comes and goes through the jungle as he will and moves at his own pace. I will do my best to convey the urgency of your request, along with your questions, whether to the tiger or through an intermediary."

"Thank you, Sita," replied the headman. "It is good to know that you are still a daughter of the village, even though you have chosen to live elsewhere and leave your friends behind."

"It is obvious that I still care for my friends, or I would not concern myself with this matter."

"Indeed, you speak truth, Sita. Come back quickly."

"I do not know how the tiger will answer your questions, or whom he will send with the answers. I do not know if he will answer you at all."

CHAPTER

20

When Sita reported her conversation with the headman to the Prince of Tigers, there was a slight smile on his face, but she was not certain if the smile was cynical or sad.

"Is that all?" he asked.

"Yes," she replied. "They said they could not make a decision without knowing your conditions."

"Very good. I will wait a few days so they will realize that this is a serious matter for me as well as for them. Then I will require you to write something for me."

"Why would you think that I, a humble girl from the village, know how to write?"

The tiger was almost inscrutable but looked slightly amused at the same time. "We have been together for many years," he said. "I know nearly everything about you."

"You might be surprised," Sita responded, but secretly she was rather proud that the Prince of Tigers had found her worthy of such applied study. She had also studied him, but she did not feel that she knew her subject quite so well as he claimed to know her. But what did it matter? Life was certainly finite, but there was plenty of time to learn more about the tiger—they had not talked enough about what his cub and youth years had been like, for example. What she did know was that the two of them had spent some wonderful years together. She had never really expected to have a happy life; she had merely hoped that if it became necessary to marry, her husband would be a kind man. Instead, she had met the Prince of Tigers, and life had become much more interesting, even exciting. She enjoyed teaching him almost as much as she enjoyed learning from him. Daily, she was immersed in beauty, something that was important to her. She had borne him two beautiful sons who depended on her to nurture them on many levels. There were challenges, of course, but she would never have exchanged her new life for the old or wished that her life had continued to flow in more traditional channels.

The tiger dictated his terms, which Sita found rather surprising. She knew they were kindly meant, but she did not understand why they were important. She wrote them on a tattered sheet of paper (or possibly it was a piece of skin) she had found in one of the palace rooms.

A few days later, when a boy who herded the village bullocks returned from a rather open area of the jungle where they had been grazing, a woman noticed something tied to the horn of one of the bullocks. She called to her husband, who removed the packet and took it to the headman. He unrolled the piece of cloth and unwrapped what turned out to be the message from the tiger. It said: *The land around Sita's hut at the edge of the jungle must be hers forever. The village must build a stone cottage there. It should have at least two rooms. There should also be a shed near the house. If these things are done, the village will have my protection again.*

"We will tell the tiger we accept," the headman said after a quick meeting with the men of the village. A few of them had suggested that perhaps this entire transaction was a ruse Sita had employed to gain security for herself, but they were shouted down by the others, and the headman agreed as well.

"We have known Sita since her birth," he stated. "She has always been difficult to deal with, but never once has she made a choice that would make her life easier. She would never agree to, let alone instigate, a plan to enrich herself through deceit." But the headman did not know to whom he could communicate that the village was willing to accept the conditions the tiger had demanded. Sita was no longer present in the village, and he knew of no other way to send a message to the powerful tiger except through her. He finally decided that the village needed to demonstrate in a tangible way that they were willing to accept the bargain and keep their part of it.

The headman took a formal vote among the men; they voted that two hectares of land located at the edge of the jungle (including the land where the current hut stood, and measured from the game trail that went into the jungle) should belong to Sita and her heirs forever. They cleared a space—removing the hut that was already there took very little time—and drew out the outline of Sita's new house on the ground. Akshat had gone hunting (unsuccessfully) for chital in the jungle, but he found a great pile of stone, clearly from some long-abandoned house or temple, that they could use to build the house. Although it was a simple house, the rooms were larger than customary, and they took care that the walls were strongly built, and the thatched roof fit tightly and did not leak. They were not as careful about the shed, but it was a fine place to keep animals or store dried ears of maize.

Two days after they hung the doors and shutters, a wild pig that had been raiding the gardens for the last month was found dead behind a row of beans; obviously it had been killed by a predator. Also, there was evidence that another pig had been killed and carried away. Everyone was happy. The tiger was back—he had dispatched two enemies to the livelihood of the village and had even left them a pig that they could roast and share among the members of the community. And although it was not something they discussed, they were also proud that they had kept their part of the bargain and done a workmanlike job establishing Sita's property and building her a sturdy house. Once again, things were as they should be.

CHAPTER

21

Ashok and Arun had been healthy babies and thriving toddlers; as they moved into boyhood, they lived happy and active lives. They ran shrieking through the empty palace rooms. They crept about the yard, hiding behind bushes and leaping out at each other with sudden screams. Sita discouraged this sort of play with anyone but each other—they had really frightened her once when Arun leaped on her back while she was weeding the pumpkins. The Prince of Tigers never turned a hair at their antics, but he was so unresponsive to their attempts to frighten him that they soon ceased to even try.

Sita was watching Ashok and Arun gallop around the garden one afternoon when suddenly something went wrong with her eyes. As she described it later that evening to the tiger, it was as though both boys were surrounded by a reddish haze or mist that kept her from seeing them clearly. She repeatedly blinked, but the haze was still there; more puzzling was the fact that it clustered around the boys—when she glanced back at the palace or up at a *gidh* hanging high in the sky with outstretched wings, her vision seemed normal. After a few minutes, the mist began to disappear, and she could see her sons clearly again. She saw the dimple in Arun's left cheek and the bruise on Ashok's leg from when he had tripped over a root and fallen down three days before. She worried a little about her eyes and what might be wrong with them but was too busy to think about it for very long.

Two weeks later, a more extended episode occurred. This time, the reddish haze surrounding the boys was visible, but the boys also appeared distorted in shape, definitely not like their normal selves. Sita had never heard of manifestations like these before. Certainly, her aunt had shared with her many stories and examples of various medical and psychological conditions she had observed, but what was happening to Sita did not fall into any of these categories. She didn't even share what she viewed as waking dreams or hallucinations with the tiger this time. Why should both of them have to worry?

The third time it happened, Sita knew she should have understood much more quickly. After all, she was the mother of Ashok and Arun, and mothers should understand their sons. But how could she understand something that fell so far outside her previous experience? She had entered into a folktale and was finding the conventions of this new world confusing and problematic. She had taken a step like this when she decided to move to the jungle with the tiger, but that felt easy and natural, while this latest development did not. She now understood what the tiger had felt when he looked at the baby boys and saw that they were human babies and not tiger cubs.

Now she was seeing her sons in a new and disturbing light— they were entirely tiger cubs as they raced about, play-fighting and snapping at each other's waving tails. When they were tired, they stumbled into a tangled knot and fell asleep. As they lay there, breathing evenly, relaxed in their slumber, the change crept over them and they were boys again, but like their tiger-cub counterparts, they were tired out from their play—breathing deeply, sleeping deeply.

Sita knew the tiger would be happy that Ashok and Arun were strongly tiger as well as strongly human, but she felt that their ability to change shape would cause them problems no matter which world they were living in. And the thought was ever in her mind in spite of the fact that she had lived with the tiger for a number of years now:

How could I, Sita of the village, have given birth to tiger cubs?

Sita was right about the tiger's response to her tale—he was delighted. "How many times hast thou seen our tiger cubs?" he queried.

"Only once, my husband. Before that, the images were not clear. But now, I am sure it will happen again, and soon."

"My Sita, I was happy with our sons already—how could I not be? They have been wonderful man-cubs, sturdily built, strong, intelligent, and daring. But I am more happy than I can say that they are true reflections of both of thee and me. I did not know the meaning of family before we were together. Now I have feelings I never thought to have. No, that is not right. I did not feel I was missing anything before, because I did not know. But now I do. My Sita, my wife, I love thee. I love our man-cubs. And I love that we are a family."

This was a very emotional speech for the tiger, who turned his head slightly away as he spoke the last few sentences. Sita had not come from a home (or a village) where emotion was freely expressed, so she understood how difficult it must be for him to utter these words. She softly stroked the cheek turned towards her, but she said nothing. She had expressed her love to her husband many times, as he had to her. His declaration this time, however, had a special meaning—that he did not regret his choice, that he had fully understood and accepted the concepts of love and family, and that he realized his life would have been incomplete without his wife and sons beside him.

As the man-cubs grew older, they slowly learned to control the transformation from boy to cub and back again, and the transformations now occurred quite quickly (almost in the blink of an eye, Sita thought). The reddish haze that had accompanied the early transformations was, to Sita's relief, absent—it had made her uneasy from the first time she had seen it. It was clear to Sita and the prince that their sons tended to change when they were excited or angry, although they did so on many other occasions as well. As they calmed down, they resumed the shapes they had previously abandoned.

Perhaps even stranger to Sita than the transformation itself was the issue of clothing. If the boys were wearing dhotis or loincloths when they transformed to their tiger phase, they were wearing exactly the same clothing when they became human once again. She puzzled about this for a long time but finally concluded that there was no answer—at least not one she could understand. When Ashok and Arun were older, both parents asked their sons about these transformations, but they soon realized that questioning the man-cubs was an exercise in futility.

"Dost thou know when thou wilt change?"

"Sometimes."

"Dost thou ever try to change?"

"Not really."

"Dost thou ever try to *not* change?"

"Doesn't work."

Sita and the tiger decided they would have to be patient. Perhaps when the man-cubs were older, they would be able to explain more about their unique abilities. Then again, they might not understand any more than did their parents about why and how these changes occurred. The ability they possessed might be a wonderful gift. On the other hand, it might prove to be a terrible curse.

22

One day, Sita heard a tiger approaching the clearing in the jungle. She knew it was not the Prince of Tigers. She would already have felt his presence if he were near. Anyway, his footsteps were so silent that she usually heard nothing until he was standing beside her, uttering his usual fond greeting: "My Sita." No, this was someone else, a stranger, someone who was asking for permission to approach the Ananta Palace. It sounded like Shira's voice, but there was a beseeching tone about it, one that hardly reflected what Sita knew Shira to be. *What reason could there be for the new humility in her tone? Why would Shira seek permission for anything?* She was known throughout the entire region for her arrogance, selfishness, cruelty, and sharp tongue; furthermore, the prince had forbidden her to come anywhere near the Ananta Palace ever again. *It must be someone else.*

"Enter, whoever thou may be," said Sita. "What dost thou need, and is there any way I can help thee?"

To Sita's surprise, it *was* Shira who came meekly out of the jungle. Her pale-orange coat, once silky and glowing, now looked dull and tarnished, and the tigress was limping badly.

"What has happened to thee, Shira?"

"I was gored by a *nilghai*, a blue bull—I was stalking him when something distracted me, and I did not focus strongly enough when I made the leap. His horns may be small, but he ripped open my paw with one of them. Now the wound is infected."

"Please let me help thee. I can drain the infected area and put a paste of leaves on it. It will hurt for a while, but then it will gradually heal."

"It is a kind thought," Shira groaned, "but it will be useless now. The poison has spread. I can feel the pain and weakness and swelling throughout my entire body. I know that I will die before long. I did not come to ask for help for me, but I have a great favor to ask of thee."

Sita was astonished. Why would Shira come to her for anything, least of all a great favor?

"What wouldst thou ask of me?"

"I have twin sons. I would ask thee to take them and raise them as thy own."

"Why me? Surely thou must know other mothers in the jungle who could help thee."

Pain and the knowledge of her approaching death might have made Shira humble, but it had not totally tamed the tigress, or stamped out her penchant for causing trouble wherever she could. An evil smile spread across her face. "And wherefore dost thou suppose I should come except to the household of the father of my cubs?"

"Thou speakest falsely," Sita said evenly. "The Prince of Tigers has not been with thee."

"Thou dost not know because he chose not to tell thee. But thou knows how often he is away. Indeed, he is out hunting, but what he is hunting for is perhaps unknown to thee."

"Thou speakest falsely," Sita repeated. "My husband's heart and mind are mine, as mine are his. If he had encountered thee in the jungle, he would have told me."

"Think what it pleases thee to think" was Shira's rejoinder, but she sank to the ground as she spoke, and Sita could see that she was very ill indeed.

"I will forgive thee the lie because thou art trying to protect and provide for thy sons," Sita said seriously. "I will take thy sons and raise them as my own, but I must know who their father is." She did not explain why this was important, but she wanted assurance that the cub's father was not a man-eater or vicious in any way, as the cubs already had one parent who was known for her unpleasant personality and evil character. Although she had already agreed to take the cubs, Sita wanted to know just what she and the Prince of Tigers could expect as the cubs developed their own personalities and characters.

"It was Manju," Shira answered sulkily. Although Manju lived east of where Sita and the prince were, he was known far and wide as being unusually mild and good-natured, so much so that the jungle dwellers usually referred to him as "the amiable Manju." The thought flashed through Sita's mind that his mild personality was what had allowed him to get mixed up with Shira, but she would never say it.

Shira clearly knew what she was thinking, even though Sita had tried to school her face so that her thought process was not evident.

"Manju is good, and I think his cubs will be like him," Shira gritted out in a low, scratchy voice. "If I could have been more like that . . ." She closed her eyes and did not finish the sentence. "I thank thee for granting my request. My son's names are Vasu and Vanada."

She looked so tired and sad that Sita started forward. Perhaps she could do something to alleviate Shira's pain, but the tigress shrank away from her touch and got to her feet. "It is too late for either help or friendship," she said. "The cubs are waiting just beyond the clearing. I will send them to thee and tell them that from now on, thou wilt be their mother." Without further words, she turned and limped slowly away.

Sita stood on the palace steps, watching the denizen of the jungle whom she liked the least of any she had met, and wondered at how her anger and disgust had turned to sympathy and pity when Shira was in pain and needed help. Then Sita saw two cubs, younger and smaller than her own, running towards her. She sat on a step so she would not be bowled over by their antics as they jumped at her and leaned against her. Sita knew the cubs were young and thoughtless. She also knew they would soon be saddened by their mother's disappearance, but for the moment, they were too excited by new experiences and exotic surroundings to notice that she was leaving. For just a moment, she saw Shira looking over her shoulder, drinking in her last look at the cubs she had borne. Then Sita was so caught up with welcoming the lively and enthusiastic cubs that she did not notice her old enemy and would-be rival slip into the concealing green of the jungle, whose leafy arms quickly enfolded her.

CHAPTER

23

The Prince of Tigers was not at all happy when he returned from the hunt and discovered that the number of cubs at the Ananta Palace had doubled in the two days he had been gone. As he entered the clearing, he noted that his sons were in their tiger form and that they were romping and playing with two cubs who were clearly younger. He had never seen these cubs before, but they seemed to be very much at home.

"Sita, what is this?" he roared. "What has happened here?"

The four cubs froze in their tracks. Ashok and Arun cowered— they had so rarely heard their father's angry roar that they thought something terrible must have happened. Vasu and Vanada, the smaller cubs, were terrified by this menacing stranger, and both tried to become invisible by diving into a little lantana bush that was clearly too small to shield them. Then Sita emerged from the palace, and they abandoned the lantana and dashed to her side, leaning against her legs.

"Perhaps I should ask thee this question, my lord," Sita said calmly. "What has happened that thou should use this tone of voice that is so strange to us? Didst thou step on a sharp stone? Hast thou been wounded in the hunt? Did a sambar score thee with his horns? What unguents should I bring to salve thy wounds? Please tell me, my lord, and I will fetch them quickly."

The tiger shot a sharp glance in her direction, but Sita controlled her features with an effort, and the confused but concerned look did not leave her face. "Thou appears to be very tense," Sita said, stroking his side and running her hand over his neck. "Wouldst thou like a massage?"

The prince began to relax. He realized he was being managed, but he had to admit that Sita's subtle approach, diverting instead of confronting, had been successful. He was no longer angry but grew more and more curious about what event had happened during his short absence that had miraculously produced two lively cubs.

As Sita lovingly examined his paws for thorns and massaged his shoulders, she told the prince of Shira's visit and of her agreement to take responsibility for Shira's cubs. Then the tiger was angry again, but not for long. Both he and Sita had hoped for more man-cubs, but it had not happened. Now, as he lay on the verandah of the palace, feeling full and sleepy, with his coat clean and combed, watching four cubs playing tumble and tag in the clearing, he felt that life was good indeed. But a worry still nagged at the corners of his mind.

These cubs were Shira's cubs, and he had known Shira for years. Setting aside the brief time they had spent together, he had never seen anything in her to admire, or even like. She was bad tempered and mean, even cruel, to practically everyone with whom she came in contact. Other jungle dwellers did their best to avoid her. Tigers do not kill for sport; they kill if they are hungry. But Shira would sometimes go out of her way to strike at or bring down an antelope or deer, even if she had no need of food. He had once seen a chital dragging a leg because Shira had swiped at it and then gone her own way. She had not killed it, but assuredly the next predator that saw it would do so, as it was no longer able to escape through its natural speed.

The Prince of Tigers saw that Sita believed Shira's story, but the cranky tigress had never seemed in the least to be a motherly type. He even wondered if Shira had persuaded a gullible Sita to take care of them so that the tigress would be free to do as she liked. He mentioned this possibility to Sita, but his wife was firm in her belief that Shira was near death and her appeal to one she viewed as a rival for the prince's attention was solely out of true concern for her sons.

He noted that Sita was truly happy to have Vasu and Vanada as part of their family. Like many mothers, she felt her children were growing up too quickly and was delighted to have younger cubs dashing around the Ananta Palace again.

For a few days Sita was concerned that the cubs would miss their mother, but she need not have worried. It was as if Vasu and Vanada instantly recognized her loving and nurturing nature. They turned to her as flowers to the sun and happily absorbed all the affection she showered upon them. One or both always followed at her heels or leaned against her. It was not long, however, before they enlarged their social scope. At first, they had been slightly leery of their older foster brothers. Sita and the prince wondered if they found the man-cubs' transformations unsettling; perhaps they were afraid when their brothers were suddenly boys instead of tigers. It was puzzling at the least, but it was not long before they were following Ashok and Arun almost as constantly as they had followed Sita. They would nuzzle her, asking for a quick pat or cuddle, but then they were on their way, following their new heroes. Vasu was drawn to the more flamboyant Arun, while Vanada admired Ashok, sometimes even trying to walk like his new elder brother.

There was really only one spot of difficulty in the cubs' transition to living with a family in the Ananta Palace instead of in the jungle with only their mother—adjusting to the presence of Nagaiah. Vasu and Vanada were terrified of the great snake. When they saw him, they immediately slunk away. Their fear and aversion was very evident to the family circle because Nagaiah had long since become a part of that circle. Ever since Sita had brought two goats back to the old palace in the jungle, the relationship between Nagaiah and the family had been completely friendly, even affectionate. Initially,

Sita had carried a bowl of milk to the underground room every day, but Nagaiah said he would prefer to come upstairs to drink it. He enjoyed spending time with the Prince of Tigers. Sita thought Nagaiah probably believed that he was co-ruler of the jungle with her husband, but she also considered the king cobra to be her greatest friend, even greater than Mor. Mor was a friendly gossip, and she was always glad to see him and chat with him, but Nagaiah had ideas and, after his long years of isolation and silence in the underground room, was eager to discuss a multitude of things.

It took longer for Nagaiah to accept Ashok and Arun. He found their boisterous ways rather annoying, and he often appeared disgruntled as he watched them at play. But after they began calling him Uncle Nagaiah, the king cobra unbent considerably and developed undeniably protective feelings towards the young inhabitants of the old palace. It was not long before Ashok and Arun were playing games that involved jumping over Nagaiah's stretched-out body. Two months later, even Vasu and Vanada were bold enough to join in the games, although Vasu leaped back quickly when he accidentally bumped into Nagaiah when the snake was drinking milk from his bowl. Nagaiah turned his head and stared at the cub. Then he lowered his head and resumed drinking, but Vasu was noticeably quiet the rest of the day.

With the assorted individuals and the resulting level of activity, a normal house would have been bursting at the seams, but there was plenty of room at the palace for everyone—and everyone was happy. Even the goats were happy enough to produce large quantities of milk, although they sometimes became upset, their eyes widening in alarm, if Nagaiah or any of the tigers came too near. Sita milked them every day, and they were relaxed and generous under her hands. Once, when she was ill (a most uncommon circumstance), Ashok took over for her and quickly learned to be an expert milker as well. Nagaiah was particularly pleased at this; he had assumed that if Sita were unavailable for any reason, he would have to do without his favorite elixir.

CHAPTER

24

Several happy and peaceful years had gone by, but on this particular day, the Prince of Tigers was worried, a feeling that was quite new to him. He had not often needed to be worried. For as far back as he could remember, really since he had been a small cub, everything had gone right for him. After all, he was the prince. He had always been large and strong for his age, and had early demonstrated that he understood and was capable of all the things that are necessary in a tiger's life. He could move through the jungle so quietly that the grasses were not disturbed by his movements; not a wisp of breeze changed its course because he was passing by. His hunts were usually successful ones, and he had foiled those who wished to do him harm.

Yet now he was worried, and he showed it in his gait and demeanor. He slouched along, not paying attention to his surroundings. He still made no noise—he was too much a tiger to ever forget to move in silence—but there was no spring in his step, and he walked with his head down instead of alertly raised with eyes moving from side to side. The tiger was lost in his thoughts, and they were not happy ones.

The Prince of Tigers was completely happy in his life with Sita and their sons. He had never regretted his decision to take a human wife; he could not imagine living with anyone else but Sita. They had been together for years, but the happiness they had found together had never dimmed. He knew she was occasionally lonely when he was away hunting in a distant part of the jungle, but she never complained, and he was anxious to return to her also.

One example of their devotion occurred the previous week when Sita found him asleep in a tall clump of lantana bushes. The sun was shining, and the golden blossoms gleamed as brightly as his coat. The clump was a little way from the Ananta Palace and not one of his usual haunts, but Sita always felt his presence if he was at all near. She nestled up against him but did not sleep; instead, she thought about their life together in the jungle and how different it was from what her life would have been. Sita was glad she had refused when the villagers tried to persuade her to leave her hut and truly become one of them, and she had never ceased to be grateful that the tiger had chosen to intrude upon her world. Her life since that moment had been like living in another world, and she never tired of it.

When the tiger awoke, he stretched and said, "I must indeed trust thee completely—I did not even awake at thy arrival." Sita put her arms around him and felt his heartbeat, steady and strong, thinking that it was like the heartbeat of the jungle, something that she could always depend on and that would go on forever. They sat together then until the shadows crept across the jungle. Talking had always been important in their relationship; today they talked about their early days together, remembering their surprise and joy at finding each other, reliving important moments—the decision to live together, the hunt for a permanent place to live, and the surprising things they had learned about each other.

The birth of the man-cubs had only cemented their relationship more firmly. He believed that he and Sita had been good parents, teaching their sons about their double heritage and what would be required to be successful in either group, animal or human. They were both concerned about the boys' future, and how their ability to transform would affect them in the coming years, but he had confidence that Ashok and Arun would be able to overcome these problems. He had been slightly alarmed when Vasu and Vanada were introduced into the family circle, but the cubs had been remarkably easy to raise. The Prince of Tigers knew that Sita regarded them as her younger sons. He doubted that his commitment was quite as strong; still, he was happy to have them as part of his family and living at the Ananta Palace. Undoubtedly, Vasu and Vanada fit into the family so well because Manju, their father, was such a lovable and kindly fellow and they took after him; the prince shuddered to think what life would have been like if the cubs had modeled themselves after their mother.

He decided not to hunt today. If he followed his usual schedule of hunting, feeding, and resting, today he should be checking this part of the jungle, and perhaps stalking the sambar stag he had sighted a couple of days ago when his stomach was full and there was no need to kill. Even if he did not see the sambar at all, the prince knew it would not be that difficult to obtain a chital or muntjac for dinner. But he was only mildly interested in the prospect. Today was a time to think and plan, not hunt.

He made his way to the Vista Rocks, the top and side of a high hill along a huge nullah that, instead of being covered in trees and vines, was comprised of a series of wide, stone ledges and flat-topped boulders. Although this was a spot favored by local tenduas, the prince scanned the area and found no evidence of them. Like the leopards, the tiger enjoyed taking advantage of the sun's warm rays, and—had he known the word—he would have described himself as a devotee.

The prince stood atop the hill and let his eyes rove across and down both sides of the nullah to the valley as he searched the landscape in all directions. He saw nothing to disturb him. He cocked his head and focused on the sounds of the jungle. All was quiet; that is, there were the usual sounds of moisture dripping from the trees, insects humming, and the *peelak* pouring out melody from his distended, golden throat. A troop of langurs lounged in a banyan tree. Their lookout, an old female, peered this way and that. She saw the tiger but realized from his stance and behavior that he was not a threat; clearly, she saw no danger anywhere, as she was silent.

The Prince of Tigers lay down on his favorite ledge. Even though the sun was pleasantly warm on his coat, he did not allow himself to doze, but the idea was a tempting one. He could not sleep this morning; he needed to stay awake and think. The prince was worried about the future. Several things had recently occurred to him, and he did not know how to put them into perspective. The chief of these was his realization that although he considered himself in his prime, he was most likely about fifteen years old, and thus would probably not live longer than five more years. He had observed that humans lived much longer—often many years longer than tigers—unless they were unfortunate enough to encounter an angry cobra or meet up with an elephant in musth. Actually, many things could considerably shorten a human's life, like disease, floods, muggers—the list was long. But the point was, he might die in five years, while Sita, older than he in actual number of years, was quite likely to live many more years without him and his support.

The prince had always viewed himself as taking care of Sita, protecting her when she needed protection and teaching her about the jungle. He remembered the first time he had brought her to these rocks; no one called them the Vista Rocks then. Sita had smiled with delight and clapped her hands, saying, "But this is wonderful. You can rest comfortably, but at the same time, you have this beautiful vista before you. You can watch how the river runs and see such a long way down the valley. It is like you can see the whole world. It is so beautiful that I could stay here forever." Then she suddenly said, "What is that little pavilion on the mountain across the valley?" and he thought, *Maybe she will never truly be a part of the jungle; maybe she will always be too tied to human things.*

He was glad he had kept these thoughts to himself, as his concern proved to be misplaced. Sita had become a true part of the jungle, but, somehow, she had also managed to keep a connection to her original place and people.

Still, the tiger was worried about Sita and the life she would have that would undoubtedly stretch well beyond his own. He was also concerned about the man-cubs. Although they were developing more slowly than if they had been fully tiger, they seemed older in man years than the time they had actually been alive. He wondered how it would all turn out. And although both his sons had become more skillful in controlling their transformations, Arun was becoming reckless.

The prince had observed his son when the man-cub did not know he was being watched. One day Arun had been trotting in tiger form down a main trail about halfway between the palace and the village. The prince, walking softly parallel to and about thirty yards from the trail, heard a man walking towards Arun; soon the two would meet. There was a slight bend in the trail, so they could not see each other yet, although the prince knew that Arun had to be aware of the man's approach. Then, just before he rounded the curve, Arun transformed into a young man. He greeted the stranger and identified himself as coming from a distant village. He did not linger, and the man passed on but was still in sight when Arun resumed his tiger shape. Fortunately, the man did not turn around; still, the prince was troubled. As a caring father, he felt it was only a matter of time until the young man-cub got into serious trouble. An individual who was both man and beast needed to realize that his position was precarious at best and always dangerous. People had been burned for less.

The prince did not have the same fears for Ashok. The firstborn twin had always demonstrated that he possessed good judgment. It was not that he refused to have fun—Ashok had a good sense of humor, and he could give as good as he got—but he never carried a joke too far. He seemed to sense what the limits were and acted accordingly, even though Arun mocked him for being too sober minded. It was more difficult to assess the characters of Vasu and Vanada; theirs were still in the process of formation.

Puzzling over these matters, the prince did not feel sleepy. Regal as always, he lay on the warm stone ledge as though it were a throne, his head high. Focused on his thoughts, he did not notice activity in the pavilion across the valley or hear what might have been a humming bee that flew so close to him; neither did he feel its powerful sting. But his green eyes closed, his lordly head sank slowly until it rested on his massive paws, and the Prince of Tigers slept the sleep that would last forever.

CHAPTER

2 5

Sita did not worry when the Prince of Tigers did not return that night or the next. As a predator who hunted game, it was necessary for him to go where the game was. There was no guarantee that he would find chital or sambar nearby and that his hunt would be over quickly. If the herd of chital moved to a different part of the jungle (or even beyond the jungle), the prince would have to follow to be successful. In this way, their lives had always been separate. He was a hunter and was sometimes gone for days at a time, while Sita remained at the Ananta Palace, keeping everything in order and tending her garden, cultivating the plants that would become the food she ate and that Ashok and Arun ate when they were man-cubs and not hunting with their father. Vasu and Vanada had tried imitating their brothers when Ashok and Arun ate kaddu and dal, but the experiment had not been successful. They were, of course, totally tiger and needed a tiger's diet to remain healthy.

Not for the first time, Sita regretted that she had not made more friends among the jungle folk; actually, her only close friends were Mor and Nagaiah. Her relationship with the rest of the jungle inhabitants was certainly not hostile, but, wrapped up in her husband and children, Sita had forgotten her original intentions and had not taken the trouble to learn more thoroughly the language of the jungle and make more friends. She was proficient in tiger talk, but past the vocabulary and grammar that was the same or similar to tiger talk, her command of jungle language was still somewhat basic. She should have set herself to become more fluent, but she had depended on the tiger to let her know what was happening around her; now, however, the tiger was not here, and as the days passed, Sita needed reassurance concerning his whereabouts and safety. She talked to Mor, but he did not often stray far from the palace environs, and he knew no more than Sita where the prince might be.

"Ashok," she asked, "could you perhaps ask Cheel if he has seen anything unusual while flying over his territory? Perhaps Haathi has heard something—I remember your father said nothing happened in the jungle that he did not know. But if the news is bad, Tabaqui would be sure to tell us." She did not truly believe there would be bad news; she mentioned the siyaar as a joke because the Prince of Tigers had always looked down on him. His view was that Tabaqui was nothing more than a gossip, particularly when there was bad news to spread abroad.

"Of course, Mother," Ashok said. He was more concerned than Sita. Securely cocooned in her love, she had not noticed that the prince's step was not as springy as it had been in days gone by. But Ashok had noticed and wondered if his father was sick or had a festering wound. He certainly did not think of him as old, but he worried about the changes. Now Ashok's anxiety was sufficiently great that he transformed in front of his mother (something he had not done for some time as he knew it still made her a little uneasy) and loped away on the trail the prince had taken when he left on the last morning his family had seen him.

But Ashok learned nothing as he searched the jungle for news of his father. Arun went to the far corners of their jungle, and even Vasu and Vanada joined in the search, walking the trails and asking all the jungle folk they met if they, or anyone they knew, had seen the Prince of Tigers. The answers were different in some ways, but in the end, they were always the same.

"Yes, yes, plenty of times, but not lately."

"He was in the grove of big teak trees."

"No, at least not for a while. It has been some time since he came this way."

"I saw him talking to Haathi last week. Or maybe the week before. Sometime, anyway."

"Perhaps he has gone elsewhere to a different part of the jungle."

"He was walking on the track that leads north."

"Maybe the game in this jungle has diminished, so he decided to go somewhere else to live."

"Without telling his wife and family?" Ashok asked, at which the informants were embarrassed and slunk away.

A few were bolder, however, and intimated that male tigers were hardly known for being family men, at which Ashok drew himself up so fiercely, and looked so much like his father, that the doubters fell silent and regretted their remarks.

Arun, Vasu, and Vanada had no better luck in their search than Ashok. They knew they would have to report their failure to Sita, and they dreaded seeing the look on her face when she realized that her husband and their father was likely gone forever. They had discovered no reason for his absence, but they felt certain that he was not coming back.

After consulting with each other, the four young tigers assembled at the palace at the same time. None of them wanted to tell Sita that they had failed to find any information about their father, and each felt he needed the support of his brothers—they did not know how Sita would react and what support they would need to offer. Ashok, as the eldest, delivered the news. "Mother," he said, "we have searched far and wide, from one edge of the jungle to the other, and from all the corners to the precise center. Nowhere have we found any trace of our father. As no one has seen him or heard any word of him, we must all accept that he is gone, and it is almost certain that he is gone forever."

Sita had been sitting when the boys came to speak with her; now she rose, and her bearing was proud and erect. "I am the wife of the Prince of Tigers," she said. "I will wait here for him for as long as it takes him to come home."

Sita developed a routine that did not include the presence of her husband. She planted a larger garden than usual and spent so much time clearing, weeding, and hoeing that she became even thinner. She went to the village more often and spent time chatting with Anila and Mitali. It was good to see her old friends, but Sita had another purpose as well—she hoped that her questions about what was happening in the village and the surrounding countryside would glean some news related to the missing Prince of Tigers. She tried to slip the questions into conversation as unobtrusively as possible.

Anila did not perceive Sita's strategy, but she realized that her friend was laboring under some great strain—she vibrated with tension. Mitali thought Sita was stranger than ever, that she had spent too much time living in the jungle or wherever it was she had chosen to live. Both of them urged Sita to return to the village, but this was a tired argument between them that covered old, familiar territory without providing new perceptions or leading in new directions. Back at the Ananta Palace, Sita stood on the balcony, watching the camagadara flight at sundown, but the view did not seem nearly as beautiful without the tiger to share it with.

In her concern over the prince's extended absence, Sita did not notice that Arun was restless. Whether in human or tiger form, he constantly prowled the forest, apparently searching for something, even though he might not know what he was searching for. Arun could not stay in one place; he was always on the move and was absent from home much of the time. He transformed from man to tiger and back again with increasing frequency. Sita had known that Arun was reckless in this regard, changing almost within sight of people, but now it happened so often that had she been more alert, she would have wondered if he had lost control over himself and his transformations. Was he deliberately choosing to transform? Or had he somehow reverted to when he was a child and did not have a choice—at any given moment—whether he would be a tiger or a human?

Always sensitive to Arun's moods, his twin noticed. Ashok was perpetually worried; only Vasu and Vanada were happy and healthy and did not require his concern. Though quite certain of the cause of his father's protracted absence, he could not quite relinquish the desperate hope that his father might be alive after all. He also worried about his mother, who had lost weight and looked more haggard every day that her lonely vigil went unrewarded. Now he was worried about his brother as well. Arun was acting in such a reckless fashion that Ashok saw nothing but trouble ahead for him, if not for the whole family. Sooner or later, someone would see Arun transform from human to tiger, and they would burn him as an abomination. Or they would see him as a tiger and kill him anyway.

Ashok presented these likely possibilities to Arun, but his brother only laughed. "Oh, Ashok," he said, his eyes shining with mischief. "Thou art so serious. I am only having fun. And I can tell thee, thou needs to have more fun. I think fun would be good for thee, my beloved but most sober brother."

"Arun, please," Ashok protested. "Think of our mother and what thy loss would do to her if something happened to thee. She has not been herself since our father disappeared; if thou were to be caught or killed, she would never recover."

"Nothing will happen to me. I am too quick for the headman of the village, even if he has obtained an old blunderbuss. Thou may sound like my father, but thou are not—remember that thou art only my brother. And I assure you, Ashok, thou wilt have to deal with thy brother for a long time yet." And Arun laughed his joyous laugh.

But, of course, he was wrong.

CHAPTER

26

In spite of Sita's initial determination to stay in the Ananta Palace, she felt increasingly sad and lonely. The two man-cubs and Shira's twin cubs (though not really cubs any longer) were in the jungle, and she found the crumbling ruin that was the Ananta Palace unendurable without the Prince of Tigers. She felt traces of him everywhere. As she moved across the great carpet where they had slept at night, she expected to see him stretching lazily. As she went out on the balcony where they once sat together and looked down into the courtyard and watched the man-cubs play, she could hear the man-cubs shouting, "Father, look! See how far I can leap!" As she walked the jungle trails, she knew she was walking where he had walked so often, and she imagined she could still see his paw prints. As she bathed in the pool, she remembered how the tiger loved the water and their happy romps there when his plunges into the pool caused such great splashes. As she worked in the garden, she knew that, at any moment, he would step out into the open, saying, "My Sita, how I have missed thee these many weeks."

Memories are supposed to bring comfort, but Sita's were driving her mad—perhaps because she did not know what had happened to the prince and there had been no specific sense of closure. She hardly talked and she never hummed anymore. If this was grief, she did not understand how others appeared to bear it more gracefully.

One evening when Sita was by herself (her sons were all off hunting), she suddenly realized that she was sitting on the steps of the palace, holding her head in her hands, and rocking back and forth. She was appalled. She had always been reserved and not particularly emotional. But that was before she met the prince. He had unlocked all her emotions, and those very emotions were now free to besiege her foundations. The next day, she moved back to her house (no longer a hut) at the edge of the jungle.

Sita was really quite comfortable there. The tiger had insisted that the house be made larger and more comfortable on the off chance that the two chose to stay there occasionally. At Sita's request, Bhasker now added two rooms to the original two and replaced the thatched roof, which had suffered damage during the monsoons. To complete the job, Sita went to the city and purchased rugs and furniture. Yes, she was physically comfortable. But she found it was also helpful to be around people and listen to what was happening in the village and nearby.

She and Anila often sat together and talked as they mended clothes or spun yarn from the silky hair of goats, descendants of those Sita had purchased when Nagaiah allowed her to take the bracelet from his hoard; she always kept two at the Ananta Palace to provide the milk that Nagaiah loved, but she had hired one of Anila's sons to take care of the small flock she brought back to the village.

As they talked, Sita heard about Shekhar's death; he had been almost eighty years old—a tremendous age. He should have just not awakened one morning; unfortunately, his hut (made of mud bricks) had collapsed during a particularly heavy rainstorm, and his death was sudden and violent.

Kanika's granddaughter had died in childbirth. The baby had lived but was sickly. The father hoped to marry again—a wife could care for the baby. Was Sita interested? Sita found herself interested— not in the widower who needed a wife, but in hearing the stories that Anila told of the people in the village. So many had had terrible things happen to them, had lost the ones they loved. She was not the only one whose heart ached.

One day, Sita walked back to the Ananta Palace. Ashok and Arun had come to her house to see her occasionally, but she had not seen Vasu and Vanada since moving to the village, and she missed them. Luckily, they were home, lying side by side in the palace courtyard. They were so glad to see Sita that they reared up, placing their paws on her shoulders and licking her face with their rough tongues. In his enthusiasm, Vanada knocked her down. Vasu tried to arrest Sita's fall by interposing his body between her and the ground, but Vanada lost his balance, and all three fell in a laughing heap. Sita was touched by their affection, realizing how much she had missed them and how much mutual love was present in their rather unorthodox relationship. She still thought of them as cubs (and they often acted that way), but in reality they had outgrown that designation; she had raised them as the sons of the Prince of Tigers and herself, and they were nearly grown.

Ashok came into the clearing midafternoon, and she threw her arms around his neck. It was really a wonderful day, marred only by the fact that Arun was not there. The three tigers walked with Sita back to the edge of the jungle. Vasu and Vanada, of course, retreated into the bamboo, but Ashok transformed and did not leave his mother until she was safely in her cottage.

After he left, Sita went out to the verandah, thinking to sit there and reflect on how the day had been a happy one, the first happy day she could remember since the disappearance of the Prince of Tigers. At once she realized that something was happening in the village. She could not hear what was being said, of course, but there was a buzz of voices, and people who had been working in the fields were rushing down the path towards the village. She called out to them, but they did not pause to answer, merely hurried on.

Sita was puzzled. What could explain this frenzy of activity? It was like a great beehive, the hum audible from a distance. Suddenly the answer to the puzzle leaped into her mind because it was obvious, if nonspecific. *Something important must have happened while I was in the jungle, but what could be this important?* She would go to the village and find out.

The loud buzzing was centered in the village square; it seemed like the entire village was standing there in the dusk, talking. A few lights were already lit, and she saw some people gesturing wildly. Sita could tell they were agitated, their voices constantly rising, but from excitement, not from anger or fear.

"Where have you been?" Mitali asked. Sita did not answer, so she continued, "Of all the days for you to go off roaming!"

Roaming was the term the villagers had come to use for the times when Sita went into the jungle. Usually, they did not even notice her absence; if they did, they decided that she was roaming. Sita felt they also believed that she did not have all her wits, but she did not mind as long as they were incurious about her activities. She wondered how they referred to the years she had been largely absent, but they appeared to have forgotten them; now she was just Sita of the village again, even though that title hardly took into account her ongoing decision to live her own life and not be an integral part of the village.

"Why, did something happen?" Sita asked.

"Only the most important thing that's ever happened here! The maharajah himself was here. I saw him with both my eyes."

"How did you know who it was?"

"By the way he was dressed, of course."

"Oh, Mitali." Anila had joined them and wanted to have her say. "You know that his servant announced him by his title when they entered the village. He came with a whole train of servants, Sita," she continued. "They were all dressed well. Some were driving oxcarts, and some were riding in the carts, although some of the carts were filled with all kinds of things. The maharajah himself rode on an elephant with some other men. I don't know who they were, but they were clearly very important."

Mitali could hardly wait to get in a few more words. "That's right. I remember now. I just forgot it when I saw the wonderful satin coat he was wearing. Honestly, Sita, it was the prettiest shade of yellow, and—"

Anila continued, paying no attention to Mitali's interruption. "The servant also thanked the village, on behalf of the maharajah, for having a wonderful jungle to hunt in so close to our village. He mentioned the section of the jungle where the hunt happened, and it's actually quite a way south of the village; I guess he doesn't really know our jungle. Anyway, they hoped to find a tiger there and they did. They shot him, so the maharajah and his men were very happy."

Sita felt her heart contract. *Could the maharajah have shot the Prince of Tigers as he returned from wherever he has been for so long?* Her heart was not beating faster, but each stroke was like a blow slamming against her entire body. She was glad of the darkness that hid her face. Her mind was filled with terror and dismay.

"Was it a big one?" she managed to ask brightly.

"Yes, a truly big one," answered Mitali. "I think it took six men to carry him. He was tied to a strong pole to make it easier to carry him, and another man walked behind to keep the tiger's tail from dragging on the ground. They put him into one of the carts."

"So he was dead?" Sita knew this was a stupid thing to say. If the tiger were not dead, he would not be tied to a pole and hauled about by men but would have escaped into the underbrush, or perhaps clambered down into a nullah to evade the men who were hunting him.

"Oh yes, as dead as anything. The maharajah was so pleased. It seems he has a big room in his palace where he has animals that he has shot and then had stuffed so they can be on display and the important people he invites to his palace can see the big kills he has made."

Anila chimed in, "Even though he was dead, I could see that the tiger was a very handsome one. He was unusual, too, because he had a strange mark on his chest."

Sita felt cold all over. "What kind of mark?" she asked.

"I do not know how to describe it," Anila replied. "But the teacher said the mark was like a prashn chinh."

Sita did not know how she kept from shouting her terror aloud, but she had to act in a way that would not arouse comments or questions. "I walked a long way today and I'm so tired," she managed to mutter. "I'm going to go home now."

"No, no," the sisters chorused. "Today has been so exciting! I know everyone will be talking about it for hours. Someone may have more to tell about the maharajah and his retinue."

"I think they will still be talking about his visit tomorrow. I can learn all about everything then. I am really tired now and am longing to go to bed and have a good sleep."

Sita slipped away into the darkness. She was in a fog as she walked to her house, seeing nothing and hearing nothing, along the way. But when she opened the door, she saw immediately that Ashok was there, waiting for her. She saw the pain in his eyes and heard the terrible words he spoke. "Mother," he said softly, "have you heard?"

CHAPTER

27

When Ashok confirmed what she was already certain of, Sita collapsed. She fell on her charpoy and wept. She refused to eat. Anila and Mitali came to see her every day; they could see that she was not well. They brought little bites of this and that to tempt her appetite, but she was not tempted. They related many gossipy little stories, hoping to divert her, but Sita was not diverted. It took every bit of the energy Sita could summon to keep the source of her distress hidden from her friends. "I feel terrible," she groaned. "I do not know what is the matter with me." When she wondered aloud if what was wrong with her was contagious, the two women stayed away, although they continued to send her food.

Most of the time, Sita locked herself away with her memories. She remembered giving birth to Ashok and Arun in the jungle. No one was with her to help her then; even the Prince of Tigers was absent. It was just Sita and her sons, as it had been for much of their lives because of the tiger's frequent absences. Now, Arun was gone. He had been heedless and reckless, but he was her man-cub whom she had given birth to and raised. She would never see him again. She would never again witness his little naughty acts, followed by his provoking smile (no matter whether human or tiger), or hear his petulant, angry voice when things went wrong. She would never stroke his orange coat, admire the dramatic black stripes, or run her fingers over the question mark on his chest again. Arun was gone.

Ashok stayed with her. He brought her cool water to drink and searched in the jungle for her favorite fruits. He stayed in his human form, and nobody from the village seemed to care or wonder about his presence. In truth, the villagers had long ago realized that he was Sita's son. They were not certain who the father might be, and it was too bad that Sita had produced a bastard child, but it was hardly surprising given her family history and her erratic life. Some said there was a second son as well, but his visits to the village had been less frequent, and few wondered why he did not appear when Sita was so unwell.

Ashok was responsible for recalling his mother to an interest in life, and his method of doing this was very simple. He sat on the floor beside the charpoy where she lay. He took her hand in his, and he said six words: "How did you meet my father?"

Sita thought back to the days before she had met the tiger. She had been happy growing up with Bhima, even though they were poor; she had liked their semi-independent life and learning about plants and how they could be used, and she had enjoyed the stories Bhima told her. That life, however, seemed drab in contrast with the times when she first felt the presence, followed by long conversations with the tiger and the deeper relationship that had developed. Sita began to tell Ashok the story of the Prince of Tigers and herself, and how they had decided to spend their lives together in the jungle. Ashok sat without moving, still holding his mother's hand. He was astonished. Sita had rarely talked about these things before and never in such detail. Ashok was not certain what it meant to him, although upon hearing how the village had attempted to force her into the mold they felt a young woman was destined to occupy, he felt anger towards those individuals who had mistreated her by trying to prevent her from following her destiny. He realized what a courageous step it had been for Sita to leave everything familiar behind and what an amazingly unusual individual the Prince of Tigers had been.

These conversations with Ashok signaled the beginning of Sita's recovery. It was not like her to be passive and defeated, and her friends rejoiced when she once again started to assert herself. They were quite surprised, however, at what Sita decided to do.

Her plan was simple. She had decided to go to the maharajah's palace and try to get work there. Anila and Mitali—and through them the rest of the village—believed that Sita had decided to do this because she was sorry to have missed the maharajah's visit to the area on his hunting trip. It had been a tremendously exciting time, probably the most excitement any of them would ever know, and Sita completely missed the occasion. And because of her illness, she had even missed the aftermath. For several days following, nothing else had been talked about; the posture and clothing of the maharajah, the size of his retinue, the speeches made, etc., were surely worthy of the hours and days of recollections and analysis that had ensued. But through her illness, Sita had missed all these discussions as well.

Small wonder that she should wish to have part of the glory, although they did not believe that it would really happen. *They* had seen the maharajah up close; even if she were taken on as one of the army of household servants at the Primrose Palace, she would probably never see him at all.

Sita ignored the comments and speculations. Only Ashok knew her real mission—that she was hoping to prove that the handsome tiger with the distinctive mark on his chest was not Arun, though on one level she knew that it must be him. First, however, Sita decided to return to the Ananta Palace and focus on her preparations, although these were few and simple. She gathered up a parcel consisting of two saris and a package of chapattis, and she set off through the jungle.

✗o

After arriving at the palace, Sita collected a few more belongings. Although she planned to take only practical items, she wished to have something to remind her of the Prince of Tigers, their sons, their adopted sons, and their life here. At last, she asked Ashok to go to the underground room, give her greetings to Nagaiah, and ask if the king cobra would allow him to take one of the jewels to Sita, something she could hold in her hands that would be a physical reminder of the happy years that were now gone.

When Ashok returned, he brought Nagaiah's salutations to Sita and a large, unset emerald that the great snake had selected for her. Sita held it in her hand and stared into its verdant depths. It was like looking into the jungle where the eye became overwhelmed by the many shades of green: grass, ferns, and leaves, brighter in sun, darker in shadow—all of the shades contributing to the feeling of being immersed in the green of the jungle. It was like looking into the eyes of the Prince of Tigers; his eyes might signal love, anger, challenge, puzzlement—she could think of any number of emotions she once read in his eyes—but those eyes were always green.

Sita closed her fingers over the emerald for a moment, then tied it into a corner of her sari. Nagaiah had chosen the perfect gift, and she felt ashamed that she had not gone to see him herself.

Sita descended the treacherous stairs. Nagaiah was waiting for her at the bottom.

"I am more happy than I can say that you have come yourself," he said. "I will miss you when you are gone."

"Do you understand why I must go?"

"Of course. You would not be Sita if you did not continue to search for your loved ones."

Nagaiah reared up straight to his full height, and Sita wrapped her arms around him, something she had never done before. He dropped his head onto her shoulder for a moment, then withdrew into the shadows as Sita slowly climbed back up the stairs. She knew with certainty that she would miss him too.

She walked to the village and left it the same way she had when she went to the city the first time, years ago. She asked for a ride in Udit's bullock cart and once again paid him a few small coins for the ride. When they arrived at the city, she again bade him farewell and walked away, soon lost in the crowd of people who were pushing and hurrying in every direction.

Sita's journey was not yet over. The maharajah's Primrose Palace and huge estate were many miles farther, out in the countryside. She headed in that direction, uncertain how she would gain access to the grounds, let alone the palace itself. Then a cart stopped, and someone asked if she would like a ride. The cart was mostly filled with bags of millet and other grains, but several palace servants were riding as well, perched on the bags, and to Sita's surprise, the servants were friendly and talkative. In response to their questions, Sita said she was from beyond the city and that someone had suggested there might be work as a maid at the Primrose Palace. Her new companions said she might be hired to sweep and mop, or something like that. There was no possibility of working as a maid to the maharajah's wives, and probably little chance that she could help in the kitchen.

Sita was content with this information; she had no desire to be a servant to a grand lady who would doubtless be displeased with everyone around her, especially those who served her. Sita would be content with the simple tasks she already knew how to do, and what they were did not matter to her. Menial tasks faded into nothingness alongside her true purpose.

CHAPTER

28

What surprised Sita the most was that in the Primrose Palace, no one was ever alone. There were always people coming and going, their scurrying feet making a sort of *shush-shush* sound on the carpets and a *slap-slap* on the marble floors. She wondered how she would ever learn her way about the palace—which of the marble hallways she should follow when she was directed to find a missing fan or take a message to a fellow servant. Usually, however, her responsibilities were limited to cleaning a certain area of the palace, the area where the maharajah's wives and waiting women lived. Daily she swept and scrubbed the marble floors and dusted the tables and chairs. Other servants were surprised that she had been given so much responsibility so soon, but Sita had early shown that she was quick and thorough with her duties; the man who supervised the cleaners was pleased to find how dependable she was.

Sita did not mind the work; what she did mind was that her work did not give her any reason to be near the maharajah's museum. She had not forgotten her intention to enter this room and see if, indeed, Arun was there—not a living Arun, merely an object that represented him, but still, in some sense, Arun, the son she had loved so dearly and lost forever. And perhaps it was not Arun at all but some stranger, another tiger who just happened to be large and beautiful with an unusual (or even similar) mark on his chest.

Sita's chance occurred when an important visitor came to the palace and the maharajah organized a fairly local shoot for this man. Everything was immediately chaotic in the palace; the servants' everyday jobs were done less thoroughly than usual as they strove to deal with additional duties for the duration of the visit. Food had to be cooked in the kitchens, then conveyed to the jungle, wherever the hunters happened to be at that time. Duties were shifted and reassigned. The man who oversaw the museum was instructed to help convey the food. He was tall and strong and could carry large hampers of victuals and lift them safely in and out of the wagons. Sita was directed to omit her usual duties; instead, she must see that the museum was in perfect order. Every inch should be swept, scrubbed, dusted, and polished because the maharajah might show the museum to his guest after the shoot.

Sita trembled as she gathered her cleaning materials and walked through the halls and rooms of the palace until she reached the museum. She had discovered its location a week after moving to the palace but had never had a reason to be in its vicinity until today. Now if anyone asked what she was doing in the museum, she could say truthfully, "The *khansama* sent me." After hearing those magic words, her questioner would go away, saying nothing more because, among the servants, the khansama's word was law. This afternoon, she would be free to investigate Arun's fate.

Sita approached the door to the museum. It was very tall, with an embossed sheet of metal laid over the wood. Her hand shook as she pulled the door open and looked straight ahead to the end of the room. The light fell slantingly through the windows, and she saw Arun at once. He had been posed sitting. His tail had been caught in mid-switch. He looked alive—his coat a deep, rich orange, the prashn chinh visible on his chest. His eyes looked fixedly to his right, seemingly focused on something, whether a blowing leaf, a chital

fawn, or a strutting peafowl. Only his immobility and the fact that
he was sitting in a large glass case spoiled the illusion that Arun was
still living and breathing, a young and vigorous male tiger—her son.

Almost against her will, Sita looked left to see what Arun was
looking at. She stopped breathing, feeling as if all the blood had
suddenly been drained from her body. Her eyes would not focus,
yet she was in no doubt of what she and Arun were looking at. The
Prince of Tigers stood there, appearing alert as always. He was not
smiling the smile Sita loved to see; instead, he had the grave look
of a prince who is known to be wise and must make the judgments
required of him as the ruler of the jungle. He looked majestic.

Sita could not help herself. She rushed forward (knocking over
the mop bucket as she ran) and fell on her knees before the glass that
held her husband frozen in its grasp. She wept. She knocked her head
on the floor. She knew she was making an outcry she would not be
able to explain if she were discovered, but the pain was too great for
her to be silent. It was inconceivable that such agony should not be
given the liberty to escape her small body. Sita finally sat up close
against the case, running her fingers across the glass and talking to
the prince as though he were able to hear and understand, as though
he could respond.

"Thou hast been gone so long," she murmured. "And with never a
word to me. Didst thou not understand how I have missed thee? How
I have needed thee? How miserable I have been without thee? I know
that thy sons and all of thy subjects could say the same, but my pain
and longing are deeper than any. Didst thou not realize, my prince,
that my life would be forever barren and empty without thee?"

The Prince of Tigers did not answer. Although he was staring
straight at Sita, his eyes did not change expression; not a whisker
moved, and he did not reach for her as he would have in the old days
when so many times he had reclined, holding her to his chest with
his great paws. Yet Sita kept talking, weeping, crooning to him, as if
to somehow break through the heavy glass barrier of death that lay

between them and recall him to her side once again.

Then Sita suddenly became aware that she was no longer alone with the prince and Arun. Yes, there were other animals there that she had ignored, animals that had also been collected by the maharajah through his skill with a gun. Now, however, the room was filled with people as well. There was a short man, gorgeously attired in a suit of light-green satin with a large diamond on his breast. Sita had never seen the maharajah except at a distance, but she assumed this was he—he had an air of command as if the entire world belonged to him. Following this man were two others: one Sita had often seen the maharajah listening to respectfully; the other was tall and thin and pale, dressed relatively plainly in a khaki suit, decorated on the chest with some bright ribbons. In addition, the two were followed by a large number of the maharajah's senior retainers and counselors.

Sita had been sobbing off and on for an hour, and her face was streaked with dust and tears. Her hair had fallen down from the knot she twisted it into every morning. She was crouched on the floor (*almost like an animal*, the maharajah thought) and apparently talking to the exhibit within one of the cases. This woman had been assigned to clean the museum; instead, it was filthy. A pool of water had collected by an overturned bucket, and she had left smudges, fingerprints, and tears over two of the cases—the two that held the maharajah's most prized exhibits.

The maharajah was proud of his museum, and he had been looking forward to displaying it to his visitor. Instead, everything appeared to be dusty and in disarray, a disgrace. Central to this unpleasant scene was the weeping, probably demented woman. The whole thing was a spectacle—and a highly distasteful one at that. "Woman!" he bellowed. "What are you doing here?"

Sita slowly got to her feet. Her mind was muddled by her discovery, and she tried to clear it; she attempted to stand straight and signal that she should be taken seriously and her words were worth listening to. She adjusted her sari and tucked her hair behind her ears before she spoke. "I know that thou art all-powerful, the maharajah who rules this kingdom," she said, "but these words must be spoken. Some truths cannot live in silence but are of such great and solemn consequence that they must be cried aloud." Sita then paused long enough to take a deep breath before she spoke the following words: "Thou hast slain my husband and my son and brought them to this place. Where else should I go to grieve for them and commune with them?"

CHAPTER

29

Yes, the maharajah had been very angry, but he had also been puzzled and intrigued on that afternoon in the museum. Who was this woman, and what was she talking about, accusing him, the maharajah of Sundara Pradesh, of killing her husband and son? What could be the meaning of her mysterious words?

It was of course irritating to have a scene like this occur when he was entertaining an important British visitor, General Arbuthnot, but he had made up for it by presenting the man with a special set of brandy glasses decorated with gold-leaf rims, and the general left the palace quite happy with the shoot, the gift, and the excellent brandy he had been served. Not being particularly interested in stuffed specimens, the man barely remembered the unkempt woman who shouted so wildly and incoherently in the museum.

The maharajah had asked Harish, his most valued advisor, whom he always kept near him, what he thought of the bizarre incident. Harish merely shook his head and indicated that women were inclined to be emotional, which tended, in his mind, to make them unreasonable.

But the maharajah could not forget the words the woman had spoken, and he did not know how to find her. She had left the room immediately after making her short but crazed speech; perhaps she had been inebriated. Everyone present had been struck dumb by amazement, and no one attempted to stop her. Perhaps they were waiting for him to order that she should be taken away and disciplined in some way, perhaps whipped, but he had been too confused and astonished to speak.

The woman must work in the palace, but the maharajah did not know the names of his servants. He didn't even know how many there were, although he thought the number was somewhere in the low hundreds. It was their job to see that the palace ran smoothly, that everything he desired to have done was done quickly, without his having to think of his request again or having to check whether his instructions had been carried out. To a lesser extent, their job was also to see to the welfare of his son, his two wives, and any relatives and friends that might live in the palace or be visiting there. The entire Primrose Palace needed to be run in such an orderly manner that an observer would be unaware of how much effort that actually took. Duleep, the khansama, was the individual responsible for maintaining this order, so the maharajah called him to his *daftar*.

"This woman who made a spectacle of herself in the museum on Thursday—who is she?" he asked.

And Duleep, knowing almost everything that transpired in the palace, answered at once, "That one is called Sita, a humble and stupid woman who was hired to do nothing more than sweep floors at the palace, as I determined she was fit for naught else. Do not be disturbed about this woman, Excellency. I have already dismissed her, as she deserved."

"No, no," the maharajah expostulated. "She must not be dismissed. I would speak with her and at once. You must bring her to me now."

Duleep tried not to squirm. "Excellency, I believed it would be your wish to have her gone. I dismissed her two days ago. I have no idea where she might be found now."

"Then you need to busy yourself finding her," the maharajah

said in the silky voice he seldom used but that always meant trouble would come to the person he was speaking to if his wishes were not carried out, quickly and efficiently.

Duleep had been with the maharajah for many years and knew him well. "Why do you seek this woman?" he ventured. "She is nothing, just a village woman with no learning, beauty, or poise."

"I will ignore your question as the answer does not concern you," the maharajah replied curtly. "Your only duty at this point is to find her at once." Duleep left the room, not certain if he was still the khansama or not. He did not know what to do. Alerting the entire staff to the problem would let them know he had somehow slackened his grasp on the mechanism of the palace and that, as a consequence, he was in disfavor. In the end, he spoke to a few of his trusted assistants, who spread the word as though they were the ones looking for the woman who had caused trouble during the general's visit.

After being ordered loudly and dramatically to leave by the khansama, who embellished his lecture with comments on her low birth and the deficiencies of her upbringing, Sita had spent two days sitting quietly behind some bales of fabric in the attic while she considered what to do. She wanted to remain near Arun and her husband, yet she had been forbidden to do so by a man of great power. Sita knew the danger of ignoring this man's command; her fellow servants had told her of individuals who had suddenly disappeared for making some error less serious that Sita's outburst, and no one knew if they had merely gone away or if something worse had happened.

Sita concluded that she would have to leave the palace. It wrenched her heart yet again. She had discovered the prince's fate and now knew for certain that he was dead; they would never again romp through the jungle, or swim in their pool, or lie close together among the jungle ferns. Still, his likeness was here, and to be so soon separated from him again, and from their son as well, was almost more than she could bear.

Yet it was necessary. She would have to return to her home, but she would not be totally on her own—she still had Ashok, Vasu and Vanada, friends in the village, her cottage, and the Ananta Palace in the jungle. She also had her memories of the Prince of Tigers—he might be dead, but the memories would always be with her. So Sita left the maharajah's palace with a group of artisans who had come to sell their wares. She had the end of her sari pulled across her face, and no one paid any attention to her. Shortly after they reached the road, Sita slipped away from the artisans and headed towards the city.

Well before she reached it, however, she heard horses coming. Sita turned aside to let them go past, but instead they surrounded her. She was frightened but stood quietly while their leader stated that she needed to return with them to the Primrose Palace. Sita was given no explanation. When she and her escort arrived at the palace, she was taken to her old room, but a guard stood outside the door all night. The next morning, he told her to follow him, and he escorted her to the maharajah.

He was sitting in what she would learn was a Western-style chair of wood and leather, one of a pair that the general had brought the maharajah as a gift on a previous visit to the palace. The other was sitting close by, but it was empty. The maharajah indicated that Sita should stand in front of him, and she moved forward until he motioned for her to stop. She looked directly at him. Sitting, it was not obvious how short he was. Today his satin suit was pale blue. Again, he was wearing jewels; she noted that they were a darker blue than his clothing.

"I would speak with you," the maharajah announced. "I want to know the meaning of what you said in the museum. Speak clearly and truthfully and tell me what I want to know."

As he spoke, the maharajah felt a certain amount of confusion. The woman before him was clearly of the most humble class. He did not remember if he had ever spoken with such a one before. Servants, yes, of course he gave orders, but he did not hold conversations with them. Furthermore, although his personal retainers were of a lower class, they did not come from the country, as this woman obviously did. Perhaps she even belonged to one of the uncivilized tribes that had never fully emerged from the jungle, although she was decently dressed in a sari and choli and stood quietly before him.

"What would you like to know?" the woman asked, as though she had not heard what he said.

"What is your name?" the maharajah said. "What are you called?"

"My name is Sita."

"That is not a common name."

"It is a humble name. Many parents prefer to give their children names that suggest brilliance or riches. My mother and aunt lived outside a village at the edge of the jungle, and they planted what they needed in order to eat. A simple name was deemed best for a girl child born into this family."

"What does Sita mean?"

"It means furrow, the furrow where seeds are planted, seeds that will grow into something that will sustain life."

"That sounds more necessary than humble."

Sita smiled for the first time. "Of course, it is both," she said. "But you must possess discernment, or you would not grasp the double meaning."

The maharajah did not know whether Sita spoke the truth as she saw it or whether she was attempting to flatter him. "I was curious to see if you knew the meaning of your name," the maharajah said. "Of course I know the meaning of the name Sita. But you neglected

to mention something else, something important. The goddess Sita
was the wife of Lord Rama. Did you know this?"

"I have always known this. Bhima, my mother's sister who raised
me, told me the stories when I was a child. But she also told me I
should focus on what was humble rather than exalted because it
would come closer to reflecting what my own life would be."

The maharajah decided to change the subject. He found the
discussion interesting, and he would enjoy talking more about the
goddess Sita—the epic heroine who had endured so much sorrow
in her life. But that conversation would not move in a direction that
addressed his central question. If rattled by a sudden shift, she might
reveal something to clarify the confusing scene that had taken place
in the museum.

"Why were you in the museum?" he asked.

"I, as one of your servants, was bidden to go to the museum and
clean it well. What I saw when I entered the room, however, made
me forget why I had come and what I was supposed to do."

"What did you see and why were you affected so strongly?"

"I believe what I said at the time explains my distress. If you have
forgotten my words, I can repeat them for you: 'Thou hast slain my
husband and my son and brought them to this place. Where else
should I go to grieve for them and commune with them?'"

The maharajah said, "I remember the words perfectly, but I do
not understand them."

CHAPTER

30

Sita stood quietly, waiting to see if the maharajah would explain the reasons behind his questions. She had expected to be frightened in his presence. He had the power to end her life with a single command, but she did not think he would issue that command. He seemed genuinely interested in what she had to say. Furthermore, it occurred to her that a woman who had been married to the Prince of Tigers should not be afraid of a mere human, even a maharajah. The latter could command her death, but the former could have accomplished it with one swipe of his paw. Yet she had never been afraid of the tiger, so why should she fear this human ruler?

"There are many things I do not understand," the maharajah continued. "I would be glad to listen if you would be willing to enlighten me."

"What would you like to know?"

"Everything," he said. "Start at the beginning. Who are you and where are you from? Who are your husband and son, and why do you hold me responsible for and accuse me of their deaths?" In truth, he was fascinated by this woman whom he found to be singularly different from anyone he had known. Partly, it was because she obviously came from humble stock yet was utterly calm; he was surprised she was not afraid of him. She spoke well and there was sincerity in every intonation of her voice and in every line of her body.

At some point, he motioned for her to sit in the other chair. Sita, unaware of what an honor it was to be allowed to sit in his presence, quickly obeyed. She did not like it; chairs had not been part of her experience, but she tried to endure this unfamiliar experience with dignity and continued speaking.

Later, he held up his hand again. "Please stop for now," the maharajah said. "But you must come again to talk to me. Each day that my time allows, you must come and talk to me for an hour. Someone will come to fetch you."

He snapped his fingers. A servant entered. "Take this woman to the women's wing," he commanded. "Give her one of the better rooms and see that she is dressed appropriately for a daily audience with me."

The servant looked surprised. He led Sita to a section of the palace she had entered every day, but only with a broom in her hand. It was clearly set aside for women of the maharajah's family, entourage, guests, and these individuals' personal servants. Women were coming and going, chittering and chattering to each other as they passed through the halls and in and out of rooms. Previously, Sita had tried to stay out of these individuals' way and keep her eyes respectfully lowered; now, she wondered who they were.

Sita felt dazed. She could not imagine why the maharajah wanted to hear about her life and experiences. And why was she being transferred to this wing of the palace from the more general underservant area? She was even more confused when she saw where she would now live, a spacious room with windows that looked out over the park surrounding the Primrose Palace. The room had carpets on the floors and a marble bathtub that a maid filled with perfumed water for her bath. The woman also brought an armload of saris. The sumptuous fabrics made Sita catch her breath. She could not imagine wearing clothes of this quality.

Nevertheless, when the maharajah sent for her the following day, Sita was wearing one of the beautiful saris that had been provided for her.

❧

From then on, Sita's life was completely different in every way. She no longer lived a hard life; she was never cold or hungry or uncomfortable. She was not even merely comfortable. Instead, her life was a luxurious one. Although the palace was cold in winter, Sita was not cold. She was wrapped in thick shawls and quilts. Her meals no longer consisted of rice and dal, some fried *aloo* or, if she was lucky, possibly a curry made with vegetables and even a bit of ground cashew nuts. Now she nibbled on the most exquisite tidbits of the finest food. If she desired something spicy, it was brought to her; if she was hungry for a sweet, she merely had to speak to a servant, and a tray of the delicacy was fetched immediately. She did not do backbreaking work in the garden where constant stooping made her body ache. She no longer swept and dusted around the palace; it had not been hard work, but it was not a task she found congenial.

In return for all this comfort and magnificence, there was only one duty Sita needed to perform. When the maharajah sent for her—and he sent for her almost every day—she must go to him, whether he was at the stables or walking among the flower beds, viewing his menagerie, or sitting in the small room that she had learned was called the daftar. Once there, he would ask her specific questions or sometimes simply request that she tell him about her previous life, without demanding or even suggesting a specific topic. After an hour, he would excuse her, and she would return to her rooms. Sometimes, he talked, made speeches, while she was his only audience. Sometimes, she spoke for the entire hour, other times, the maharajah constantly asked her questions that she must answer. She did not always know the answers.

On one level, it was a very easy life; on another, it was extremely difficult. Wandering among her memories, talking to someone about the Prince of Tigers, was a great relief. Sita had never told these stories to anyone except Ashok and a few to Arun before his death; the prince had always been a part of her life that she needed to conceal.

But sharing the memories of her husband was also very painful. And how could it be that the person she seemed destined to discuss the tiger with was the very individual who had murdered him? So Sita compromised. She responded to the maharajah's questions, but what she gave him was a carefully edited version, a facsimile—yes, she painted a picture of the prince, but in muted colors, rather like the prince who resided in the maharajah's museum. She thought she might not recognize this tiger if she met him, but the maharajah was suitably impressed.

Every day, when Sita walked back to her room, or if she took a stroll in the grounds, she considered the irony of talking to the maharajah about the Prince of Tigers. She thought about it from different angles until her head ached. Had she said too much? Had she said too little? Some days, she wanted to tell the maharajah everything; but often she wanted to close her lips and never speak again. When she saw him sitting across from her, the deep anger that he was here and her husband was not occasionally welled up so strongly that she was unable to say anything and had to take a few minutes to compose herself before she could continue.

One day, Sita was returning to her room after a walk to a gazebo overlooking a small lake. The afternoon was very hot, and she had hoped the shady nook and the breeze coming off the water would cool her flushed cheeks. She let her hand trail in the water and then patted her cheeks with her damp hand, but in a few moments she felt as hot as ever. She stood and started towards the palace when she spotted the maharajah's messenger coming through the trees.

"The maharajah would like to see you," the man announced.

"Are you certain? I have already seen him today, and he never asks me to come more than once a day."

"I cannot tell you why he wants to see you. I can only say that he specifically told me to bring you to him without delay. I went to your rooms, but as you were not there, I decided to look near the lake. I know you often come here. If I had not found you, I would have gone next to the maharajah's menagerie as you often go to see the animals that are kept there."

"All right," Sita said. "I will go to him shortly."

"No, you are to come now; I am to escort you. This was also a part of the maharajah's instructions."

Sita thought the messenger must have made a mistake, but she followed him to the usual room. The same chairs were in their usual spots. The maharajah sat in one, and he waved her to the other. She thought he looked pale and tense.

"I have something to say to you that I want you to consider seriously," the maharajah stated. "Please listen carefully."

This directive made no sense at all to Sita. She was his servant. *Why doesn't he just ask me what he wants to know?* He often told her what he wanted her to talk about—"Do more people of the village become ill in the hot season or in the rainy season? When someone builds a hut out of mud bricks, how long will the bricks last until they begin to crumble?" It must be something he thought she would be unable to answer easily. Sita nodded and leaned forward.

"Sita," the maharajah said, speaking slowly and articulating his words clearly, "I greatly admire you. You are a wise woman; every day I am struck by your wisdom and discretion. I may take another wife, and I would be pleased if you would consent to a marriage with me. It would be a great honor to wed a woman whose former husband was the Prince of Tigers."

CHAPTER

31

Sita was thankful for the education she had been given by the prince. If she had been a tiger in actuality, she would not have moved a whisker. She was a woman, but not by a blink of the eye or a movement of the mouth did she give any indication of what was in her mind.

"Your Excellency, you have given me much to think about," she said quietly. "May I be excused so that I may ponder the words you have spoken?"

"Of course you are excused. You will attend me at the same time tomorrow, and I will expect your answer then."

Sita rose. *Is it my imagination, or does the maharajah sound testy?* She bowed and left the room without haste, even though it felt as though she were escaping. She went to her room and took the emerald from its hiding place. Then she sat by the window, holding it in her hand, rolling it between her fingers and staring into its green depths. What she saw, however, was not the emerald itself—she saw the eyes of the Prince of Tigers. She looked out over the grounds for a long time, imagining the prince running across the green expanse of well-tended lawn.

Unable to sit still, she went out and meandered along the carefully graveled pathways and among the beautiful old trees that grew everywhere on the maharajah's estate except the spaces where sweeping lawns or beds of flowers had been planted. She wandered to the lake again and sat there, alone, trying to think coherently while she watched the silver fish make silver splashes. Her heart dictated what her answer must be. It would have been her answer if she had answered immediately, and it would still be her answer when she saw him again tomorrow. There was no other answer she could give. The problem she faced was not the answer itself but how to put that answer into an acceptable form. She did not wish to anger her benefactor. The opportunity he had afforded her to talk about the past, particularly to talk about the Prince of Tigers, was an important part of her current life.

People in the village knew that she had some sort of connection with a tiger, but they did not know that the Prince of Tigers was her husband or that she had borne him two sons. If she had stated this fact, they would probably have thought she had lost her wits. It was true that those deemed mad were taken care of and treated gently because they were viewed as almost holy by virtue of their madness. But Sita did not want to be treated gently or thought mad. She wanted to be respected because she was Sita, nothing more. She enjoyed the respect she received at the maharajah's palace because of her relationship with him, but she was well aware that if something happened to him, the respect would instantly evaporate.

The issues of respect and maintenance did not figure into her decision, however. Sita had decided she had no choice but to refuse the maharajah's most generous offer. Surely he knew that, should she accept, there would be whispers, contempt, confrontation (perhaps even rebellion) directed towards him, coming from other rulers, his court, and even his own household. All this would most certainly occur were he to marry someone like herself, someone from the peasant class.

Sita believed that he was indeed willing to make this great sacrifice out of respect for her. But Sita was not willing to make a great sacrifice for him. The fact that she and the maharajah could be considered friends (of a sort) was astonishing enough. Seldom, if ever, would a woman be able to find forgiveness for an individual who had killed her husband and son. Sita had not exactly forgiven the maharajah, but her great anger against him lessened as she came to understand much more clearly what his life consisted of and why he made many of the choices he did. But what could never be ignored was that she did not and could never love the maharajah.

Love was not highly valued in the culture that had produced Sita. People married for other reasons—support, security, family pressures, a skill that the prospective spouse possessed, or money that could mark the establishment of a new household or ensure the security of an old one. The Prince of Tigers, however, had changed all the ideas of marriage Sita had acquired throughout her early life. Of course, it should include the ability of the couple to provide for themselves and whatever progeny should come from the union, but a true marriage needed to be so much more. The two individuals who had agreed to this union should be happy in it—they should support each other, have like interests, learn together, and enjoy the many and varied aspects of their life together. They should love each other.

In truth, having been married to the Prince of Tigers, Sita knew that she could never honestly enter into a marriage with anyone else. The new relationship would be a sad pretense, an attempt to replicate something that could never be replicated. She had to make the maharajah understand this, without her response signaling a failure to understand the magnitude of what he was offering her—a gift that might tarnish his position and diminish his stature among his peers and fellow rulers. He might consider her refusal to be an insult, a reaction Sita wished to avoid if at all possible.

The next day dawned all too quickly. Sita had slept little, and there was a tired droop to her shoulders as she made her way through the palace to the maharajah's daftar. The servants who saw her thought she looked unhappy. *Perhaps*, they thought, *the master has grown tired of this woman. Perhaps he is going to send her away today and she knows it.*

Sita did not see these sidelong glances—her mind on the approaching interview, she noticed nothing. When she entered the daftar, the maharajah was sitting, waiting for her. Again, he waved her to the other chair, but today, she ignored his gesture and stood before him.

"Well," he said, "what have you to say to me?"

"I have thought of many reasons why our union would not be wise," Sita said softly but clearly. "However, in the end, I must and will tell you the truth. I hope you will understand and accept it as truth when I tell you that, having been the wife of the Prince of Tigers, it would clearly be impossible for me to marry another. It makes no difference that he is dead." The maharajah, remembering the terrible scene in the museum with Sita screeching out her pain, winced at the bluntness of the statement. "He is the husband of my heart, and I will forever be unable to take another. That is the truth, unvarnished and complete."

The maharajah looked down silently for a long moment. Sita knew that he was unaccustomed to being disagreed with or frustrated. She had expected an explosion, but the silence was worse. Finally, he looked up.

"Your answer is not a surprise," he said. "Indeed, I have expected it since you said you wanted time to consider my proposal. Any other woman would have thought only of what she would gain from a marriage to me—comfort, security, money, jewels—and she would have accepted immediately. All those things, but you were willing to reject them, and to do so immediately. I believe that you asked for time not because you did not know what your answer would be, but in order to couch your answer in terms that would neither hurt me nor make me angry."

"You speak truth, Excellency."

"Were you not concerned that I might order your execution, or have you punished if you refused me?"

Sita shook her head. She had thought he might be angry, but she had not dwelled on what the consequences for herself might be if she should refuse the maharajah's offer.

"I thought not. But I also expected you to say no; therefore, I have been contemplating another plan."

Puzzled but calm, Sita waited for him to continue.

"I have many ideas in my head that I have been unable to talk about to my ministers. They would not understand why I want to know certain things. Even Harish, my chief minister with whom I discuss most governance issues, is not interested in these things, but they rattle in my brain and I need to talk to someone about them. Now I know that you were destined to be the one."

"I do not understand," Sita said. "I am only a woman, and I come from a small, poor village. My background is humble."

"That is precisely why," the maharajah stated. "You can explain to me the things I do not understand. I want to know more about what my subjects think and why. You will be one of my councilors."

"I do not believe I am fitted for or prepared to hold this position."

"That is for me to decide." The maharajah sounded somewhat vexed. "It will not be an onerous position to fill, as very little will change. We already discuss these things almost every day. We will continue to talk as we do now, but the scope of our discussions will be much broader and more detailed, as well. That is all for today."

CHAPTER

32

Indeed, the changes were not great, although when Sita returned to her room after what the maharajah twinklingly referred to thereafter as the "refusal council," she was led to different rooms on a different floor of the palace. Her new rooms were, of course, still in the women's wing, but they were on the same floor as those of the maharajah's wives, and their grandeur was close in scale. To be sure, Sita had lived in large rooms in the Ananta Palace, but there, the furnishings were old and some of them had partly, or even mostly, disintegrated. The shabby carpets had still been in surprisingly good shape, but some of the hangings of more fragile material had rotted away, made more obvious after Sita subjected them to a beating to remove dust, followed by a washing. Some of the wooden furniture had been broken, and Sita's efforts to repair those pieces had not been particularly successful.

These new rooms in the Primrose Palace were so beautiful and grand that Sita felt they were hardly real. All the furnishings were more lovely than any she had ever seen. What she liked best, however, was the balcony where she could sit and look into the trees, watching the birds flitting from branch to branch, and the monkeys as they swung from one perch to another. She spent hours there but had to admit that although the view made her feel closer to the jungle and therefore more herself, it also made her homesick for the life she could never have again.

Two days after the move, the maharajah's first wife, the maharani, paid Sita a visit. She was a tall, thin, dark-skinned woman with a disagreeable expression on her face; when she spoke, Sita discovered that she had a disagreeable voice as well—the kind of voice that was so scratchy it hurt the ears. Her sari was made from turquoise silk, embellished with multicolored embroidery, but she seemed more interested in calling attention to her jewelry, constantly fingering her jeweled necklace and rearranging the golden bracelets on both arms. "I had to see the woman whom my husband thought to make his third wife," she said. "I cannot understand why," she continued, looking Sita over as though she were a goat someone was trying to sell. "You are neither young nor beautiful. It could not have been for political reasons, as you clearly come from a very low class of people. Why would he do such a thing? Perhaps you can tell me—is he losing his mind?"

Sita merely shrugged but lowered her eyes respectfully as she did so. She did not want to further anger or embarrass the woman.

"I hear that you see him every day for at least an hour. What do the two of you talk about? Or perhaps it is not what you talk about but what you do."

Sita wanted to tell the woman that she had an ugly mind and to ask why the maharani did not pay more attention to her husband, but she decided it was more prudent to remain silent.

"You appear so stupid you are not even worth speaking to, let alone having a conversation with; I can hardly believe that you are capable of speech," the maharani stated coolly and left the room.

Sita did not brood over this encounter. She had other things to think about. She did not know what the maharajah expected of her, and she worried that when he asked her the questions apparently plaguing him, she would not have the answers he needed or wanted. She wondered if she should have been more concerned about the maharani's displeasure, however, when the next day Navya, her maid, came to her with a long face.

"Whatever have you done to anger Maharani Kali?" she asked. "It may not be my place to speak, but I am worried about you."

"I have done nothing to her. I have not even spoken to her, although she was very insulting when she stopped by my room yesterday."

The maid shook her head. "She is smart, unlike Lady Indira, who is sweet but unthinking." Navya lowered her voice. "Please be careful. Do not eat anything Kali offers you, and take nothing from her servants either. Please believe me—the maharani is dangerous."

This information was sobering, particularly because Navya, a pleasant, helpful girl, was obviously frightened. Sita promised to be careful; she saw nothing she could do except follow Navya's instructions about food. She wondered, however, if the maharani was accustomed to disposing of those who angered her or those whom she viewed as rivals with *angur shefa* or even *dhatura*. Sita knew how helpful angur shefa could be when treating earache or a cough that would not go away, but she also knew that if the dosage was not correct, treatment could result in convulsions or the heart beating faster and faster until it suddenly refused to beat at all. Because of the danger involved, Sita had tended not to use angur shefa when someone asked her for something that would diminish pain in the head, ears, or stomach. And now, after Navya's warning, she realized how easy it would be to slip some chopped-up leaves of either plant into a bowl of curry; indeed, she would need to be very careful.

Sita continued to see the maharajah almost every day. He would send a summons by a servant, and she would accompany the servant back to the daftar where the maharajah waited. He often asked her questions about how the humble people lived and what they thought. He asked what crops they grew and what they did when the crops failed. He asked whether new babies more often lived or died. He asked whether the wild animals were as abundant as they had been in previous years. And he was always curious about the Prince of Tigers and the life Sita had shared with him in the jungle, but that was the one area that Sita still felt she must carefully edit.

Sita often did not understand the questions the maharajah asked or felt that her answers were not what he was looking for. However, he seemed particularly anxious to understand the lives and thoughts of the simple people who lived in the many small villages sprinkled across his domain. Sita had never been to these villages (except her own, of course), but she finally thought of a plan that might help the maharajah gather more information than she was able to give him.

"Your Highness," she said one day. "I think I have thought of something that would assist your understanding in these matters. Let us go to my village, and you can talk to the people there. Then, you not only would have my opinion but would be able to listen to a variety of opinions."

"What an excellent idea, Sita," the maharajah said, looking cheerful for the first time that day. "Let us go tomorrow."

Sita had thought she would need to persuade the maharajah to take action; immediate acceptance of her plan was not what she had expected at all. At once she mentioned several things that argued against such a speedy action. It would take time to decide on the number of people who would accompany the maharajah, both for his comfort and to demonstrate the level of prestige an individual of his station should be shown to possess. Even deciding what clothes should be worn (both by the maharajah and the selected courtiers who accompanied him) would be time consuming. In addition to transporting this selected retinue, there would need to be carts and bullocks to carry the clothes of the maharajah and his attendants, and more carts would be needed to carry sufficient food to feed this company.

Sita also thought she should go by herself a day or two in advance, in order to apprise the village of the honor in store and allow them time to consider how to respond to the maharajah's questions. She remembered how excited they had been by his previous visit, and she hoped they would stay calm enough to be articulate. After all, she often found it hard to know how to respond to the maharajah's queries, and she did not think the villagers would be any more skillful in this sort of dialogue than she.

The maharajah refused to let her precede the party, however; he insisted that he needed her by his side as a sort of translator. He was also feeling so intoxicated by the proposed expedition that he decided to visit several additional villages.

Sita had to agree that it would be wise to harvest many opinions (it was her idea, after all), but she felt sad. The maharajah knew he had shot her son Arun, but he was unaware that she had another son—Ashok. Sita was not sure why she kept Ashok's existence a secret. Perhaps she did not completely trust the maharajah. This was hardly surprising, yet since the day she had shouted out the tragic words ("Thou hast slain my husband and my son"), he had done nothing to make her distrust him. But she had looked forward to arriving early, lingering for a little time in the village, and then finding Ashok and spending some time with him, just the two of them.

She also wanted to talk to Vasu and Vanada. In contemplating the future of Shira's twins, it seemed to her that they lacked the initiative and motivation to live successfully on their own in the jungle. Although in general the tiger is not a particularly social animal, Vasu and Vanada had known nothing but the loving and supportive circle of their adoptive family. Sita worried about their future; she thought she might have a solution, but she needed to talk to all her sons before moving ahead with her plan.

CHAPTER

33

A fter the ever-swelling group left the gates of the Primrose Palace, it took four days for the bullock train to reach the village. The maharajah and the ministers he had invited to attend him on this tour of investigation rode horses or elephants. The women of his court who had decided to join the party (the maharajah's second wife and her attendants) rode in a cart wreathed with fabric veils and curtains. Servants rode in other carts, but these carts were not shielded from the blazing sun. Others walked.

Sita had asked to be included in this number, but the maharajah refused. "It would not be appropriate to your station as one of my councilors," he said. He insisted that she ride with the women of the court. This did not make Sita happy, but it was not her choice to make. At first, some of the attendants treated her with disdain, but when they saw that Indira, the maharajah's second wife, was friendly and curious about this strange woman, they quickly adjusted their attitudes accordingly. Indira had been prepared to resent Sita as a rival, but as soon as she pushed aside her *dupatta* to look closely at this woman, Indira was reminded of a beloved ayah in her father's palace. That resemblance, along with the fact that Sita was both older and less attractive than she, caused Indira to quickly fall into the habit of treating Sita as an old retainer and friend.

Indira talked a lot. She had as many questions for Sita as did her husband, but they were rather different in nature. "Did you actually grow up in a village? Why didn't you come to the palace or a city? If you lived in a village, where did you buy things like creams for your skin?" She did not ask questions all the time. Sometimes, she made comments on what she saw or about herself. "Look at the pink blossoms on that tree—I love pink, don't you? Sita, you look just like Meher, my ayah, except she was really old of course, and you aren't, not really. Look at this bracelet the maharajah gave me—I was so excited when he slid it onto my wrist!"

Indira was blessed with the gifts of youth and beauty. These were important to her, and Sita wondered what Indira would be like when, as was inevitable, time robbed her of these gifts. She was like a beautiful, indulged child who assumed she was loved by all around her. This came close to being a fact as she was basically kind and did not mistreat her servants and those around her, as Kali did routinely and quite as a matter of course. Indira warned Sita against Kali.

"She hates me because I am young and beautiful and she is not. I do not know why she hates you, but I know she does. She really, really does, and will try to hurt you if she gets a chance. I told the maharajah this and he said I should not worry about it. So I don't—I know he'll take care of it." Sita did not know what she thought about Indira as her self-appointed protector, but she certainly wished the young woman were not so talkative, particularly when they were surrounded by her women, who nodded in agreement every time Kali was mentioned. Sita wondered how many of them were in Kali's pay and would report the conversations to her. She listened to what was said but had no intention of joining the chatty Indira in accusing the maharani of evil intentions towards the other women in the maharajah's life.

When the cavalcade arrived at the village, they were greeted with surprise, delight, trepidation, and much noise. The villagers could hardly believe that the maharajah had condescended to visit them once again. But what could be his purpose? It was rumored that Sita was with him and his court. What was the meaning of this? They had hardly believed that she was living at the palace, even though they understood she was only a lowly servant, one of the countless women who never raised their heads from their sweeping. Had she transgressed in some way? Did the maharajah believe that her punishment—whatever it should be—would carry more weight if it were meted out to her in her own village? What could she have done that merited such shame, particularly as that shame would apply not only to her but also to the entire village?

Therefore, they were extremely surprised when the maharajah introduced Sita as one of his most valued councilors, who had, in fact, instructed him to come to the village in order to understand the viewpoints and attitudes of those of his subjects who ordinarily had no chance to speak.

The villagers were practically struck dumb. Sita a valued advisor to the maharajah! They themselves asked to give the maharajah their views! There was much shuffling of feet and mumbling before anyone was willing to speak up. Eventually, a number of men and even a few women actually did so. Only a few said things like they only had one goat and they wished they had two, or that they did not know how they could live because someone had stolen their only hen that actually laid eggs. Others were more thoughtful. One said that if a dam could be built across the small river that ran just south of the village, the crops would not be flooded and left to rot. Another suggested that a wall around the village gardens would prevent the depredations of the wild pigs that had severely diminished the village's food supply for the last two years.

At last, the meeting was over. The maharajah formally thanked the headman of the village for the suggestions that had been made, and announced that he and his train would be leaving the village the next day for an exploratory trip around the region, during which he would visit other villages and solicit their opinions.

"May I be excused?" Sita asked him after the villagers had streamed away, chattering about this most unexpected but auspicious visit. Some of them thought they might follow the maharajah's train to see where it went next, and to hopefully see their ruler again, but most merely wanted to discuss the great honor the maharajah had bestowed upon the village.

"Yes, of course," the maharajah replied. "Our visit here went very well. I think I have grasped how to talk to the common people now. I know you want to spend some time here in your own village. I will be coming back this way in a week or so, and you can join me then. I want to turn these things over in my mind before I talk to you about what was said today and what I will hear at other villages. We will talk after we return to the palace."

Afternoon shadows were dappling the trail when Sita, hoping to see her sons, slipped away into the jungle. Once past the jungle's edge and beyond where she might naturally see another person, Sita ran nearly all the way to the Ananta Palace; she thought of how she had sometimes run fleetly over the trail when she was racing towards wherever the Prince of Tigers was waiting for her. Sita would never run as fleetly again, and the prince would never be waiting for her again, either. Arun was gone forever also; nevertheless, Ashok was still living, and Sita hoped fervently that she would be able to see her son in the time she had before returning to the Primrose Palace. She thought it highly probable, knowing their natures, that she would find Vasu and Vanada in the vicinity of the Ananta Palace.

She stopped when she reached the clearing. Her beloved palace seemed different. It would forever be changed through the absence of its master, but it was also different because the jungle was inching towards the palace, erasing the border between the wild and the ordered. Even so, it was still the place that held her happiest memories; it was the place she saw in her dreams. Now it lay dozing in the late-afternoon sun, the stone walls darkening as the shadows crept over them.

"Vasu, Vanada," Sita called. "Are you here?" She sensed that Ashok was not at the palace, but she hoped her other sons would be there to greet her.

She heard their hoarse tiger voices answer her with only one word between them (although that word was repeated more than once): "Mother, Mother."

Then there was a great rush, and Sita was bowled over by the tumultuous welcome of her adopted sons. They play-pounced on her, they picked her up, they licked her face and arms until her skin was abraded. They were like kittens wanting to play with a parent, grabbing at her ears or giving her a little nip. Vasu and Vanada, however, were not kittens; they were full-grown male tigers, and the possibility of unintentional damage was present with every pounce and every pressure from a paw.

Throughout this demonstration, the brothers had been quiet except for their sandpaper chuffles, but Sita uttered endearments as, in turn, she petted and embraced them. Finally, the two lay quietly as she caressed their silken coats.

"Vasu, I want thee to think about something I am going to say. Vanada, thou must listen, too."

Sita sounded serious, so the twins raised their heads with their ears alert.

"I have missed thee so much," she murmured, "and I have wondered how the two of thee manage alone in the palace where there was once so much joy. Now the prince and Arun are not with us, I am gone, and Ashok is only with thee part of the time.

"We are lonely for thee and for the old days," Vasu replied, while Vanada added, "I know that tigers are said not to be social creatures, but the society of our family was very dear to us."

"I have been thinking about thy situation, and I have a suggestion,"

Sita said. "If thou wert to adopt it, it would mean a loss of freedom. Thou wouldst no longer be able to live in the jungle."

The two tigers went completely quiet when she said this. Not a whisker moved and not a muscle twitched, but they were still listening.

"The maharajah has a section of his estate that is allotted to jungle animals," Sita told them. "They are not in cages but have spacious enclosures where they can roam to a certain extent. If thou wert to choose to go there, thou wouldst always have plenty to eat, thou wouldst be safe from danger, and I would be able to see thee almost every day. Of course, thou wouldst be together—that is understood. On the other hand, if thou choose to do this, thou wouldst no longer be able to hunt, and thou wouldst not be free."

"Mother," Vasu began.

"Please do not give me an answer now," Sita said. "Think about this idea until tomorrow. Also, I have not yet suggested this plan to the maharajah. He may not agree because he may have other ideas about what animals should be in his menagerie."

The twins looked at each other. "We do not have to wait until tomorrow," Vanada said. "We do not need to talk about this; we can read each other's minds, and what those minds say is this: We want to be where thou art. We have missed thee so much. Furthermore, hunting has little appeal for us, and we have never been good at it, even though all tigers should be. We would go hungry if not for our brother Ashok, who hunts for us as well as for himself. He will tell thee this is true. We want to be together, and if thou art there also, we will be happy."

CHAPTER

34

I t was much later that night when Ashok returned to the Ananta Palace. Sita was sitting on the great balcony, looking out into the night. The dim lamp she had lit in the room behind her showed Vanada and Vasu were fast asleep, Vanada's head thrown over the back of his brother. She stifled an impulse to return to them, to put her arms around their necks and tell them that she loved them and that everything would be all right. Sita realized that they had been as worried about their future as sons of the amiable Manju could be. But there was no point in waking them. She would know nothing more until she talked to Ashok and the maharajah.

Then Sita felt Ashok's presence and knew he was nearing the old palace. She was waiting when he climbed the stairs and joined her on the balcony. She threw her arms around her son, then pulled back to look at him. Sita had not forgotten a single detail of Ashok's appearance—the straight line of his nose, the way his hair grew, the shape of his ears—yet it seemed as though she were looking at a stranger. This young man bore himself proudly, like the jungle was his to command. Ashok had always been capable and self-sufficient, but now she saw little of the cub or youth in him. Ashok had matured since she had been at the Primrose Palace, and this particular transformation had taken place without her.

"How art thou, my son?" she asked. "Thou art never far from my thoughts."

"I sometimes wonder, Mother," he said, "whether thou art too busy with the affairs of state to remember those of us who still dwell in the jungle." Sita felt a quick stab of hurt at his words. She had forgotten how impassive a tiger's face could be, and even though he was wearing his human skin, he was still a tiger. And then she noticed the twinkle in his eyes. "Of course, I know thou dost not forget us, could never forget us," he said. "But I have had no news of thee for many months. How art thou, my mother?"

"I have been worried about Vasu and Vanada," Sita said. "They have been much on my mind of late."

"I, too, have been concerned. They have never been particularly good hunters. I wonder if they would be able to support themselves if I were not here to provide food for them, and to guard our territory. Recently, a large tiger from the south decided to move here where the hunting was better than the area he had recently inherited. I met with him three times before he was persuaded to remove himself."

Ashok had always had a gift for understatement.

"How didst thou achieve this?" Sita asked.

"Through talk and threats, mostly."

"Did thou fight him?"

"Briefly. I clawed him deeply on one shoulder before he ran away, but he returned once more."

"Why did he finally depart? How wert thou able to persuade him?"

"I asked Vasu and Vanada to accompany me to meet this tiger. When, much to his surprise, he was confronted by a group of three male tigers together, he left rather speedily. But Vasu and Vanada did not like doing this. They were not prepared to fight for their jungle."

"And what about thee?"

"I would have been happy to make his shoulders match. But I was also happy to send him away without further violence. I only mention this because my brothers seem somewhat unfitted for jungle life."

"I may have found a solution," Sita said. "They can most likely become part of the maharajah's menagerie. They would never be free, of course, but they would be together in an enclosure with a great deal of space, and I would be there to help them through any difficulties. I have not yet mentioned this idea to the maharajah, although I doubt he will have any objections. I wanted to talk with thee first. Tell me, what dost thou think of this plan?"

"I think it ideal," Ashok replied. "They would then be safe. I do not think the loss of freedom would bother them too much. I think it would kill me, although it does not seem to have harmed thee."

"Dost thou see me as deprived of freedom?" Sita asked.

"Most assuredly."

"This is hard to explain," Sita began, "but since the death of thy father, things are different with me. It does not mean that I love thee or thy brothers any the less. If thy father were alive, it would be impossible for me to stay away from him and the jungle. But he is not, and thou art grown with a life of thy own. I am trying to provide for Vasu and Vanada, and they have already said they are willing to go to the maharajah's menagerie if he agrees. I think they will almost certainly be happy there. But what about thee, my son? Wouldst thou like me to look for a job for thee in the household of the maharajah?"

"Most assuredly not."

"Why dost thou speak so decidedly, my son?"

"Because, my mother," replied Ashok, "I have met a woman."

CHAPTER

35

S ita was surprised. Of course, Ashok was of an age to marry. It had been a long time since she had thought of him as her little Ashok; indeed, she had come to think of him as an exceptionally self-sufficient adult, both as a tiger and as a man. As a tiger, he was a superb hunter, easily providing for the wants of two grown males besides himself. As a human, he was logical and direct; he interacted appropriately with others but did not seem to need them or even especially desire to be around them. He had dealt with Sita's property wisely and well since she had been living at the Primrose Palace—renting out her fields, for example, so that they would not stand idle and would instead bring in a small income.

Who could she be? Sita wondered. *Who is the right age in the village? Is it the maid I've employed to keep the house? Is it a woman from another village?*

"Tell me, my son," Sita said. And so he did.

Ashok had been hunting in the jungle, unsuccessfully; therefore, there was no food for Vasu and Vanada and, of course, nothing for him either. Even though he knew his brothers would be hungry, he decided not to keep hunting but to transform, go to the house at the edge of the jungle, and eat a supper of dal and chapattis. It never ceased to amaze him that whether he was in the shape of a man or a tiger, he could hunger for the food that belonged specifically to the opposite. Although he was a tiger at the moment, he suddenly wanted lentils, while as a man he had at times craved the flesh of a freshly killed sambar, even though he was usually content enough with what other men ate.

He stopped briefly by the Ananta Palace to let his brothers know that he would resume the hunt that night or the following day. They did not seem unduly disturbed by the news of no food today. Both were in the pool, Vanada leaping about, making great splashes as if he were a cub again, while Vasu lounged closer to the edge, occasionally rolling over in the cool water.

Ashok took the path towards the village. Well before the jungle thinned, he stepped aside from the trail to transform. Every time he did this, especially when he was near people, Ashok thought of Arun. His twin had been so certain that he could easily control this aspect of his life, while at the same time he enjoyed the sense of tricking those who saw him but had no idea of his dual nature. Ironically, Arun's death had not come about because of this fact and his carelessness; from the viewpoint of the maharajah, Arun had simply been a tiger and had died as one. Ashok recognized, however, that given Arun's reckless nature, it would only have been a matter of time before his ability to transform was discovered by others . . . and the likelihood was that the outcome would have been the same.

Ashok walked into the house and called for Aditi, the maid, but no one answered. Of course, she had not expected him, so there was no reason for a kettle of dal to be simmering on the stove or a basin of water to be set out so he could bathe himself. Ashok grimaced, then picked up a bucket and headed for the well; at least he would be clean, even though he might go unfed.

The well was just outside the village, and a woman was already there. Her back was to him as he approached, but he had already realized she was no one he knew—she was too tall, almost as tall as he was. Perhaps she belonged to the new family that no one seemed to like. They had been living in the village for a few months but had not been successful in making friends—if indeed their intention had been to do so.

The woman turned as he neared. She had a full bucket in each hand, but she put them down as she watched him lower his bucket into the well. He looked at her, too. She was young and looked strong. She was hardly the ideally pretty girl, but there was something attractive about her—something familiar. Perhaps it was the way she moved—smoothly, even when she was hauling her buckets out of the well. She also projected a level of assurance that could be seen as arrogance.

Then she spoke. "You must be Ashok."

"I am. I have lived near this village all my life, but I do not know you."

"My name is Neelam. I have lived here only a short time." She moved closer then, looking directly into his eyes. And then she said the most amazing thing: "I think you are part tiger."

Unlike Arun, Ashok had always been extremely careful about concealing his dual identity; he had never expected to be unmasked, and certainly not in this brusque yet casual way. He was completely taken aback, and his answer was both scattered and accusatory, reflecting his sudden panic. "Why would you say such a silly thing? It is the sort of childish thing a baby, not yet understanding how the world works, would say. Why would you, a grown woman who looks to have all her senses, say this thing?"

She put her hand on his arm. They stood there for a moment, linked by this physical contact, staring into each other's eyes, before she said, "I can feel the tiger blood running through your veins."

Ashok stood perfectly still, but when he tried to respond, he was nearly incapable of speech. His response was mumbled (and somewhat repetitious): "Why would you say this thing? Why would you even think this thing?"

She answered him briefly, and it was like the words cut into him—how or why he could not explain: "Because I am part tiger, too."

CHAPTER

36

Ashok pulled away, but he was still looking into her eyes, and what he saw was conviction. The young woman might be suffering from some sort of delusion, but she clearly believed the words she had spoken. But what was the truth? Ashok had been surprised before, although not very often; however, now he found himself totally dumbfounded, a new experience.

Ashok knew very well that it was possible to be both human and tiger—he had grown up with this truth for as long as he could remember. He was also aware that he was quite different from both of his parents because he had the blood of both tiger and human within him. Although this duality was often difficult, sometimes even painful, Ashok also was gifted in ways he had believed with certainty—now that Arun was dead—that no one from either world could ever understand. Neelam's words—"I am part tiger, too"—had, if not shaken, certainly jostled this belief.

He swung around, spilling half the water in his bucket, and walked swiftly back to Sita's house. When he got there, he found that Aditi had returned. She offered to cook him a meal, but he refused, saying he had suddenly been called away, and she merely nodded, apparently incurious about his comings and goings. She might have peeked out of the door as he slipped into the jungle, but he hardly cared if she saw that he was going in a different direction than the village he had named as his destination. He quickly transformed, barely stepping off the path to conceal the process should someone be nearby. Then he ran.

Ashok the tiger ran through the jungle, turning from one path onto another without paying any attention to where the track might lead. Tonight, it made no difference where he was going; he had no destination. He had to run. He could not stop running, because . . . he did not know what would happen then. The foundations of his life had been shaken. He did not know how to reconcile his known life with the window that had suddenly opened a view of the unknown. A mor, shrieking at his swift approach, was so flustered that it was almost unable to flap to safety in a nearby tree, but he did not notice. A naga was lying in the path, and he automatically vaulted over it, not granting the snake a single thought. He met two woodcutters as he approached the jungle's edge farthest from his home, but he ignored them. His speed and weight would have bowled them over had they not dashed towards a nearby tree, gibbering in fear as they pulled themselves up into the branches. Ashok did not observe their flight. If he paused for a moment, he would be overwhelmed by the thoughts troubling his brain, thoughts that tended to come to him more readily when he was a man than when he was a tiger.

He thought of his father, the Prince of Tigers, the beautiful yet savage ruler of the jungle, the dispenser of justice to all who dwelt there, making decisions about life and death and who would live in his jungle and who would be expelled. He thought of his mother, the quiet but independent young woman who preferred the Prince of Tigers to any man she had ever seen, and whose life had been changed forever when a single bullet struck her husband down. He thought of his brother, who had been unable to live with the humility and caution required of him as a maturing man-cub but instead chose to flaunt both sides of his heritage.

He thought of his own struggles in trying to resolve the dilemma of his two natures, and the necessity of always hiding half of himself, no matter the circumstances. Of course, Vasu and Vanada had always known of his duality, but it was of very little significance to them—Ashok was simply their brother, no matter what shape he appeared in. Only one person in the whole world truly knew him as both tiger and man. Sita had watched him grow and change, she understood his trials, she felt the pain of his struggles—but even her knowledge was incomplete. And finally, he thought of the woman who had looked directly into his eyes and uttered the words "I am part tiger, too."

Ashok knew he had to talk to Neelam again and soon. He waited by the path until she returned from the fields, carrying a basket of aloo that she had dug.

"I would talk more with you," he said when she drew near. "When would you be able to meet?"

"Not now; I must help my mother prepare the evening meal," she replied. "Perhaps I shall take a short walk after we eat."

"Will you walk towards the jungle path?"

"I will start in that direction. I may be called back to do an extra duty, or by one who thinks it is not seemly for me to be walking alone in the evening."

"I shall wait for you where the path enters the jungle."

"If I cannot come tonight, I will come another evening."

Neelam did not appear that night or the next, but Ashok was innately patient—a predator must learn patience at an early age—and knew she would come when she could. He almost welcomed the delay; he wanted to have his thoughts in order before he saw her. Ashok had never thought seriously about getting married. He had seen the love and understanding between his parents and the great grief that overwhelmed his mother after his father was killed. But he had not thought it possible for him to marry, for him to have a love like that of his parents. He had never seen a girl for whom he thought he could have the same passion, but there were other considerations as well.

Ashok would certainly be viewed as an attractive potential husband. His mother owned a large house in good repair and a little land; in addition, he had taught himself to work with leather—he made and mended bridles and other practical items, and sometimes crafted more ornamental objects. All those things spelled economic security and would testify to his ability as a husband to provide for a family. Ashok knew, however, that these tangible attributes were as nothing when measured against the fact that he was only half human; the other half was tiger, which meant that he would be seen as an enemy to be destroyed should anyone discover his heritage. He had become adept at controlling when and under what circumstances transformation took place. But Ashok did not know how he would conceal this from a human wife on a permanent basis, or whether he would be in control at all in their more private moments.

But now, Ashok realized that he might not need to conceal the fact because it was already assumed, if not absolutely known, by Neelam. All he had to do was acknowledge her assumption, to admit his father's race. Although Neelam might have a smaller proportion of tiger blood than Ashok, it was already clear that she had a certain intuition and understanding that would not be shared by other girls—girls who grew up in circumstances where a family tree might extend to a few nearby villages but which would certainly not include a jungle pedigree.

Because of Ashok's decision to avoid marriage, he had not tended to dwell on the attributes of the young women he saw in the village or met when he went farther afield. But now, he realized that Neelam was attractive. Not in the way that was usually preferred in his culture. She was not small, willowy, and graceful; instead, she was tall and straight, and she looked strong rather than delicate. But her features were even, her skin was smooth and unscarred, and he had liked looking directly into her eyes, which were nearly at the level of his own and, astonishingly, blue. Ashok was filled with anticipation concerning their next conversation, when he would look into her eyes again.

CHAPTER

37

Neelam also looked forward to meeting Ashok again. A few days had passed since they first met. She could tell that he had been taken aback, even shocked, by her words and the fact that she had touched him on the arm; she hoped she had not alienated him by being too forward. She liked his green eyes and direct gaze; he stood straight and unafraid; he listened when one spoke, even if he did not necessarily wish to hear what was spoken.

To explain where she was going, she told her mother that she had heard a *jujube*, or *ber*, tree was fruiting, and she wanted to go and pick some fruit; she brought a *chunni* with her to carry the fruit home in. When Neelam reached the jungle path, Ashok was not there; still thinking of the man she hoped to meet, she ventured a little way into the jungle.

She had not walked very far down the jungle path when she saw the fruiting tree, further off the track than she liked to venture; nevertheless, she was pleased she had found it, particularly as Ashok had not been waiting for her at the jungle's edge. They could eat the fruit at their evening meal, or Suhani, her mother, might decide to chop it for chutney or dry it to make a sweet snack.

The tree trunk spilled into branches that began fairly close to the ground, so Neelam was certain she could climb it and collect the fruit fairly easily. She would have to be careful, however, because jujube trees are often quite thorny.

Neelam climbed the tree, but instead of picking the fruit immediately, she sat quietly in a fork, savoring the sounds and scents of the closing day. The path was within sight of the tree, and she was surprised to see a magnificent male tiger ambling down the path in the direction of the village. Tigers were not that commonly seen, and it was certainly unexpected to see one so close to human habitation. This tiger was not slinking along the trail or trying to conceal its movements; in fact, it seemed perfectly at ease as it strolled down the path, its head turning from side to side as it sniffed the air. For a moment, she wondered if it could be a man-eater but dismissed the notion; it was too beautiful, too healthy, too much at home. Furthermore, the tiger did not project the intensity of a predator on the hunt.

Neelam realized, however, the predicament she was in. She could not go home while a tiger was prowling about in her vicinity; safety dictated that she remain where she was. Although she was part tiger, she could not picture herself strolling up to a large male and claiming relationship. The thought made her smile, although the smile was a little grim. The tiger suddenly lifted its head and peered in her direction. She was certain it had seen her, but it continued on down the path without giving her a second glance.

Neelam felt she looked silly, perched rather uncomfortably in a jujube tree, although why she should be embarrassed about this she had no idea. She also felt somewhat disappointed, although she was unable to explain that either. Indeed, it was preferable for a tiger not to be hunting but to walk on by instead of coming over to the tree and perhaps standing up against it, scratching the bark with its sharp claws as it reached up for her. A man in the village who had once experienced this said it was terrifying—the tiger was so tall when it stood on its hind legs that it could almost reach the fork where he was cowering, too frightened to climb higher.

Neelam had to laugh at her fanciful imagination.

She would not be able to leave her perch unless her father and brothers came looking for her and found her; she might have to spend the night here. If the tiger did not return, it would probably be safe to go home the next morning.

It was near dark when she at last heard a man's footsteps on the path. "Hello," she called out. "I am Neelam. I am all right, but I am in the tree because there is a tiger in the area. Please be careful."

The man left the path and came towards her, and she realized that it was Ashok.

"You can come down now," he said in his low, calm voice. "You are quite safe."

"Thank you," Neelam said, trying to climb down with as much dignity as possible, a difficult job as her sari caught on thorns and ripped as she started down. Ashok helped her the last few feet. When she was standing on the ground again, she realized she had forgotten to pick any fruit. Her mother would be disappointed.

"Were you frightened when you saw the tiger?" Ashok asked.

"A little. I was glad that I was in the tree, even though I did not believe it was a man-eater."

They stood close together. There was very little light, but she saw the shine of his eyes—green, the same color as in the daytime.

"I do not understand why you were frightened at all," Ashok said. "Did you not realize that the tiger was me?"

3 8

This time it was Neelam who was shocked. Although she had felt instinctively that Ashok was part tiger (and her assumption had been essentially confirmed by his incoherent attempt at denial), it had not occurred to her that he could appear in either form—as man or tiger. There had never been any question of transformation in her family; she never knew such a thing was even possible. Perhaps the tiger strain was not as recent and therefore not as strong. Or it might simply be a talent that her family did not possess. Neelam stared at Ashok, mentally reassessing everything she had heard about him and everything she had noted herself. She had to admit that nothing had prepared her for, or even hinted at, a difference between them of such magnitude.

Neelam was bursting with questions. She had been intrigued by this young man who was somewhat apart from the village ever since she had first seen him. When he visited to make some arrangements regarding his mother's house and lands, she had thought that he carried himself with distinction. From then on, she watched for him and paid close attention if anyone even uttered his name. She had suspected that he was part tiger and challenged him as though her supposition were actual fact, but it had not occurred to her until now that he actually moved like a tiger even when he was in human form—self-possessed, graceful, and with absolute confidence.

"Ashok," she began.

"Say nothing now," he advised her. "Both of us need to think about what has just happened and what it might mean. If you had not happened to see me as a tiger, this conversation would have been greatly delayed, or it might never have taken place at all. But I think it is absolutely necessary that we meet soon and talk about what happened today."

"I must admit that your transformation was a complete surprise," Neelam replied. "Your suggestion is a good one—we both need time to think this through."

"I will walk you back to the village," Ashok said. "It is not good for you to be walking alone at night. You are safe in the jungle because you are with me, and it is my jungle. But tongues might wag if you were thought to be wandering about either alone or with me after dark."

Ashok walked with Neelam to the village square and left her to find her way home from there alone. It would not do to signal his intentions when it was not yet clear whether he had intentions or not. Ashok had not chosen to display himself to Neelam in his tiger form, but after she had seen him, it *had* been his choice to reveal himself to the young woman as a dual individual, both tiger and human. He could not determine whether this decision was a wise one or not. Only time would tell.

How Neelam reacted to this knowledge would decide whether they had a future together. If she talked about what she had seen around the village, Ashok would have to leave his own jungle and go far away. If she told only her family but they spread the news, the result would be the same. If the village gossip tomorrow and the next day was still focused on matters such as whether Akshat beat his wife for serving him burnt beans or how Dhruv had been able to afford a second cow, Ashok would know that he was safe, at least for now. But before he could even think about moving forward in a relationship with Neelam, he knew he must speak with his mother.

Sita was silent for a long time after Ashok told her about meeting Neelam and the young woman's instinctive knowledge of his heritage. He did not have to tell Sita that he hoped to marry this woman. Ashok had never spoken to his mother about his fear that he would never be able to marry or completely confide in another human being about his dual nature; Sita, however, had sensed his troubled state of mind and was sad that she could do nothing to help solve a problem that had come about because of her choices.

She understood Ashok's deep reserve, and how his situation was further complicated by his ability to transform. She had married the Prince of Tigers and never regretted her decision. However, Bhima had brought her up at the edge of the jungle, so Sita had had a smaller adjustment to make than a girl who had grown up immersed in village culture. Bhima had been a free-thinking woman, and Sita had absorbed her independent spirit; she had never known another woman with an affinity for the jungle like she herself possessed. *Would Askok ever find a mate who was right for him?*

But suddenly, a solution appeared to be at hand. A woman who herself was part tiger would be much more likely to understand, or at least accept, Ashok's dual nature; she could be a great comfort to him as well as a loving partner in his life. It only remained to discover whether Neelam was a good woman, a kind woman, and one who would make Ashok's life easier and fuller, and bring him joy. Furthermore, what would her family say to a proposed match?

"We will wait and see," Sita told her son. "I will discover what I can about this young woman and her family. Ashok, is it in thy heart that thou would want to marry her?" He nodded, but his expression had already given Sita the answer.

※

First, she talked to Anila. "Who is this new family in the village?" Sita asked. "Where did they come from and why did they move here?"

Anila shrugged. "They have been here some months—the couple, two sons, and a daughter—but I have not spoken with them. I am not sure where they came from—several villages away, I think. There was some trouble. Someone accused the wife of being a witch, and the husband beat the troublemaker. But the man who was beaten had relatives in that village who made it unpleasant for the family. So they came here."

"What is the daughter like?"

"I knew it!" Anila squealed. "You are looking for a wife for Ashok!"

"Not really. I do like to keep a lookout, though, and see who might be both available and suitable. If he should make a choice from another village, however—"

"The father is a good worker. I think they all are. But they are quiet and keep to themselves, so no one really knows them."

And therefore, as they are outsiders, no one likes them, Sita thought. She knew how stern the village's disapproval could be. They had known Sita for her entire life, yet when she chose to ignore their dictates and go her own way, few had supported her. Even now, Sita never felt that she was totally accepted by the village. They were glad for the things she had brought them, like the tiger's protection and consequence because of the maharajah's visit; those benefits faded to insignificance, however, when something reminded them of Sita's insistence on independence. How easily the entire village could become aggrieved or even hostile if individuals did not behave as was expected. *I know all too well how it feels to lack the approval of the village.*

Next, Sita went to the house of Neelam's family. It was small but neat, and the yard had been raked clean. "Welcome to our home,"

Neelam's mother said, "but it is hot inside. Would you like to sit on this charpoy in the yard where we will have the advantage of a breeze?" They sat down, and Neelam appeared, bearing a tray with two glasses of a fruit drink sweetened with jaggery.

"I cannot welcome you to the village," Sita said, "because I understand that you have already been here for some time. But I am glad indeed that you have come here. If the village is to grow and prosper, new people must choose to move here to live."

Suhani smiled politely, but the smile was a little strained. "I thank you for the kind thoughts," she replied, "but I hardly believe that your sentiments are shared by the rest of the village."

"I am sorry to hear that but not entirely surprised. I have lived here much of my life, yet I feel that, even so, I myself am not entirely accepted."

"I have in fact heard that Sita always goes her own way," Suhani said, and the two women looked at each other and laughed.

"You have heard correctly," Sita replied. "I am happy to agree with the village's decisions as long as I feel that what they want to do is the right thing. I have never, however, allowed them to make choices for me. I have always believed that how I live my life must be my own decision." She noted that Suhani looked searchingly at her. "But now I would like to talk about serious things. First, is it true that there is tiger blood in your family?"

Suddenly, the door to the house flew open with a crash. A tall, thin man erupted rather than emerged. His blue eyes were blazing, and he was shouting, almost incoherent in his anger. "Do not tell me that these rumors have pursued us once again!" he spluttered. "What must I do to cease this evil gossip? At the last village, it was not enough to pound the evil mouth until it was bloody. What do I need to do here?"

Sita did not move or speak, but Suhani quietly rose and put her hand on the enraged man's arm. "This is Sita," she said. "She means us no harm. She is herself rather an outcast here, and this is the village where she was born. Yet she is so wise that even the maharajah finds her worth listening to." Turning to Sita, she finished by saying, "This is my husband, Gokul. It is he who has had to stand up for me and defend me for all the years that we have been married. As you can see, though promising to do this was not part of the marriage vows, it is a responsibility that he takes seriously."

"If only all husbands supported their wives so strongly, the world might be a better place," Sita said. "Thank you for assuring Gokul that I mean no harm for, most assuredly, I do not." Turning to the man, she asked, "Is it true you used to drive a bullock team, and was it work that you found congenial?"

"Indeed, but this village is not large enough to provide that kind of work," Gokul answered. He had calmed down under his wife's soothing words and touch; now he was alert, wondering why Sita would ask him this question.

"When the maharajah returns to his palace, he will doubtless need a driver for a special cart," Sita said. "This cart will hold a cage, containing two male tigers. I want the driver to understand something about tigers. If he knows tiger talk, all the better, but I do not expect to find a driver who knows how to speak tiger. If I could find one who understands how tigers think and act, however, it would make the journey easier for these tigers who are going to join the maharajah's menagerie. If you are interested, please come to my house this evening and we will discuss the details."

The two stared at Sita as though she had lost her mind. Finally, Suhani got out the words "And what is your interest in these particular tigers?"

"They are my adopted sons," Sita replied calmly.

CHAPTER

39

T he couple came to Sita's house that evening; they were silent
as Aditi ushered them in and served them lentil *papadums*
and sliced mango, but their eyes were full of questions.

When the niceties had been observed, Sita turned to Gokul. "I
have a number of questions for you," she stated. "Do you want the
job as driver for the tigers? Can you make a single, roomy cage that
will fit on the bullock cart? Do you have an understanding of tigers?
Do you speak tiger? And, finally, if the maharajah decides that the
tigers need their own keeper (and provided you get along with them
during the trip to the palace), would you be interested in the job?"

Faced with so many questions, Gokul seemed incapable of
speech, but Suhani was not flustered and was able to respond. "My
husband is an experienced driver and will be happy to drive the tigers;
he can easily build a strong cage for them before the maharajah is
ready to leave for his home. But may I ask a question? Why would
you want both tigers in one cage? Will this not lead to trouble?"

"I understand your concern," Sita replied, "but it will not cause
trouble in this case. Vasu and Vanada have never been separated.
They would be miserable if they were caged separately, even if the
cages were next to each other. I expect they would fill the air with
their lamentations for this sorry state of affairs, and the journey to

the Primrose Palace would be thoroughly noisy and unpleasant for everyone."

As the issue of the cage had been addressed, Suhani answered Sita's other questions. "I cannot say that anyone in our current family has had direct experience with tigers up to this time; however, we know there is tiger blood in the family, so we have an interest and are willing to learn. I know a few words of tiger talk, and I have taught them to my husband. We will be happy to learn more if you have time to tutor us before the move."

Gokul finally spoke. "My wife has, I think, answered your questions more fully than I could do. As she has said, we have an interest and are willing to learn. If the tigers are willing to accept me as a keeper, I would certainly be willing to serve them in that capacity."

Sita was impressed by her dealings with Neelam's family. She had not yet met the sons, but Suhani was clearly a sensible woman. It was a good sign that Gokul was not angered by his wife responding to Sita's questions when Suhani was more prepared than he to deal with them. Sita had seen little of Neelam, but the girl was quick, polite, and seemed to be a good worker; she was clearly curious about Sita, but observed rather than intruding into conversations between Sita and her parents. Sita could see how Ashok would appreciate her more than a girl who talked incessantly or who made certain that she was noticed through her tinkling laugh or her studied and languid hand motions.

Sita decided to proceed with the second issue, one that she dreaded but knew she had to lay before the couple. "There is one more thing to discuss, something much more important than what has already been mentioned. My son, Ashok, has met your daughter, Neelam, and I do not believe they are indifferent to each other. This being the case, I would like you to consider whether we should arrange a marriage between them."

The couple glanced at each other but said nothing. Sita wondered if they were actively hostile to the idea or merely surprised by her direct approach. Finally, Sita broke the silence. "It is my understanding, and you have confirmed to me, that there is tiger blood in your family. If negotiations proceed, of course I would be interested in knowing more details. I can personally assure you that tiger blood runs very strongly in Ashok, as he is half tiger."

Surprise was evident on both their faces. "This is something we would have to think on," Suhani said quietly, "and of course we will have to talk to Neelam."

"I would not want to continue talking about a marriage between our children unless it is certain that this is something that Neelam, as well as Ashok, wants."

"I appreciate your confidence in sharing personal information with us," Suhani said. "I assume that this is not generally known in the village?"

"You are correct, and I do not care for it to be known. The village knows that I have some sort of tie to the tigers in the area, but they have no idea what the connection is. There has been no talk for many years, but I imagine it will be revived when Vasu and Vanada embark on their journey in the maharajah's bullock cart."

"We will talk more tomorrow," promised Suhani, and Gokul nodded his agreement.

CHAPTER

40

Life was suddenly a beehive of activity. Gokul and his sons, Bikram and Gotama, were busy building a strong, exceptionally spacious cage for Vasu and Vanada. The maharajah had sent word to Sita by a messenger, saying that he would be delayed in his return to the village as he wanted to explore his kingdom a little longer; furthermore, two of the oxcarts had suffered broken axles and the repairs were taking longer than anticipated. Sita had replied that she welcomed the opportunity to spend more time at her house and in the village; she had also explained Vasu and Vanada's situation and asked whether he would accept them into his menagerie. The maharajah's response was short and simple. "Of course the tigers are welcome at the Primrose Palace. Make whatever arrangements are necessary to ensure their comfort and happiness."

The maharajah was pleased to provide the two brothers with a large enclosure where they could prowl about without restraint. He was also happy for Gokul and Suhani to take care of them if that was what Sita wanted. The maharajah was always surprised that Sita did not ask him for things for herself. Everyone else around him was always seeking for him to demonstrate his favor by appointing them to a more prestigious position, giving them jewels, or, if they had served him for a long time, providing them with a pension so that they never had to worry about how they would live when they were too old to work.

Only Sita never asked him for anything. Yes, the maharajah had ordered that she be assigned good rooms in the women's wing, he had directed that she be given fabric for appropriate clothes, and he had even insisted that she accept a few small pieces of jewelry. But she never asked him for these things; she had not asked him for anything until she needed to provide for her adopted sons. Therefore, the maharajah was happy to agree to whatever she wanted. The palace grounds were extensive; he could afford to set aside several hectares for the twins. If Sita felt they needed people who understood them to tend them, that was fine, too. He could hardly wait to see the tigers and learn how Sita would persuade them to cooperate as they moved from freedom in the jungle to what might be luxurious but was still a prison of sorts.

Sita was aware that Ashok and Neelam had been meeting, although he had not mentioned it to her. She could tell because when Ashok came home from one of these meetings, there was a new serenity about him. Although he said nothing, happiness emanated from him. When she met with Neelam's parents, however, she felt there was still a certain reserve present, and she knew it must be linked to Ashok's tiger blood.

"I sense that you are less than enthusiastic about this match," Sita stated. "I am surprised at this because of the tiger strain in your own family. May I ask why it is so?"

"Perhaps your experience with tigers was different from that of my grandmother," Suhani said. "The recounting can wait for another time. Even though we feel we have somewhat of an understanding of tigers and believe we can be good caregivers for your stepsons, the idea of giving our daughter to a man who is half tiger fills us with trepidation."

Sita chose her words carefully. "On the one hand, of course, I can understand your concerns. On the other hand, you could give Neelam to a man who is totally human but who is dishonest, unkind, a wastrel, and who might beat her. Would that be better than if you gave her to a man who indeed is half tiger but who does not possess any of the distressing qualities I have mentioned? Furthermore, I believe that he loves and values her for herself."

Neelam's parents were silent.

"I might also ask how many times you have been approached by a parent or a matchmaker who is asking for Neelam's hand?"

"This has never happened."

"It is happening now, and I hope that you will give it serious consideration. Ashok would be a good husband to Neelam, and their financial position should be fairly secure." Sita paused, wondering how they would answer.

"It is not that we are against the match," Suhani finally said. "It is just that we are worried. We have met Ashok, and he seems like a fine young man. But what if at some future time . . ."

The three talked for a long time. At length, Sita felt their objections were melting away, and by the end of the evening, all were in agreement that their children should marry. Sita knew, however, that the shift of attitude was more likely connected to Neelam's wishes than the arguments Sita had put forward for the marriage. Apparently, Neelam was happy in the same way that Ashok was. She glowed, and before long her parents were actually delighted that such a good match had come about so easily—especially after feeling like outcasts wherever they lived. Sita could be considered a well-to-do woman, and she had a powerful protector. She had merely asked the maharajah, and suddenly both Gokul and Suhani were employed; it was also likely that jobs for Bikram and Gotama would be found at the Primrose Palace. Of the family, only Neelam would be left in the village, but she had mentioned that Ashok had another home in the jungle where they intended to spend much of their time.

Sita was elated that Ashok had suddenly and unexpectedly found a woman whom he obviously loved, and who was clearly over the moon about him. Her parents had come to approve of Ashok as a prospective son-in-law, and although the family had suffered some financial reverses (because of the necessity of moving multiple times), they had clearly been saving for the day Neelam would be married, and she would go to her husband with several silver bracelets. In less than a week's time, the village priest would mumble a few words over the young couple, and a feast would be prepared for the entire village. Then Ashok and Neelam would go away into the jungle, where he planned to take her to several beautiful and romantic spots, after which they would spend time alone at the Ananta Palace. They would return eventually to Sita's house but had not set a day to do so.

A few days before the wedding, Sita paid a visit to the old palace. She intended to find something to give Neelam, something to let the girl know how happy Sita was that her new daughter loved and appreciated Ashok for himself. The name *Neelam* means "sapphire," and Sita rummaged through the mound of jewelry and trinkets in the underground room, seeking a piece she remembered. At last, she found what she was searching for—a necklace made from a thin sheet of silver, beaten fine and twisted into shapes of leaves and flowers, with a single large sapphire hung at the bottom. Nagaiah, who had been watching the entire process, nodded his approval.

"Thank you, old friend," murmured Sita. "You have ever been generous to me."

"And why not?" the great snake replied. "Not only are we friends of long standing, but you love the palace as much as I do. I have been surprised that you have been able to stay away so long. We are growing older, but our memories of the Ananta Palace and the time we have spent here together with our loved ones will always warm our hearts."

They embraced as they had done when Sita left for the Primrose Palace. She noted that Nagaiah appeared much older, but she said nothing; she wondered if she would ever see him again. Sita wrapped the necklace carefully in paper and left it with a note to Ashok, asking him to give it to Neelam with her love when they returned to the palace from their jungle honeymoon.

After the wedding was over and Ashok and Neelam were gone, Sita spent her last night at Ananta Palace with Vasu and Vanada. Then, well before light the next morning, the three began their long walk to the village. For some reason, the young tigers' farewell to their childhood home closed a chapter of family history much more conclusively than did the marriage of Ashok and Neelam. Ashok would continue to live in the jungle of his birth, but it was unlikely that Vasu and Vanada would ever return to where they had been not only born but also raised to adulthood.

The twins, however, were unfazed by similar thoughts and seemed to regard leaving the jungle as a great lark. As Sita followed the path towards the village, they gamboled about her as if they were cubs again, batting at flowers, galloping after shrieking peafowl, and pretending to sneak up on her as she walked through tall grass. All too soon, they emerged from the jungle and stood together by her house. Gokul was there with the cage on the cart. Boards had been laid to form a ramp from the ground to the cart bed so that Vasu and Vanada could easily walk up and into the cage. A small audience from the village watched, their eyes round in amazement.

Sita walked up the ramp and called to her sons. They followed her into the cage and immediately began to sniff around the corners, ignoring the bullocks, who were rolling their eyes in fright as Gokul kept them calm with difficulty. "My sons," Sita said. "I must leave thee now. Gokul and Suhani will be riding with thee to thy new home; they will ensure that food for thee is plentiful and good. I, of course, am also going to the Primrose Palace in a few days; I will assuredly see thee soon."

Sita's tears fell as she watched the cart drive away. The bullocks were still uneasy at the contents of their load, but Gokul continued to speak soothingly to them, and it seemed unlikely that they would bolt. Vasu and Vanada continued to investigate their temporary quarters and found everything interesting. A few villagers lingered nearby, their mouths hanging open in surprise. Although it was known that Sita was linked somehow with tigers, it was still astonishing to see her actually get into the cage with two male tigers, pat them lovingly, and address them in an unknown language that sounded not at all like words but like some sort of guttural gabble. The villagers were confused and perplexed, and in their uneasiness they forgot they were on the way to their fields and returned to the village instead, anxious to report what they had seen.

CHAPTER

41

In fact, there was little or no commotion in the village resulting from the departure of Vasu and Vanada. The village decided that the witnesses must have fabricated or exaggerated their tale—in spite of the fact that Gokul had been seen by many driving a bullock cart, with Suhani on the seat beside him and two impressive tigers being conveyed in an outlandishly large cage. The villagers would have to wait to discover the truth until the couple returned from wherever they were taking the tigers; however, Gokul and Suhani did not return, and Bikram and Gotama walked out of the village in the direction of the city that same afternoon. Neelam and Ashok had also gone away, so there was no one to clarify what had happened, and the event was quickly forgotten. They could have asked Sita herself, but judging from the past, they did not think she would take kindly to being questioned.

When the maharajah returned, Sita left with him and his attendants. She told Anila that she did not know when she would return, and in fact the village did not see her for many months. The villagers were hoping that the maharajah might pay them another visit and talk to them again. It was amazing to them that he comported himself more like a person than the godlike creature a maharajah must inevitably be. He had asked their opinions and listened attentively while they offered them. Although he was dressed so that he looked more like a doll than a man, he had spoken courteously and thanked them for helping him to improve his rule. They were not certain what this meant, but it sounded important, and they were filled with pride that they had been given the opportunity to contribute. It added to their individual and collective sense of importance, and they were at peace. They did not necessarily credit Sita for giving them this opportunity, but it would have made no difference to her; her reward was feeling that her suggestion to the maharajah might possibly bear fruit and the lives of the poor might be improved.

Now that Sita was back at the Primrose Palace, she missed Ashok very much and was sorry there had not been enough time to get to know Neelam better. But she also felt that a certain weight which had oppressed her all the time she was gone had lifted the moment she slipped into the museum where the Prince of Tigers was waiting for her. She knew it was foolish, but she related to him everything that had happened while she was gone; both he and Arun seemed to listen attentively. She told them that Ashok was married and happy at last, and that Vasu and Vanada were now living close by on the maharajah's palace grounds. Housed in his menagerie, they were now quite near to their adoptive father and brother, although they were not likely to ever see them.

Sita visited the twins on an almost daily basis. Because of this, she came to know Gokul and Suhani quite well and learned to admire their independence and their devotion to each other. Although no relationship, in her mind, could ever be the equal of what had existed between the Prince of Tigers and herself, Sita was pleased to note that Neelam's parents spoke to each other with respect and seemed to share everything. Sometimes they did not even speak; a searching look at each other was all they needed to convey their thoughts. This reminded Sita of how she and the tiger had often communicated. A mere movement of his whiskers or ears, or a twitch of his tail, often told her what he was thinking, and he had repeatedly said that he could gauge her mood by the position of her hands or how straight she held her back. It pleased her that Ashok had married into a family who also put a high value on communication, and she knew he would be the happier for it.

Vasu and Vanada were settling in well. They were happy with the mini-jungle that had been provided for them, walking its trails and prowling through its bamboo thickets as though they were in their old milieu. There was plenty of the kinds of food they liked. A pool had been dug for them, and they enjoyed playing in the water. They did not miss hunting for their own food, having done very little of it in their lives. The Prince of Tigers had provided for them when they were young, and Ashok took over the duty after his father's death. Now Suhani and Gokul fed them and saw to all their needs. The maharajah occasionally went with Sita to visit them, but he chose not to go into their enclosure. He was amazed at Sita's fearlessness in doing so and at the obvious affection displayed between the tigers and his councilor—he had trouble thinking of her as their mother.

Of course, the transition of Vasu and Vanada from the jungle to the menagerie had its awkward moments. One day, a keeper who had thought the two tigers were confined elsewhere so that he could install some new plantings was taken by surprise when he rose from the bed of marigolds, dusted off his hands, and suddenly noticed the head of a tiger protruding from the shrubbery. Vanada, delighted that he had found a new friend, pranced playfully towards the terrified man, who dropped his gardening tools and fled to the gate as fast as he could run.

On another occasion, Gokul had been called away to perform a task elsewhere, and a different keeper discovered Sita in the enclosure with the two tigers. He opened the gate just as Vanada was licking Sita's face, while Vasu made mock charges at his brother.

The keeper thought Sita had strayed into the area by mistake and was being attacked by the tigers. He called a number of his fellows, who rushed into the enclosure, armed with laathis, hoes, and ropes, while one carried a battered musket.

Suhani came running when she heard the commotion. Both she and Sita begged and pleaded and explained that Sita had raised these particular tigers and that they meant her no harm. It was only when Bikram and Gotama arrived on the scene and Sita invoked the maharajah that the men retreated, still shaking their heads in confusion, not knowing whether to believe what they had seen or what they had been told. They had not believed the women's story, which sounded quite fanciful, but now it had been vouched for by men; also, unlikely as it seemed, if the maharajah had given his permission to this silly woman to go in the tiger enclosure, who were they to disapprove? None of them wanted to displease the maharajah of Sundara Pradesh.

After that, Sita tried to visit very early in the morning when no one else would be present, save Gokul and Suhani. Gokul was usually already at work, but Suhani and Sita often sat together and talked, sometimes in the enclosure with Vasu and Vanada, who might come strolling up at any moment, and sometimes in the couple's house. Suhani told Sita about her grandmother, a beautiful girl who was seduced by a tiger. Unlike the Prince of Tigers, however, this individual did not want a family or seek permanent ties. He soon left the area, and Suhani's grandmother never saw him again. *So that is what my husband meant when he said some tigers are not trustworthy*, Sita thought.

Suhani was curious about what living in the jungle had been like. She could not imagine being in an environment so different from the small villages where she had spent her entire life. Moving to the Primrose Palace had been a big adjustment for her, even though she and Gokul had a house of their own and did not have to live in the palace that was always humming with the activities of the hundred or so people who did live there.

Sita enjoyed these chats and was glad she had grown close to Ashok's mother-in-law. Suhani's family had always been very reserved because of their peculiar circumstances and the fact that they had moved so many times; as a result, Suhani had never had a friend and was similarly delighted to find one in Sita. Furthermore, there was another benefit of Gokul and Suhani residing at the Primrose Palace that Sita had not foreseen. The maharajah had employed both of Neelam's brothers. Bikram was one of the maharajah's messengers; if he was sent in the general direction of the village, it was now easy to send letters to Ashok and Neelam and receive word from them as well. Gotama was his father's assistant, but when work was slow, he would sometimes take a few days and go to the village as well. With this frequent interchange of messages, the two palaces did not seem as far from each other as they once had.

The twins adjusted to their new keepers very well. Although they had not known Gokul and Suhani for long, the couple were kindly and felt affection for their charges. Sita continued to tutor Neelam's parents in tiger talk, and their vocabulary was now reasonably extensive. They conversed with Vasu and Vanada every day, and the twins responded positively to their interest, rubbing against Gokul when he brought their food and chuffing loudly when Suhani scratched behind their ears. Sita was very pleased that her plan had worked out so well for all concerned.

CHAPTER

42

Something was wrong with the maharajah; he had never been a large man, but now he suddenly seemed quite small. He was aging very quickly, and Sita saw changes in him all the time. Not every day, it was true, for sending his manservant to fetch her was no longer a daily occurrence. She still saw him two or three times a week, but they no longer met in the daftar; now she saw the maharajah in another room where he reclined on a low divan while they talked. Their sessions were also shorter because even when the maharajah felt well enough to meet, he tired quickly. He still asked her questions about how the humble people talked and felt, and for her reactions to the decisions he must make.

One day, he asked her about animal life. It seemed to him that the wildlife was less abundant in his kingdom than it had been in his youth. Did she feel this was a sign that the world was getting old and was no longer productive?

"No, Your Excellency," Sita replied. "I believe the world is still as fertile and productive as ever, save the fields where the same crop is grown year after year until the soil has become exhausted."

"Then, what is the answer?"

"I wonder that you can ask me that. Let us say that there are eight tigers in a certain area of the jungle. If Your Excellency or another maharajah goes there with his elephants and gun bearers and he and his friends shoot four of these tigers, are there not half as many as there were before? Now there are four tigers. Even if the females reproduce (and it is possible that no females are among the four), there will doubtless be another shoot before the cubs are mature. Thus, the number of tigers grows ever fewer."

"I had never thought of a shoot in those terms," the maharajah said slowly. "I had always thought the wildlife present in the country was limitless, inexhaustible. But now that you say this . . ." His voice trailed away.

"The same is true of waterfowl," Sita continued inexorably. "When your friends come, you take them to the jheel to shoot. At the end of the day, hundreds of birds—perhaps more—lie dead, and for what purpose? Some are eaten, but no one eats the flesh of the heron or the bittern. It is a great and sad waste, Your Excellency."

"Do you have a suggestion to combat this waste?"

"I may, but it would only cut down on the waste, not cause it to cease."

"Come and tell me tomorrow," the maharajah said. "I will ask my son, the *maharaj kumar*, to be here, and you can tell him as well. I am too tired to talk more today."

Sita noticed how pinched and gray his face looked. She also noticed that he clutched at his stomach as he called for his servant to bring him more medicine. Sita had been making tea for him from vasa bach leaves, but it was obvious that her herbal medicines were now unable to dull the maharajah's pain. He needed something stronger.

The next day, the maharajah looked a little better. Jaya, the maharaj kumar, who appeared to be about Ashok's age, was with him when Sita arrived. The young man had been sent away to school; she had heard that he had modern ideas, but she did not know what this meant. His face twitched a little when Sita entered the room—he was trying to hide a grin but was unable to do so.

"So, this is the councilor on whom my father depends," he said, laughingly, a touch of derision creeping into his voice. "Where did he find you? In the marketplace, selling herbs?"

"I am embarrassed for my son to make such statements when he lacks proper knowledge," the maharajah said softly. "But we will let him hear for himself. Tell me, my son, after you came home from university, what was your first recommendation when we discussed what we could do to improve the lot of our subjects?"

"Father, you know very well what I suggested," the young man protested, "but I am happy to remind you. I said that there were many things we could do to help our subjects, but perhaps the most important thing we could do is see that they are taught to read and write. This would lay the foundation for increasing the level of education in the future."

"Sita, what did you tell me several months ago?"

"Your Excellency, I said that not knowing how to read or write was crippling to your subjects. That many villages existed where perhaps only one person could do so, or perhaps there was no one who could do both, or even either. This makes communication very difficult, and as a result, people are isolated from each other."

The future maharajah looked at Sita more attentively. "Is this true?" he asked. "Did you really recommend this course of action to my father?"

"Indeed I did. I believe reading and writing are most important."

"Do you yourself read and write, or is it something you wish you were able to do?"

"I can both read and write."

"How did you learn?"

"I was taught by my aunt. I do not know how she learned or from whom."

"Enough," interrupted the maharajah. "Today I want to hear an idea that Sita has about our diminishing wildlife. Sita, you said you would have a suggestion for me today. Please proceed."

"Your Excellency," Sita said, "after thinking it over some more, I am not convinced the idea is sound."

"My son and I will be the judges of that. Proceed."

"First of all," Sita began, "I am not talking about those who hunt for food. People in the villages who eat meat feel very lucky indeed when they happen to obtain an animal for food. This does not happen every day, or every week, or sometimes even every month. They do not possess the weapons to kill these animals. If a man brings home a chital for food, it might be because the animal stepped in a hole and broke a leg. It is then not able to get away and he has been able to kill it with a stick or a hoe, or even a laathi if he happened to be carrying one. You can see that this circumstance would not happen often."

"Certainly not," agreed the maharajah, trying to visualize a villager in a dhoti and puggaree pursuing an incapacitated chital.

"I know you employ hunters to provide for those of your court who eat meat."

"It is so."

"I am not talking about that either. I am talking about the culture of *shikar*—when animals are hunted and shot not because of something necessary such as food but for no practical purpose."

The maharajah dropped his eyes; he knew that this train of thought had begun with his killing of the Prince of Tigers.

"Your Excellency, may I ask why you hunt?"

"Well, I was taught to use a gun at an early age. I have always been a good shot."

"So there is no real reason, except to exercise your skill?"

"I suppose so. I mean, there are other reasons. It is a good way for men to get together and talk. I learn a lot about what is going on in different principalities from conversation at shoots. Also, it is pleasant to display one's trophies of the hunt, thus demonstrating a high level of skill."

Sita could not help flinching at this bald statement, but the maharajah, caught up in defending his attitudes and actions, did not notice.

"Father, is the demonstration of skill indeed the chief reason for the shoots?" Jaya broke in.

"Yes, my son."

"I do not believe it is a very good reason, Father. Many times, most of the planning is done by your *shikari*. He determines where the shoot will take place and how the beaters will be organized. There is very little left for you to do save to sit on an elephant or a machan and shoot an animal that is walking or running towards you. This animal is frightened and confused; it has been pursued and directed by the beaters into a position where you can have a clear shot. I am not certain how much skill this takes."

The maharajah looked somewhat abashed. "Be quiet, my son. I want to hear Sita's suggestion."

"Your Excellency, when you had a visitor from another country last year, the man who has been here several times, General . . . I forget his name, he brought you a gift—a strange sort of box that made a sound like a twig snapping when you pressed a button. I do not know its name."

"It is called a camera."

"Does it take skill to use it?"

"To use it well."

"I have seen what I think you call photographs that have been somehow formed by this camera. Some of them look so real it is as though the animal itself is standing there, looking at you. Does it take skill to get that close to a wild animal?"

"I would say it takes great skill and a certain amount of luck."

"Then why not try to demonstrate to people the skill that is required in order to take a picture of the animal? The picture would be the trophy, and the fact that you were able to take the picture would show a high level of skill."

Jaya sat looking at Sita in amazement. His mouth was slightly open. "It is a wonderful idea," he finally said, "but I do not know whether it will work. Shooting is so much a part of the culture of our nobility. It is worth trying, but another problem is that there are only a few people who possess a camera."

"But that would be part of the plan," commented Sita. "Only the ruling class would be able to do this at first (probably for a long time), but that would make it more attractive to others."

Sita turned to the maharajah to see what he would say, but he had fallen asleep. He looked very small, huddled under his cream satin quilt embroidered with brightly colored birds and flowers.

CHAPTER

43

After that day, Jaya was usually present at the meetings between Sita and his father, and those meetings were no longer two-person conversations. Jaya was full of ideas about what could and should be done in the future. Sometimes the maharajah participated, but more and more, he became an observer. He often listened attentively, an expression of pride on his face as he noted his son's interest in the task of governing that lay before him in the not-too-distant future.

As his malady grew stronger, the maharajah grew weaker. Sometimes he was too tired even to listen, and Jaya would ask Sita to meet him in the daftar so they could continue their discussion. Sita could see that although he loved and respected his father, he was also eager to commence the practical application of the ideas he had been refining through his years of education, his personal observations, and his recent conversations with his father and herself. The maharaj kumar knew he was building on the foundations his father had laid, but he also realized that the maharajah was too tired and ill to move forward—it would be Jaya's responsibility to carry out the plans they made.

One day, the maharajah felt a little stronger. He asked his manservant to prop him up in a sitting position on the divan so he could talk more easily; he almost seemed like his old self. Jaya did not come that day, and the maharajah spent most of the hour talking about his two wives and his son.

"I am glad that Jaya will be the maharajah of Sundara Pradesh after me," he exclaimed. "In many ways we are alike. We are both concerned with how we should govern, and we have many ideas of how to improve life for our subjects. I have ideas, but I have not been granted the time to put those ideas into operation. Jaya will have the time. Although I believe that I have done well, I feel certain that he will be a better maharajah than I have been."

They sat comfortably without speaking for a few minutes, listening to the rhythmic calls of the doves going to bed early in the trees surrounding the Primrose Palace.

"It is hard to believe that Jaya is Kali's son," the maharajah finally said. "I must tell you that I married her for political reasons; the amount of land and money that came with her were, I regret to say, more attractive to me than she was. I always tried to be kind, but no doubt she sensed my feigned interest in her was less than sincere. In any event, she has always chosen to be unpleasant or worse, so it has been impossible to develop any affection for her. How Jaya turned out to be not only kind but genuinely concerned about others I do not know."

Sita nodded but said nothing. She thought of how often she had compared the maharani to Shira in her mind (although Kali was not beautiful), in the way that each cultivated her ill nature and took pride in her disagreeable ways.

"Did she ever threaten you or cause you any trouble?" the maharajah said, directing a sharp glance at Sita.

"She was insulting, but I did not mind that. My maid warned me to neither eat nor drink anything that came from her hands. I decided that Navya's advice was good, but the maharani did not come near me again."

"That is good to know. I warned her that if anything happened to you, she would be held accountable and suffer a terrible fate," the maharajah said. "I felt sad to talk to her as though she were a criminal, but I know she is capable of almost anything.

"It is true that Jaya seems nothing like her."

"I sometimes think that he got his intelligence from Kali, but his kindness comes from Indira, even though she is not his mother."

"I have never seen Indira be unkind to anyone," Sita stated.

"That is true—Indira is excessively good natured as long as she has pretty saris, beautiful jewels, and sweets to eat," the maharajah said with a twinkle. "When she is in that mood, I find her very restful to be around."

That was the maharajah's last good day; after that the pain in his stomach grew ever greater so that he often called for opium to ease the pain. During the last weeks of his life, the maharajah did not ask Sita any questions about what the people wanted, or how his household could be run more efficiently, or how best to be a good ruler. He did tell her that he had instructed his heir to investigate more fully the matter of a dam for the village and, if it seemed like a good idea, to proceed with building it. But in general, the maharajah appeared to realize that his days of ruling both his household and his state were in the past, and he was content to pass the reins of power to Jaya. Now he could ask questions about what he wanted to know for himself, and he did. He asked Sita to tell him yet more about the Prince of Tigers.

Sita had always concealed as much of this subject as possible and simplified what she had chosen to reveal. She talked freely about aspects of the village and the jungle but felt it was wrong to discuss her beloved husband with the man who had murdered him, always adroitly evading explicit questions about the prince, turning the conversation in other directions. The maharajah had sensed her unwillingness and had not pressed her; perhaps he also felt tension in this unusual situation.

Now, however, Sita felt differently. The maharajah was clearly dying, and he had been her benefactor, even her friend, for years. What harm could it do to tell him of old times that were gone forever? Initially, she had felt it was a protection to Ashok that the man who had killed both her husband and one of her sons should not know of the existence of another, living son. But again, she no longer feared that the maharajah would act against either her or those who belonged to her. Therefore, she decided to grant this last wish of a dying ruler by telling him many previously untold stories about the Prince of Tigers and their life together in the jungle.

Sita had never told the entire tale before. She had told some stories to Ashok and Arun, long ago when they were young. She did not think that Arun listened very carefully—he had not asked any questions—but the telling had come so shortly before his own death that perhaps he hardly had the opportunity to consider what points needed clarification. Sita knew that Ashok had absorbed the stories she told and, of course, learned much more when she was ill after Arun's death. She knew he still thought about the stories because Ashok occasionally asked for more details or wanted to know the result of some event she had related. What, for example, had happened to the young man who thought it was his right to marry Sita, even though he did not acknowledge that it was her right to be respected or even considered his equal?

Sita always answered Ashok's questions, but they came at intervals; weeks, months, or even a year might go by without him saying something that led her to speak about the prince and the past. Furthermore, his questions were always focused on a specific topic or issue. So now it was a tremendous relief to Sita to talk and talk—to talk for hours—if the maharajah was not feeling too much pain and could listen while she filled her mind and her speech with images of the Prince of Tigers and their life together.

The maharajah listened quietly. Like Arun, he did not ask questions, but for different reasons. For Arun, it was like long-ago history being passed on. Even though this history was vitally important to his very existence, history was in the past and therefore not relevant in his view. But the maharajah felt he was gaining a true and complete understanding of Sita for the first time—understanding her independence, her need for freedom, her complete acceptance of a totally foreign lifestyle, and the power of enduring love.

In spite of his respect for Sita, his belief in the wisdom she offered, and his affection for her, the maharajah had always been puzzled that she had so easily rejected him when he offered to marry her. Perhaps she had not understood what a sacrifice it would have been in the eyes of his entire kingdom if she had agreed to his proposal. The maharajah had to admit, though, that he had not previously understood Sita's depth of emotion for and the strength of her commitment to the Prince of Tigers. There could never have been enough room in her heart for another husband, whether man or tiger.

The maharajah died early one morning, well before dawn. Sita was not with him, but she had seen him the night before. He was so weak he could hardly speak, but he managed to say three words: "I am sorry." The maharajah did not need to say what he was sorry for; it was obvious to Sita that he was apologizing for the tremendous holes in the fabric of her life for which he was responsible.

His manservant and Harish were with him, though, so he was not alone. Harish remained by his master's side, gazing on the man he had come to regard as a son, while the manservant hastened to spread the news. The entire Primrose Palace was buzzing in no time, and Sita was awakened by the noise as the word was passed. Courtiers began to wail, and all the servants were asking each other about what changes would be made and how these changes would affect them.

Sita spent no time weeping and wailing; she went directly to the museum. Seated beside Arun and the Prince of Tigers, she made her farewells to both. She remembered her shock when she had first discovered her lost loved ones there, and she rejoiced that, for the last several years, she had been able to spend time with them every day. She tried to banish the thought from her mind that if it had not been for the maharajah's desire to demonstrate his skill, she might have spent those years with her actual husband and son instead of the replicas that resembled them so closely. And she was even separated from the replicas by sheets of glass.

Less than an hour later, Sita was ready to leave the palace forever. She went to the menagerie to spend some time with Vasu and Vanada and say farewell to them. She had not seen them as often since the maharajah entered the final phase of his illness, but she was also aware that she was no longer as important to them as she once had been. They were accustomed to the easy life that was provided for them and had transferred some of their affection to Gokul and Suhani, who cared for them daily and had become very fond of their charges. Both had produced cubs with female tigers in the menagerie, but they were content in the company of each other, showing no signs of becoming attached to their mates or offspring.

Gokul and Suhani were sorry to see Sita go, but they were not surprised. They knew that although the old maharajah's son respected Sita and her ideas and each felt they worked well together, Jaya and Sita did not share the same relationship she once had with his father. Jaya had asked her to continue as one of his councilors, but Sita told him she needed to return to the jungle.

Gokul and Suhani assured Sita that they loved Vasu and Vanada and would continue to care for them and watch over them. They found their life with the twins a satisfying one, and they were happy that both Gotama and Bikram worked for the palace. If for any reason the situation at the Primrose Palace changed so that they felt Vasu and Vanada would no longer be safe and happy, they would contact her as quickly as possible.

They asked her to tell Neelam that they thought of her daily and repeated what they had often said before—they were grateful their daughter had found such a man as Ashok, a good man who loved and valued her. Sita responded by saying that she had come to think of Neelam as a daughter and she valued the home that had produced such a woman—one who was exactly the right wife for her son. Neither mentioned the qualms Neelam's parents had originally felt about giving their daughter to a man who was half tiger.

Then Sita, dressed as humbly as when she had come to the Primrose Palace, simply walked away. She did not ask to be conveyed to her village, or even to the city. She had decided to leave behind all the appointments of her room that the maharajah had ordered for her, the sumptuous saris and cholis that had been made for her, and the minor jewels he had given her. She felt certain that his wives would indulge themselves in a frenzy of grief over the maharajah's death, even though they had been unable to spare the time and make the effort to spend an occasional hour by his bedside while he was ailing but still alive. She thought it probable that they—certainly Kali, anyway—would look around for an object to direct their grief and anger towards, and who better than the simple village girl who had so bewitched the maharajah that he had offered to marry her? They might accuse her of stealing those things the maharajah had given her. It was better to leave everything behind.

The emerald Sita had brought with her, however, was hers, and she rewrapped it in a corner of a scarf in the small parcel she carried. Sita had forgotten that Nagaiah had chosen it for her as a reminder of their jungle home. More specifically, it represented the Prince of Tigers and their life together in the jungle; she could never be parted from it. Now she and the green jewel were going back to the green jungle, and she felt at peace.

CHAPTER

44

Sita spent a few days at her house. The original hut—a small, cramped, one-room dwelling perched at the edge of the jungle—had become by steps a rather large and rambling house. First it was replaced by a two-room stone structure built by the men of the village as part of the bargain they made with the Prince of Tigers to protect them and their fields; later two more rooms were added. The maharajah decided after his visit to the village that the house was too small and mean for one of his councilors and the house had been further enlarged. He had paid for the improvements and additions, but the on-site decisions had been made by Ashok and he had seen that they were carried out to his specifications. Now Sita owned a comfortable house with a number of rooms, built of stone and timber; it was ready to receive her whenever she came to the village and she knew Ashok and his family also spent time there.

The village had also grown, but it had spread out in the opposite direction. The house might have been located in the village by now except for the agreement made so long ago between the village and the prince that she was to have two hectares of land around it forever. The headman who had made the pact was now dead, but Indian villages have long memories. After years of being looked down upon, Sita was now treated as a person of consequence, although that probably had more to do with the fact that she had been associated with the maharajah, a rather more distinguished connection than being in some mysterious way linked to a tiger.

Anila was glad to see her, of course, and they talked over things old and new. Anila was a grandmother four times over now, as each of her two children had produced two children of their own. Although Sita had told her little of her life away from the village, Anila knew that Ashok was Sita's son and that he had married Neelam, the daughter of the outcast family. But then they had all gone away. Ashok and Neelam appeared in the village occasionally and sometimes lived in Sita's house for a while. More often, however, they were someplace else; Anila supposed it was wherever Sita had lived when she disappeared for long periods of time, but she did not ask. Sita had always deflected this type of question, and Ashok did not seem like a man one could interrogate.

Sita knew that Ashok and Neelam had two boys, but she had not known that Neelam was expecting a third child. Anila did not know whether it had been born yet, and she tut-tutted over why Neelam had not chosen to return to the village for any of the births. Her words reminded Sita why she herself had not wanted to move into the village—where everything one did was picked over and discussed by everyone. She had wavered when it was time for her sons to be born, wanting to be in a familiar place among familiar faces when the birth occurred. In the end, of course, Sita had borne her man-cubs in the jungle. She had no doubt that Neelam had done the same, but hopefully without Sita's doubts and misgivings.

When Sita entered the jungle, taking the old path she knew so well, she felt she was home again. When she heard the song of the peelak, her heart sang in unison. She spoke to a *chuha* she saw sniffing about the roots of a banyan tree, but though she used the language of the jungle, he hurried off, doubtless startled by hearing the jungle tongue coming from the mouth of a human. A small group of dholes ran past. She was surprised to see them as they had not hunted in this part of the jungle for many years; she hoped they were not returning. The dholes ignored Sita and she was relieved—there was good reason to fear these relentless hunters who made no friends outside their own pack.

It was a long walk, but Sita was not tired. Ahead was the Ananta Palace, her home and that of the Prince of Tigers. She was glad Ashok and Neelam had chosen to make it their home as well. When Sita entered the clearing, she saw two young boys playing in the open space and stopped to watch them. First, they were chasing a butterfly; then they were chasing each other. Although they were not twins, Hari and Bala were close enough in age and looked so similar that it was easy to imagine that she was seeing Ashok and Arun once again, young and happy, with no worries of what life might hold for them in the future.

They were getting closer and closer to the pool in their play, and Sita wondered if they knew how to swim yet. Suddenly Neelam rose from where she had been weeding in the garden, a baby on her back. Clearly, the baby she had been expecting had been born. "Boys, do not play too near the pool," she said. "Thy father has not yet taught thee the ways of water."

Then she saw Sita. "Welcome, Mother. It is good to see thee. Too long have we been without thy company."

Sita moved forward, and the two women embraced. "I am ever grateful that thou art my daughter now," Sita said.

They spoke in tiger talk, which Neelam had picked up very easily. Sita wondered if this was due to her tiger blood or if languages were simply easy for her. In either case, Sita felt proud of her daughter-in-law, who fit so easily into the family that she and the Prince of Tigers had established.

"I expect Ashok home tonight," Neelam said. "He is out hunting."

Sita had been curious if, married to a mostly human wife and without the need to provide for his foster brothers, Ashok might abandon this part of his heritage. Apparently, that was not the case.

"He will be very happy to see thee. He has been worried about thee of late," Neelam added.

Ⅻ

Indeed, Ashok was happy to see his mother, and he hugged her with a fervor he seldom displayed. "We have been missing thee," he cried. "When the baby, our little daughter, was born, we thought thou might come to bless her, but we were disappointed. Mother, do not stay away any longer."

Sita's heart was warmed by the love she felt from both her son and his wife. "I have returned," she said simply. "This will be my home for the rest of my life—here, where I lived so happily with the Prince of Tigers."

Then both of them began to talk at once.

"We were hoping . . ." began Ashok.

"It will be wonderful . . ." said Neelam.

"I want thee to know . . ."

"Thou can teach . . ."

Then all three laughed at the boys' antics as Hari and Bala romped around the room in their excitement at having a visitor and their need to always be darting about like the energetic man-cubs they were.

When the baby, perhaps alarmed by this excess of emotion and jollity, began to cry, Sita took her in her arms. "I never had a daughter until thee, Neelam," she said, "so I have never had a small daughter. I will be very happy if I can be part of this little one's life. How hast thou named her?"

"Her name is Priya," said Ashok. "We would have named her Sita, but for us, there can only be one Sita."

Sita smiled and jiggled Priya on her hip; the baby stopped crying immediately, staring up with wide-open eyes at this stranger—her grandmother (though she did not know it), whose touch was gentle yet firm. "It is so good to be home," Sita said.

It was indeed good to be home. It was good to sit on the balcony of the Ananta Palace and chat with Mor again, although it was a different Mor. He had a thousand questions to ask about the Primrose Palace, and while Sita answered them, his wives crept close to listen; they clucked in astonishment at the strange and wonderful things they heard. Sita went to the underground room to pay her respects to the new Nagaiah. Ashok had told her that her old friend was dead, but his nephew had come to take his place as guardian of the treasure. Ashok introduced the two. The young king cobra was courteous but not friendly, though he was certainly less menacing than the old Nagaiah had been the first time Sita met him. She knew she would miss her conversations with Nagaiah; it seemed unlikely that she would develop a similar relationship with his successor.

Sita was soon caught up in many of the old duties, except they felt different now. When she worked in the garden, Neelam was usually working there also, and the two women talked as they hoed the beans or planted *khira* together. It had been a long time since little ones tumbled about the old palace, which now echoed with running feet, shouted dares, and snippets of song. It was like Sita was reliving the childhood of Ashok and Arun, yet Neelam's boys were very different from her own. Ashok had always been responsible and somewhat solemn, while Arun was happy and teasing, never expecting to be called to account for his transgressions. There was not as much difference in the personalities of these boys. Hari was older, so he was a little more daring, but Bala was determined that he would not be left behind, whether they were climbing trees, jumping into the pool, or running races across the clearing. Both man-cubs were sturdy and healthy and forever on the move. It seemed to Sita that they were always competing with each other, but their competitions were basically friendly. They ran and jumped and played until they were exhausted, then collapsed into a tangled heap and were instantly asleep.

All three children were growing fast. Sita had been very curious whether or not the man-cubs would be able to transform. They changed occasionally, but they could not manage it unless they concentrated hard, signaled by wrinkled foreheads and expectant expressions. Sometimes, the alteration stalled out in the reddish haze; then, Hari and Bala disgustedly resumed the form they were in when they tried to initiate the process. Priya had shown no signs of being able to transform at all, but she was still young, mostly following her mother and grandmother around on her fat little legs. Sita thought that only her eyes gave a hint of her tiger heritage. They were not the same green as the Prince of Tigers' eyes, but they were definitely green in color, a deeper shade than Ashok's.

Ashok stopped beside his mother as she sat on the balcony with mending in her hands. "I have to go to the city," he told her. "I would like to go farther and visit Vasu and Vanada, and I am carrying messages from Neelam to her parents. Would you like to send a message to the young maharajah as well?"

Sita agreed this would be a good idea. She wrote,

> *It has been a long time since I left the Primrose Palace, but I have heard only good news of your reign. People say you are like your father in that you care for the people you rule over. I think of your father fondly and often, and of the years I spent in his employ.*
> *Sita.*

"That is short and simple," teased Ashok. "Where are all the flowery phrases such as 'Your always devoted servant,' and 'May Your Excellency reign forever'?"

"The young maharajah knows me," Sita replied. "If I wrote things like that to Jaya, he would not believe it was written by me and would arrest you as the bearer of a false message, doubtless sent by someone attempting to deceive him for some evil purpose."

Ashok and Neelam laughed. "You are right, Mother," Neelam exclaimed, and Ashok added, "If this maharajah has half the wisdom of his father, he would indeed recognize instantly that a letter that used all those flattering and toadying phrases (or even if it were filled with the polite forms that would be included if a writer from the marketplace were involved) would not be a letter written by a woman who was known and celebrated for her wisdom and her plain speaking."

¥o

Ashok was indeed going to see his foster brothers, and Neelam was anxious to have news of her parents. Neither of these, however, was his chief objective, although he carried out both errands before he approached the maharajah with Sita's letter.

Suhani and Gokul were delighted to see their son-in-law; they could hardly remember a time when they were concerned that Ashok might not be a good husband because of his tiger blood. Ashok gave them Neelam's message and some nuts she had sent from the jungle. He answered their questions about the children, how tall Hari and Bala were and whether little Priya was talking much yet. He said that, yes, Sita was well, but she appeared to be aging. Ashok then asked about Vasu and Vanada; he was astounded by the news he received.

"Vasu is much the same," Gokul said as he and Ashok walked towards the tiger enclosure. "He is happy with the life he is living and sees no reason why it should ever change. But Vanada is a different story. This spring, when a young tigress was put into an enclosure with him, it was like he fell in love. He did not want her to leave, and when she was put into a separate pen, he moaned and carried on until she was returned to him. The whole situation was awkward because the brothers have always shared the same enclosure. But it looks as though Vanada has decided to be a family man.

"Bikram and Gotama helped me build a temporary barrier across the middle of the twins' enclosure. Vasu is now by himself, and

Vanada is sharing his space with Farha. This was necessary as Farha will soon deliver cubs and I felt it was not advisable to have cubs in the same enclosure with a male tiger that was not their father. Of course, if this were a normal situation, it might not be safe to house them with their father either . . . but Vanada has decided he will not be a typical male tiger."

"Frankly, I do not understand this at all," Ashok said. "Of course, my father challenged the order even more dramatically, but he was a truly unique individual. Generally, this is not the way tigers behave. They do not live in a family circle, but it is true that Vasu and Vanada's upbringing was highly unusual, as they did."

"You and I know this, and Vasu knows it too. But apparently Vanada does not know it, or if he does, he has decided to alter the usual pattern for tigers to a different one that he prefers. Vanada has chosen to live his life according to this new plan," Gokul responded.

"What about the tigress? Did she not find the situation unusual?"

"At first she did, and she was very unpleasant, snarling and lashing out at Vanada whenever he came near. But now I think maybe she is accepting it."

"I am more surprised than I can say," commented Ashok. "Did Vanada talk to you about all this?"

"He tried, but maybe he can explain it to you more clearly. We talk daily about the usual things like food and water and a new ball to play with, but this thing is much more complicated. I am sure Vanada will be able to talk more easily to you."

"We will see" was all Ashok said, but he was worried. *What would lead Vanada to act so out of character for a tiger? And why would he choose to do anything that would separate him from his beloved brother?* He had never been separated from Vasu, and both had declared their mutual intention for this situation of togetherness to continue always. *What has changed Vanada from the easygoing son of Manju? And what could have caused him to demand a change in the life that he freely chose for himself?*

Ashok pondered these questions, but by the time he approached his foster brothers' enclosure, he had reached no conclusions.

"Vanada," Ashok called out as he unlatched the gate to the couple's enclosure. "Where art thou, O my brother?"

"Ashok." Vanada yawned as he emerged from a clump of bamboo, but he quickly rushed to his brother's side, stood on his hind legs, and put his paws on Ashok's shoulders. "It makes me happy to look at thee. Thou hast not visited my home before. What brings thee here today?"

"I brought some things from Neelam to her parents," Ashok replied. "I bear a message from our mother to the young maharajah. And, of course, she sent her love to you and Vasu."

Vanada immediately wanted to know all about Sita and whether she was happy to be at the Ananta Palace again. Although he was perfectly at ease with Gokul and Suhani and had grown very fond of them, no keepers, however friendly and sensitive, could entirely take the place of his foster mother.

"Gokul has told me something that surprised me very much," Ashok began.

"Oh, thou must mean about Farha. I know what thou wilt say, that this way is not the way of tigers."

"Thou speakest truly. Indeed, it is not the way among tigers— they do not generally live together in a family situation. But how did this come about?"

"It is indeed strange," said Vanada, "and I am not sure that I can explain it to thee in a way thou canst understand."

"Wilt thou try?"

"Of course I will, Ashok; I would not keep my reasons a secret from thee. I should tell thee that, indeed, I miss Vasu and all the good times we had together. I had never thought to be separated from him for any length of time. But all I can say is that when I saw Farha, I suddenly remembered our home in the Ananta Palace. I remembered the devotion we daily saw between our parents, and how happy our family was then. And I thought, *Is there any reason why I cannot have this happiness for myself?*"

"I understand thy desire because I have always carried it within myself," Ashok replied. "I never thought to know the same happiness that our parents had, and I know how fortunate I am to have found it. Neelam had always known that the possibility existed, even though she did not expect to find that happiness any more than I did. But what about Farha? She would have grown up knowing that tigers tend to be solitary. Thy desire to establish a family must have been a great surprise to her, and perhaps not a pleasant one."

"Thou art right, my brother. But let me call her and she can tell thee herself how she feels about our living arrangements."

Vanada made a sound that male tigers sometimes make—not a cough, not a roar, but a sound of questioning or supplication. It was answered immediately; in a few moments, a young tigress appeared. Her body tensed and her eyes opened wide in surprise when she spotted her husband in apparent conversation with a man other than Gokul.

"Who is this stranger?" she asked.

"Farha, I have often spoken to thee of my brother, Ashok," Vanada replied. "This is he."

Her astonishment was evident in her expression. "I did not realize that thy brother was a man. I assumed he was a tiger as we are."

"Ashok is both man and tiger," Vanada said proudly. "He is the son of the Prince of Tigers that was and of my beloved Sita, who became my mother when I was yet a cub. Someday, perhaps thou wilt see Ashok in his tiger form. But when he is in the world of men, it is safer for him to appear as a man."

Farha looked searchingly at Ashok but did not respond.

"I must ask thee a question, Farha," Ashok said. "It is most unusual for tigers who mate to continue living together in amity and happiness. Dost thou feel that this is possible for thee and my brother?"

"I can hardly believe it myself," Farha admitted. "It took me some time to become accustomed to it, but it is true. I have come to enjoy this life. I used to be lonely often, but now, I am never lonely as Vanada is always here with me. We talk together and are companions in everything. Soon our cubs will be born, and then all of us will be together. Even though I have never heard of a male tiger interacting with his cubs and teaching them, I am sure that Vanada will be a wonderful father."

Ashok left Vanada's enclosure feeling a great sense of relief. He was pleased that both Vanada and Farha were committed to what he could hardly help regarding as an experiment; it was fortunate that the pair involved did *not* regard it as such. Instead, both were eagerly looking forward to their future together as a tiger family, no matter how unorthodox that might seem. Ashok had to acknowledge that Vanada—like himself—had been raised in a situation even more unorthodox than the one Vanada had chosen for himself.

He next went to Vasu's enclosure, curious about what Vanada's twin would have to say about this strange turn of events. He soon discovered that Vasu was not happy at all.

"We have been together every day since the day we were born," Vasu complained, "and were together in the womb even before that. Why must Vanada seek to change the natural order of things? He is a tiger and should strive to act like one!" Vasu raked his claws across the gate to his sleeping quarters, leaving deep scratches in the wood. It was obvious he was angry, but Ashok felt he was also hurt and confused.

"Both of us realize that the Prince of Tigers did not act according to the natural order of things. If he had not behaved in a manner quite unnatural to tigers, I would never have been born, and thou wouldst never have had Sita as thy foster mother."

"It is true," groaned Vasu. "But I am lonely, and I miss my brother. And I will never understand the choice he has made."

"He has told me that when he saw Farha, he remembered how happy we all were in the old palace and instantly wanted to have that kind of life for himself. Of course, he will not be able to replicate the life we had, but I believe he means to do so as far as is possible."

"It is true we were happy then," Vasu admitted. "I miss those days too. But what I miss now more than anything else is spending time with my twin. We used to saunter around our enclosure together, talking about this and that. If we were tired, we lay down and slept. If we were hungry, we went near Gokul's quarters and called for Suhani. We played together in the pool and sometimes fought the mock battles we have engaged in since we were cubs. Now none of those things happen." Vasu groaned and hid his face in his paws.

"Would it please thee if, in addition to the individual enclosures that thou and Vanada now have, there was another, joint enclosure, where thou and he could spend some time together, as in former days?" Ashok asked.

"I still want the former days, not some pale imitation," Vasu replied. "But it is good of thee, my brother, to think of this solution— it would be better than the total separation that exists now."

"I will see what I can do," promised Ashok.

CHAPTER

46

After a brief conversation with Gokul, Ashok proceeded to the maharajah's palace. He gave his name at the entrance to the palace and stated that he had come to consult with the maharajah on a matter of business. He refused to give any further details except to a personal attendant of the ruler.

The servant he said this to felt like laughing in the young man's face. Who did this upstart think he was? But there was something about the way Ashok held himself and the confidence with which he spoke that led the man to send for Harish at once. The old minister did not arrive for an hour, but Ashok waited patiently, asking no questions and showing no signs of unrest. He stood by the open window and gazed out over the palace grounds. He wondered how many times Sita had done the same thing, feeling homesick for the jungle and wishing she were away from the scurrying feet that constantly ran to and fro in the palace. Ashok had been here for only a short time, but already he felt confined—it was not exactly like being in a cage, but there was a definite sense of restriction.

When he heard footsteps, Ashok turned and inclined his head to the approaching minister. "If it may please you," he said, "I am Ashok, the son of Sita, former councilor of the old maharajah. She has sent a message to his son, the current maharajah, and charged me to deliver it into no hands but his."

The old man studied him at length. "I can see that you have a look of Sita about you," he said. "Even though you are humbly dressed and appear to have walked a long way, you are not afraid to look directly into my eyes. You speak well and your speech has the ring of truth. Come with me."

They walked for a long time as they traversed a hall, climbed the marble stairs, and continued to the room that the old maharajah had used as a daftar. The room was just as Sita had described it. The desk was still there, and there were still two chairs. The minister motioned Ashok to one of the chairs. "This is where your mother used to sit when she attended the maharajah," Harish said. "His Excellency will be with you in a few minutes."

Again, Ashok waited, but it was not long until a young man strolled into the room. His clothes were not extravagant, but the fabric was clearly not what was sold in the bazaar. Ashok rose, but the maharajah motioned for him to be seated.

"I am told you have a message for me," he said, extending his hand. Ashok silently handed him Sita's note, and the maharajah read it in silence.

"It is good to hear from Sita and to see her hand again," the young maharajah said. "You are her son?"

"I am."

"I did not know that Sita had a son. She never mentioned you to me. If she told my father, perhaps it was near the end of his life, and he was too ill to pass the information on to me—I know he would have found it interesting." The young maharajah felt a little miffed. His father had shared with him practically everything he knew about Sita, but this was a significant omission.

"I cannot say for certain why she would have kept my existence a secret, unless she was afraid that the revelation might result in additional pain for her."

"You are daring," said the young maharajah. "Nevertheless, I can see why her mind might turn in an unfortunate direction, given past history."

"Given past history," agreed Ashok.

"I must wonder, however, why this is the first time I have heard from your mother; furthermore, this message does not contain anything that necessitated its being delivered personally by you. It could have been delivered by anyone. Therefore, I must ask you if there is some other reason for your presence here, some request you have to make that you felt was best made in person. You probably realized that I would be more likely to grant that request if it was, in a sense, authorized by a woman for whom I have a great deal of admiration and respect. Somehow, this all seems less straightforward than I am accustomed to think Sita is."

"You are perceptive," remarked Ashok.

The maharajah nodded in agreement and watched the young man from the jungle closely. *Why does he approach me, and what does Sita's son hope to gain through this audience?*

"I told my mother that I was coming in this direction on business," Ashok began. "I told her I planned to see my brothers and suggested that she might like to send a message to you that I could carry myself. She was happy for the opportunity to communicate with one whom she remembers fondly and always speaks of with respect."

"So, what is your purpose?" the maharajah inquired. "What do you seek? Are you hoping for employment in the palace?"

"Not at all," Ashok replied. "I am happy in the jungle now; furthermore, I am certain that I will never want to leave it. But you are correct in assuming that I am here for a particular purpose. I have two things to ask of you. The first is small, but the second is not. The second is extremely important to my family, and I hope, with all my heart, that you will choose to grant this request."

So I was not wrong, thought the young ruler. *Of course he wants something.* To Ashok, he said, "Tell me what you want, and I will see whether it is possible to grant your wish or not."

"I will ask the small thing first," Ashok said. "Of course, you know that my foster brothers are part of your menagerie and live in the grounds of the palace."

"I knew the twin tigers were Sita's foster sons, so I should have realized that they would be your foster brothers, as well. Are you requesting something for them? Jeweled collars, perhaps?"

"Not at all. I am requesting something quite different. When Sita asked your father to accept them in the menagerie, they were housed together, as was their wish. Now things have changed between them. Vasu wishes his life to continue as it is now, but Vanada wants to have only one mate and intends that they shall live together."

"Strange, but interesting," the maharajah said, leaning forward and steepling his fingers together. "Please continue."

"Gokul has attempted to separate them by placing a temporary barrier across their enclosure, but the twins are unhappy at being completely separated; therefore, I would like to discuss a possible solution with Your Excellency."

The maharajah was intrigued. "This sounds amazingly like family discord among humans. Please tell me how you would address this matter."

Ashok explained his idea of remaking the one large enclosure into three—a good-sized one each for Vasu and Vanada, and a third area between them with gates that opened into the others; then, the brothers could spend time together as they had done in the past. "When Vasu and Vanada desire this, they can ask Gokul to open the gates and allow each of them to pass into the joint enclosure, where they can talk and meander about as they were accustomed to do."

"A brilliant idea," the maharajah responded. "There is plenty of room so all their needs can be met. We can easily make the tiger enclosure larger and redesign the area so that all three sections will be comfortable and spacious, particularly the one for Vanada and his mate, who will be raising a family. I am fascinated by this shift in the natural order of things. What did you say the tigress is called? I am amazed that Vanada was able to find a tigress who shares the same unusual perspective that he holds."

"Her name is Farha. Apparently, she did not initially favor this idea and was very unpleasant, but I believe that my brother can be quite persuasive. Farha is very happy now."

"Good. I want Sita's foster sons to be happy here. But what about Vasu?"

"He is not happy, but the reorganization of the enclosure will be helpful to him; hopefully, he will adjust to the separation from Vanada in time."

"I will order the carpenters to begin work on the enclosures at once. You were right—this is a small thing. Now, what is the important thing you wish to ask me?"

Ashok hesitated. He did not know how best to introduce this delicate subject. "My mother is growing old," he began.

The maharajah nodded. "I could tell this from her letter," he said. "Although she has always formed her characters very well (and still does), yet I could detect a slight trembling of her hand when she wrote the letter."

"It is true, Your Majesty. And as she grows more frail, she dwells more and more in the past, remembering the happiest times of her life, when she was living with my father in the jungle."

The maharajah was surprised. He had expected that Ashok would ask for some position in the palace for which he was not fitted or, even more likely, a pension for Sita. He did not think the first option would work out very well, although he was willing to try it for Sita's sake. He was perfectly willing to grant the second—he had offered Sita a pension before, but she had refused it. Now, however, it appeared that Ashok had something else entirely on his mind. "What would you have me do?" he asked.

"My mother misses my father, the Prince of Tigers, with a pain that is incredibly strong—its sharpness has not been diminished by time. And while she sits in the jungle, grieving, the body of her husband stands in your palace (seen only by a few) in a glass case that must be dusted every day. This is the boon I ask—that although you cannot restore my father to Sita, you can send her what is left of him."

"This is a strange and most unusual request."

"It is, but being able to look again upon the face of her beloved husband would make my mother very happy."

"What about the body of your brother?"

"Of course I would like to take both my father and Arun back to their home in the jungle. But I thought it might be more difficult to persuade you to part with the Prince of Tigers, the centerpiece of your father's collection as I understand it, than with his son; therefore, I decided to go straight to the heart of the matter, even though I realize that this is probably the most difficult part of my appeal for you to grant."

"You are right. The Prince of Tigers is the centerpiece of the museum, my father's trophy room. But this collection was his passion, not mine. It would gratify me to send the Prince of Tigers and your brother to Sita, as you believe it is so important to her. I owe her much, both for the evil my father unwittingly did to her and for the good with which she repaid him (and me as well) over the years when she served as a voice of wisdom in the palace."

So the maharajah's agreement to the return of Arun and the Prince of Tigers to the jungle was easily obtained. Far more difficult was deciding how the transfer would be accomplished, and the two men discussed a variety of plans, none of which seemed practical.

"They could go in a cart as far as the village," Ashok said slowly, "but what would happen then? The path into the jungle is narrow and would not admit a cart and bullocks. We would also need a large group of men to lift the cases out of the cart and put them where they will reside in the future. Furthermore, the location of our home in the jungle has always been secret, for reasons I am certain you understand. It is not acceptable to have so many people know where and how we live."

"I have it!" shouted the maharajah suddenly, leaping to his feet. "We will use elephants! Each tiger can be placed on the back of an elephant. The elephants can lift the tigers wherever it is that you want the cases to be placed."

"It might work," admitted Ashok.

"A few people will still have to know the destination, but not nearly as many, so I will choose men that I trust. Furthermore, we will skirt the jungle and approach from a different direction. If someone is seeking to know where the tigers are being taken, this will confuse the issue," the maharajah continued.

So it was decided. The Prince of Tigers and Arun would be conveyed by elephants to the Ananta Palace, and Sita would once again be surrounded by her beloved husband and both of her sons, the dead as well as the living. It only remained to make the preparations, one of which was for the maharajah to photograph the two tigers. Even if they would no longer reside in the museum's collection, he would have a record of these exhibits that had been of such importance to his father. The old maharajah would have been quite surprised to know that the figures of the prince and Arun— the most important displays in his collection—would be replaced by photographs.

CHAPTER

47

The young maharajah had only one condition for the transfer of the most important exhibits from his father's museum to the long-deserted, crumbling palace in the jungle—he must accompany the expedition and be present when the transfer was made.

This condition caused Ashok some worry. Sita had always carefully preserved the secret of the Ananta Palace's location; only the family and other jungle dwellers knew where it was. Now it would be revealed not only to the mahouts but also to a small retinue, and even the present maharajah himself. Ashok did not know how Sita would react to this intrusion, but he believed (or at least hoped) that in her joy at being near the Prince of Tigers and Arun once again, she would be willing to forgive his surrender of her privacy and security. Her separation from her husband and son had been Sita's chief regret as she left the Primrose Palace to return to the jungle; somehow it had seemed to her like an abandonment of those closest to her heart. She had also left Vasu and Vanada behind, and though her heart was heavy without them, she believed the twins were happy in a life that best suited their personalities and needs.

Ashok took all possible precautions to ensure that the exhibits of his father and brother were handled gently and not damaged, and to preserve the security of the old palace's location. The journey took over a week, much longer than was strictly necessary. The party went many leagues out of their way in order to avoid the city, skirt the jungle, and enter from a direction far away from the village, thus avoiding Ashok's usual route to the Ananta Palace. Although the maharajah's retinue was always quite small compared to how his father had traveled, Jaya slashed it further. Only six elephants (and their mahouts) entered the jungle; they were needed to carry the two tigers, four servitors, and the maharajah himself. Ashok sometimes walked when looking for a trail leading in the right direction but usually rode with Jaya, and the two men talked for hours.

When they finally reached the Ananta Palace, Ashok asked the group to wait until he could talk to his mother and explain what was happening. He found Sita sitting on the lower verandah, watching Hari and Bala try to teach Priya how to walk through piles of leaves without making any noise. She smiled to hear her grandsons explaining to their sister that every true tiger should be able to do this. Priya was happy to follow her brothers through the leaves but refused to stop kicking them because she wanted to hear them crunch.

"Mother," Ashok greeted her. "I am happy to see thee well."

"Ashok, my son," Sita replied, "I am happy to see thee back in thy rightful place here at the palace. I have missed thee sorely, as has thy wife."

"I have also brought somebody to see thee."

"Who?" Sita's face showed alarm. Everyone she loved except Vasu and Vanada—Ashok, Neelam, and their three children—was here at the palace, and she did not think the twins would choose to return. Yes, she loved Anila, her oldest friend, but even Anila had never been allowed to enter Sita's innermost heart with all its secrets.

Ashok turned and signaled Jaya to approach. When Sita saw him, her astonishment was great. "Your Excellency honors us," she said, bowing.

The maharajah bowed in his turn. "My dear Sita, it is good to see you once again," he said. "I wish to congratulate you on having such an excellent son. Not only is he wise, like his mother, but he is also a generous man; in addition, he is a good negotiator."

"What do you mean? What has Ashok said or done to deserve your praise?"

"He has convinced me that certain exhibits that were in my father's museum would reside more peacefully and appropriately here in the jungle." Sita was not sure of his meaning, but her heart began to pound; whatever the maharajah meant was, she knew, of great importance to her.

The maharajah waved his hand, and several elephants emerged from the jungle into the clearing. All six bore howdahs and their mahouts on their backs, but the first two elephants were carrying what appeared to be large boxes covered with canvas, looking rather like tents; the other elephants carried a few men she did not recognize. Sita still could not make out what the maharajah was getting at. She felt confused, not only by his presence but also by the intrusion of elephants and strangers into the remote solitude of her home. Of course, she had seen *haathiyon* file across the clearing many times, but those animals were part of the jungle, while these were working elephants that did the will of man. And she had never seen a stranger here, only members of her family and other jungle dwellers.

Then the maharajah reached up and pulled some cords that drew the canvas away from what it covered. Sita could now see what it was that the first two elephants were carrying: glass cases, each containing a beautiful male tiger. They were the same cases and the same tigers she had sat beside every day she was at the Primrose Palace. She had talked to them as though they were alive. She did not know whether they could hear and understand—from some faraway afterlife—what she said, but she had daily reported to them what was going on around her, and always assured them of her ongoing love. Now they were here at the old palace in the jungle, the very spot from which each had ventured forth on what was to be the last day of his life.

"It makes my heart glad that your husband and son will now be with you," the young maharajah was saying. "This is where they should be, where they belong."

"But what about the museum?" Sita heard herself saying, and thought how silly she sounded. "These exhibits were among the favorites of your father."

"It is true, Sita," the maharajah said, "but this is their rightful place, in the jungle where they ruled. Furthermore, I will not forget them, and I have kept something to remind me of the two tigers I regarded with such awe when I was a boy."

"What have you kept?" Sita wondered if the maharajah had removed some hair from the tigers to be woven into embroidery or wound with wire to make a piece of jewelry.

"Here," he said and handed her a folder that held three photographs. One was of Arun and another of the Prince of Tigers, photographed by the maharaja after removing them from their glass cases so there would be no glare. The prince stood and Arun sat in front of some lantana bushes Sita recognized from the palace gardens. They looked so natural she could imagine the photographs had been taken when the Prince of Tigers and Arun were alive, although she knew that could not be true. Besides the individual pictures of the two tigers, there was another where they were posed together, Arun seemingly gazing at his father with admiration. Sita looked confusedly from the photographs to the elephants and the burdens they had conveyed for such a distance. The mahouts and the maharajah's servants were carefully lowering the cases to the ground.

"These pictures are for you as well as the exhibits from my father's museum," Jaya said. "I well remember when you advised me to turn to the camera for my specimens, and I have done so. I have kept copies of these for myself, of course, to remember not only the

Prince of Tigers and his son but also to remember the woman who always gave both my father and me good advice, and who had much to do with how I see the world."

The rest of the afternoon was a blur. The maharajah had also brought Sita a chest that contained all the things she had abandoned when she left the Primrose Palace. In addition, he took a picture of Sita by herself, one of Sita with the Prince of Tigers and Arun, and one of Sita and her family—Ashok, Neelam, Hari, Bala, and Priya. Meanwhile, the elephants lifted the cases (with some difficulty) to the balcony; from there the men struggled to carry them to the spacious room where the family spent much of their time. At last the operation was finished, and the maharajah and his men departed, Ashok accompanying them to be sure they took the right trails and did not become lost.

Sita sat quietly in front of the glass cases, facing her husband. She hardly noticed that Neelam and her grandchildren were in the same room. "At last, Prince of Tigers, thou hast come home to me," she murmured.

CHAPTER

48

Of course, there were many things to talk about when Ashok returned and for many days after. Sita wanted to hear all about Vasu and Vanada. She was sorry that the close fellowship between the twins had been altered, but at the same time, she was happy Vanada had made a choice she felt would ensure his future happiness. Sita was surprised but pleased he had chosen to follow the example of the Prince of Tigers with regard to his domestic life. At this point, she had forgotten that she and the prince had sometimes disagreed about things; she recalled their life together as ideal, and remembered her husband as being practically perfect.

Ashok sometimes teased her gently about her memories. "Dost thou not remember, Mother," he would say, mischievously, "how angry thou wert when my father dragged home the remains of a sambar and left smears of blood all around the front door of the palace?"

"I remember," Sita said rather grimly, "but a slip of that kind was exceedingly unusual for the Prince of Tigers. Generally, thy father did nothing that merited my disapproval."

Ashok decided not to mention other times when Sita and the Prince of Tigers had held different attitudes about how life in the Ananta Palace should be ordered. He remembered that the disagreement about adopting Vasu and Vanada had gone on for quite some time, although his parents rarely spoke of it, at least when he and Arun were present. Sita was sympathetic with Shira for trying to provide for her cubs; she knew how she would have felt if her own man-cubs had been left motherless. Therefore, Sita had been the one to agree to keep them, without even consulting the prince; he, on the other hand, had initially wanted nothing to do with the twin cubs, afraid that in personality and character, they would be like their mother. In fact, the discovery that they were like their father, the amiable Manju, had relieved both foster parents, who came to think of the cubs as their own.

Sita wanted to hear news of Gokul and Suhani, and Neelam had many questions about her parents as well. Ashok said they were well and looking forward to the birth of Vanada and Farha's cubs. Sita also asked after some of the servants at the palace, and she was curious about the museum now that its centerpiece was missing.

"My father and Arun are not truly missing," Ashok reminded her. "The maharajah has copies of the photographs he gave thee. He is also going to have an artist paint large pictures, using the photographs as models, so the paintings will truly resemble Arun and my father; these paintings will be hung in the museum. The Prince of Tigers will still be the museum's centerpiece, with Arun at his side, Mother."

"As he should be," Sita replied, a little tartly. She could not understand why anyone would care about other exhibits when the Prince of Tigers and his son were present, whether in a photograph, a painting, or as a mounted specimen.

Ashok had been right when he thought that having the Prince of Tigers present in the home would bring Sita joy. As she had done in the museum, she often talked to him, both relating news about the family and nearby jungle friends and recalling the early happy days of their acquaintance and life together. Ashok and Neelam noted that she was living more and more in the past, but not entirely so. Suhani had promised to send word when Farha's cubs were born, and Sita definitely looked forward to receiving that news. She was delighted when Ashok returned from a visit to the village with a letter from Suhani in his hand.

Only a single cub had been born, but she was healthy and thriving. In spite of Farha's expressed confidence in her mate, she had been somewhat uneasy when Vanada insisted on sharing in the cub's care, but he was proving himself a devoted father. In fact, he spent so much time with the cub that he had missed several of his appointments with Vasu, who, not understanding his twin's devotion to this helpless and mewling new addition, watched mournfully through the gate from the shared enclosure, occasionally calling out to remind Vanada that he was waiting.

I am sure that when the newness wears off, Vanada will remember he has a brother, too, wrote Suhani, *but for now, he is completely focused on the new cub. Her name is Farah, she has a sweet little face, blue eyes, and her coat is very pale—I would call it a cream color. I am certain, however, that Vanada does miss Vasu; hopefully, it will soon occur to him that his brother is unhappy. Vasu will be happier when Vanada starts visiting the shared enclosure again; he will always be miserable without his twin.*

"This will happen soon," Sita predicted to Ashok and Neelam, after reading Suhani's letter. "They are too close to be completely separated for long. It is simply that the new cub is so important to Vanada. Now the family he looked forward to is complete, and he can hardly see past this fact. But soon he will notice Vasu's sadness and ask Gokul to open the gate so that he can spend time with his brother again."

"Art thou certain?" Neelam asked. "Art thou not afraid that Vasu and Vanada are growing farther apart all the time?"

"I suppose it is possible," Sita replied, "but I do not believe—no matter what their choices—that either one will ever abandon the other. Each would be incomplete without the physical and emotional closeness to each other that they have known all their lives."

Ashok spoke up then. "I agree with Mother. I speak not as a parent (who may project his own wishes onto what he witnesses) but as a brother who observed Vasu and Vanada daily when they were young, and has had recent conversations with them both. Furthermore, I myself am a twin and know all too well the pain and grief that accompanies separation, particularly if that separation is permanent. Their devotion to each other remains strong, even though they have chosen different paths. Vanada has not forgotten his brother—Vasu will just have to be patient."

CHAPTER

49

Ashok and Neelam were sad to see Sita growing more and more frail. She asked Ashok to remove the glass that surrounded the Prince of Tigers so she could sit closer to him. She spent much of the day there, talking to him, recounting a hundred things that had happened to her or the boys after his death.

Most of these tales were not new—she had told them to him before. His lack of response was not new either, but it had never prevented Sita from talking to him; however, Neelam noticed that after several months, Sita spent less time talking to the prince and more time just watching her grandchildren. Neelam encouraged the children to play near their grandmother, and to listen to the stories she told them about what she had seen and experienced after she moved to the jungle to live with the Prince of Tigers. They listened, but Neelam did not know whether they were truly learning from what they heard. Neelam also tried her best to see that Sita was as comfortable as possible.

Ashok had guessed what would make her happy and had facilitated bringing his father to the old palace, but it was no longer enough to have the facsimile of her husband there. She had been so happy to see him in their home that she had initially not grasped all the implications of having the prince nearby in his present form. She realized now, however, that no matter what she told him, no matter what words of love came from her lips, he would never answer. He would merely continue standing there, his head raised as he gazed into the distance.

Although she had always known that the prince was gone forever, in her happiness at seeing him again, she had somehow believed that he was really back again. The renewed knowledge that he would never truly be back was devastating. Sita, once more plunged into grief, became weaker.

One day, Sita asked to be carried out to the second-floor balcony so that she could look out over the jungle and smell its scents. Ashok lifted her tiny body; she weighed next to nothing. Her eyes seemed dim, and Ashok was not even sure that she could see into the green depths of tangled foliage that had framed her life. He wondered whether she was living in her memories rather than reacting to what was around her now—the sun filtering through the leaves, Hari and Bala playing with a couple of *nevala* in the green shade, the bright flowers planted around the palace and Priya wandering among them. He laid her gently on the rug where she often stretched out for a nap. He had noted that she was sleeping more and more lately, almost dazed when she was awakened to eat food that she barely touched.

"I think she is very close to death," Neelam said softly. "Art thou going to carry out thy plan?"

"It is the last thing I can do for her while she yet lives," Ashok replied, watching his mother as she fought for breath.

He left the balcony while Neelam knelt by Sita, speaking softly to her mother-in-law and raising her body slightly.

Suddenly, a magnificent male tiger strode onto the balcony. "My Sita," he called loudly. "Art thou not going to welcome me home? When thy husband has been kept from thy side for so long?"

Sita raised herself to her knees and held out her arms. "My husband," she cried. "The Prince of Tigers! Thou hast finally returned to me. At last." Her voice broke on the last word, and she sank back on the rug.

She did not feel Neelam's arms around her or see the tiger she had thought was her husband transform into her son. Together, Ashok and Neelam held her as her breathing slowed and finally ceased.

Sita had been an independent young woman and a village outcast. She had been the wife of the Prince of Tigers and borne him two man-cubs, one of whom had died early, while the other developed into a thoughtful and caring man. She had accepted two tiger cubs into her home and mothered them as well. She had been the councilor to two maharajahs. Her life had been a full one, but she had never ceased to mourn the husband who had been taken from her so suddenly and pointlessly. Now she had followed him into death.

Ashok burned the bodies of his parents the day after Sita's death. Together on the verandah, overlooking the jungle where they had shared so many happy memories, was, he felt, an appropriate place for them to go through the final rites together. He did not know whether they would be reborn or, if so, as what entities, but it seemed to him that if they were purged together by the sacred fire, they had a better chance of being together in their next lives.

Neelam was not certain that his thinking was correct, but she recognized the love that lay behind it and said nothing.

She helped him move the Prince of Tigers, who still stood, with his head raised, looking into the distance. Ashok imagined that perhaps he was looking into the next life. Sita was propped up with pillows and leaned against the Tiger. She looked even smaller beside his bulk. Ashok and Neelam took dry logs and built a loose wall around the couple, although it was quite low in the direction they were facing. Ashok wanted to be sure that they could see the jungle where they had lived together so happily.

Ashok lit the pyre, and the flames soared up, taking no notice of the two who were so quiet within the circle of fire. The jungle dwellers wondered at the sparks and smoke ascending from the old palace; there was often a cooking fire there, but these flames meant something different.

The Prince of Tigers, because of the process he had been put through after his death, burned more readily than Sita; at last, however, nothing was left of the two but ash and pieces of bone. Ashok swept these remains into a pottery jar. He walked to the waterfall and strewed the ashes across the water where they were washed over the lip of the falls to vanish into the roiling water below. They would be distributed along the edges of the river—Sita and the Prince of Tigers would always be part of their jungle. Then Ashok walked slowly back to the palace where Neelam was waiting to comfort him.

Although they had witnessed Sita's growing weakness, neither of them had been able to envision a life without her; now they knew they must live without Sita's guidance and love. The two held each other's hands as they went to look at their sleeping children. In their tiger forms, Hari and Bala lay sprawled out on the carpet, breathing deeply as they prowled in a dream jungle. Priya was curled into a tight little ball; she whimpered softly as though she already missed Sita's arms, which had so often enfolded her and held her close. Then Neelam brewed tea, and she and Ashok sat and talked of Sita and consoled each other until the sky began to lighten and they realized the new day was at hand.

EPILOGUE

When he suddenly jerked awake, the young reporter realized he had stopped taking notes a long time ago. It felt as though Chandra Devi had been talking forever. Even in his sleep, he had heard her voice rising and falling, although he could not now remember any of the actual words she had spoken. He wondered if he had dozed through any important parts but then decided that was unlikely. What he dimly remembered of her story seemed so strange, so fanciful, so, so, well, *inconceivable*—it was some mishmash about tigers, although he hardly knew what.

He could never use what he had heard as a story for his paper anyway. His editor wouldn't waste time reading it, let alone editing it; he would merely fling it back on his desk, perhaps with a strongly inked *"Unacceptable"* scrawled across the first page. The reporter had been hoping to unearth a story, but instead had acquired this jumble of tigers and cobras and maharajahs and palaces . . . and a woman named Sita, or Mita, or some such name. No, there was nothing for him here.

The reporter wondered how he could extricate himself from the situation without giving offense. After all, this woman had spent the bulk of the day talking to him, even though he had been unable to stay awake. She deserved his respect, although the parts of the story that he dimly remembered could not possibly be true. Perhaps it was some fantastic tale she had heard from her ayah as a child; she might have taken that story, embellished it in all sorts of ways, and passed the end product on to him as something that had actually occurred in her own family.

"Thank you very much, Mrs., uh, uh, Mrs. Devi," he said. "It was a very interesting story, and it was good of you to take the time to tell it to me."

She still sat in her chair, looking like a small goddess in her silken sari and with the jewels in her ears, and around her neck, and on her wrists. She did not acknowledge his words, just continued to sit quietly without moving a muscle, staring past him.

"Thank you for talking to me," he tried again.

Then she turned and looked at him. She was not smiling, so why did he think she was amused? He had noticed her green eyes earlier, but now he saw that the green was deeper, and there was an intent aspect to her eyes that he had not noticed before. They almost glowed, and for a moment, he had the strangest feeling—as though she were watching him as a predator would observe its prey. It made him uneasy. Then she stood up, her back straight, and walked slowly and silently into the house, closing the door behind her.

Well, that's the end of it, thought the reporter. *A wasted trip and all that—wish I hadn't heard about Murchison in the bar that night; if I hadn't, I wouldn't be in this mess now. I was really hoping to get something good here. I was also hoping the editor would pay for it, of course, but I doubt that will happen now. And what will I do about the car?* He walked back towards the village, noticing how dark it had become in the moments since he had left Chandra Devi's house, wondering what *had* happened with the car, and hoping he would not have to spend another night on the charpoy in the goat shed.

Acknowledgments

First of all, reading was important in my family, and there were always books around to read. When my brothers and I were small, our mother, Bertha Scott, read to us; some of my favorite books date from my childhood. She and my grandmother, Lillie Booth, were also great storytellers. The detail and color my mother added to Bible stories made them come alive, while my grandmother told wonderful tales of her childhood in Nevada. I begged her to tell the ones I loved most over and over again.

Other contributors to my love of books were David and Ione Hyman, and Avis Deiss. David and Ione gave me children's classics and books on art and music. Mrs. Deiss, a local elementary school teacher, would bring me a large box of books at the end of the school year so I would have plenty of books to read during the summer months.

Lois Stoops, a high school English teacher, inspired me to write better than I thought I could, and to revise even after I thought the job was done.

And favorite authors who were part of the writing process? Of course, my debt to Rudyard Kipling is both huge and obvious. As a child, I loved *The Jungle Books*; as an adult, I had to wonder how the stories would have been different if the main character had been a girl, and if she had been given a choice between the world of the jungle and that of man. Jim Corbett taught me about tigers' intelligence. I thought of Charles Dickens in the village scenes where characters insist on talking whether or not what they say makes sense.

A big thank-you to early readers of the book (Linda Strahan, Elizabeth Moritz, Pandora Villaseñor, Claudia Wiggins, and Sharon Churches) who gave me suggestions and advice that helped to improve it on so many levels.

Kudos all around to John Koehler and his team of talented professionals, particularly Hannah Woodlan (editing) and Danielle Koehler (beautiful cover art and interior design). John assured me that publication would happen, and he guided me through the entire process; as a total neophyte in the world of publishing, I needed that guidance (as I'm sure he guessed) to move forward.

And finally, no end of gratitude goes to my family, who have been incredibly supportive during this journey. My husband, Vernon, extricated me from more technological snafus than you can imagine. He and our son, Andrew; our daughter and her husband, Stephanie and David; and our grandchildren, Natalie and Dylan, have been with me all the way—giving me time and space to think and write, celebrating with me when I worked out some problem in the plot, shaking their fists at the agents who saw no promise in my submissions, and always ready with a word of encouragement or a hug when I needed one. I am incredibly lucky to have all of you in my life.

Glossary

ANIMALS

baagh	tiger
bandar-log	monkey people; here used interchangeably with langurs
bhalu	sloth bear; feeds on insects and fruit
camagadara	bat
chital	medium-sized deer, white below and golden-brown spotted with white above; also known as spotted deer
chuha	rat or mouse
dhole	Indian wild dog
haathi	elephant (plural: haathiyon)
krait	an extremely venomous snake
langur	a type of monkey
mugger	freshwater crocodile; an aggressive predator, both in the water and on land where it occasionally ambushes its victims
muntjac	small, reddish-brown deer with darker face; also known as barking deer due to the calls it makes
naga	snake, more specifically a cobra. A naga may also be a mythical being who is half cobra and half human and may assume either form at will.
naja naja	Indian or spectacled cobra
nevala	Indian mongoose
nilghai	largest Indian antelope; also known as blue bull
sambar	large, native Indian deer with a shaggy coat, mane, and sizable antlers
siyaar	golden (or Indian) jackal
tendua	leopard

BIRDS

cheel	black kite, a bird of prey that both hunts and scavenges
gidh	white-backed vulture; a scavenger
mor	peacock
peafowl	general name including both peacock and peahen
peelak	golden oriole
val kuruvi	Indian paradise flycatcher

CLOTHING

choli	item of women's clothing; blouse that is worn with a sari
chunni	woman's scarf or shawl that is worn over the head
dhoti	item of men's clothing; a long piece of fabric wrapped around the lower body, through the legs, and tied at the waist
dupatta	veil or shawl
puggaree	long length of thin material wrapped around a man's head; different patterns of wrap reflect different cultures and traditions; also referred to as a turban
sari	item of women's clothing; a long piece of fabric wrapped around the wearer, forming a skirt; the end of the fabric is sometimes used as a scarf or partial veil

DESCRIPTION/TITLE

ayah	nurse or maid
beaters	men employed to direct game towards waiting hunters by means of noise and motion
gulam	slave
khalanayak	villain
khansama	major domo or butler
maharaj kumar	heir (usually son) of a maharajah
maharajah	regional ruler of a principality (a "princely state")
maharani	chief wife of a maharajah
mahout	elephant driver
shikari	hunter or hunting guide

FOOD

aloo	potato
chapatti	flat bread made from wheat and cooked on a griddle; a staple of the peasant diet
chutney	many types of relish or dipping sauce, usually made from vegetables, yogurt, etc.
dal	soup or stew usually made from lentils (or other legumes) that have been dried and split
groundnuts	peanuts
jaggery	traditional, unrefined sweetener made from sugar cane juice or palm sap
kaddu	pumpkin
khira	cucumber
lentils	a type of legume commonly used in soup or stew; chief ingredient of dal

maize	corn
papadum	crispy, thin, round cracker; often made from lentils
suran	yam; also known as jimikand

FURNITURE

charpoy	light, portable bed, usually consisting of a frame strung with rope; sometimes employed as a machan
divan	low couch or sofa to sit or lie on
howdah	"carriage" on an elephant's back to carry people; sometimes called a "castle"
machan	platform constructed in a tree from which to shoot game, especially tigers

GEOGRAPHIC ENTITY

jheel	shallow lake or reservoir, often man-made
hectare	approximately two and a half acres
nullah	small, steep-sided valley or canyon; usually dry except during floods
Sundara Pradesh	principality ruled by the maharajah

MISCELLANEOUS

ananta	forever; without end
anna	Indian coin of small denomination
bazaar	marketplace

chuffle   low gravelly sound made by large cats who
                cannot purr and make this sound instead;
                chuff (v)

daftar   office

garbhanaal   umbilical cord

monsoon   rainy season in India, lasting for three to four
                months; much, if not most, of the year's rainfall
                occurs during this time

musth   recurring phase when the elevated levels
                of testosterone in bull elephants result in
                aggressive behavior

prashn chinh   question mark

shikar   expedition to hunt animals for sport

shoot   expedition to hunt game

uple   fuel made of shaped and dried cow dung; also
                called dung cake

TREES/PLANTS

angur shefa   plant in nightshade family; although used
                medicinally, leaves, berries, and particularly
                seeds are toxic when ingested and can lead to
                convulsions and accelerated heartbeat

bael   tree whose fruit is used for food and traditional
                medicine; also known as Bengal quince

banyan   species of fig tree, one of the group termed
                strangler figs; over time the banyan can spread
                laterally to cover a large area

choola   local name for a slow-growing, medium-sized
                tree sometimes almost covered by deep-orange
                blossoms; also known as dhak or flame of the
                forest

dhatura	also from nightshade family and also used medicinally, but more toxic than angur shefa; also known as thorn-apple
jujube	tree whose fruit is used for both food and traditional medicine; also known as ber
lantana	a common (although introduced) flowering and invasive plant; the flowers are often mixed red and orange
maniphal	small tree whose flowers attract many butterflies and moths; the seeds are used to poison fish
neem	Indian lilac; used to treat skin disease, repel insects, or as a spice
sal	slow-growing deciduous tree that has religious significance; also an important source of lumber
shatavari	species of asparagus used to treat indigestion and ulcers; its name means "curer of a hundred diseases"
teak	common hardwood tree
vasa bach	rushlike plant that grows near water; used to treat a number of ailments, and as an ingredient in food and perfume; also known as sweet flag

WEAPON

bhaala	lance
laathi	a heavy stick, usually made of bamboo and sometimes tipped or strengthened with iron; often carried by police as a truncheon

CPSIA information can be obtained
at www.ICGtesting.com
Printed in the USA
LVHW101627081122
732650LV00008B/1066